The Pyn Papers

C. C. Ellis

Edited by David G. Cylkowski, Ph.D.

Associate Editor............. .... C.B. Cylkowski

Technical Consultant............... .... R.M. Haas

Cover Design: "The Eagle Soars"...... C.C. Ditri

A *Whitewood* Publication © 2013

Introduction

I met Miss Pyn in the springtime in a world astonishingly alive with new shape and shadow, fresh hue and fragrance. It was, as Miss Pyn's chronicler, C.C. Ellis, might well have written, that one spring day with gently warm and perfectly still air and sky couple-colored yet clear -- that day so wonderfully bright that occurs when lilac-time and rhododendron-time meet in a fleeting embrace and the roses give promise of becoming their very best. It was a day perfect for discovery.

For months I had been away from my home in the States, away from college and my students, reading in dark, gray libraries at Oxford and Cambridge. Then for weeks and weeks I had been in London crowd-wrestling, entombed each morning and evening on the Underground, sometimes moving, too often not. Between my daily adventurous encounters with the Underground, I could be found at the third table from the door closeted in the manuscript room of The British Museum Library reading scientific papers devoted to arboriculture, the products of fourteenth and fifteenth century scholars and scribes.

Anyone who has been environed for days, let alone weeks in London -- jumping on and jumping off the Underground each morning and evening, with the incessant recorded voice bellowing "Mind the gap" at every stop, and then reading manuscripts or not reading manuscripts -- will understand the consuming and urgent need I felt for a ride, even for only a single day, into the English countryside.

It happened in Hampshire. My colleague, driver and guide -- only recently retired as Department Head of the English Literature Faculty of a prestigious school in Hammersmith -- accompanied me on pilgrimage to Jane Austen's house at Chawton.

En route, I noticed a hand-lettered sign announcing an auction to be held at a house on, it turned out, an unmarked car path somewhere off Pickaxe Lane. I suggested to my friend that during our return journey we might stop by for a look-in. She concurred.

After a refreshing visit to Miss Austen's home, we enjoyed, in the Austen House Garden, a memorable picnic lunch provided by my friend. After a post-luncheon modest pint of Grey Friar's best bitter at the pub over the road, we did in fact find the auction in a comfortable Victorian country home stuffed with treasures gleaned from Georgian, Victorian and Edwardian eras, all far too costly for a wandering scholar, especially one on leave.

One curiosity, atop a handsome mahogany credenza, did interest me -- a smallish stack of what appeared to be old papers and magazines, some with late nineteenth and some with twentieth century dates on them. While most of the auction-goers admired crystal chandeliers and pewter candlesticks, I rummaged through the pile of printed and handwritten bits, snippets, and pieces of former times that someone had wished to retain and remember.

An old magazine piqued my scholarly inquisitiveness. It was an 1886 issue of *The London Illustrated News* lavishly picturing, with detailed iron etchings, an age which celebrated the gentile occupations of the equestrian course and the operatic circuit. The most recent paper was not very old at all. Dated January 1986, its headlines proclaimed "American Spacecraft Explodes." What different worlds were capsulated here in but one hundred years of print; what an unusual, perhaps unique, inquiring mind dared to seek and very likely found kinship with both these worlds?

I continued looking through the stack of papers, which everyone else apparently thought was just a pile of debris. After a time I found one, then another, and then many more -- sixteen in all -- yellow pads of legal-sized notepaper covered with what appeared to be a contemporary hieroglyphic, a unique shorthand consisting largely of peculiar abbreviations and squiggles, swirls, and curlicues of the kind some medieval scribes used to double letters or indicate frequently used inflections. I thought the pages might reveal a kindred spirit, one familiar with scribal practice. So I examined the papers closely.

Some of them had a word or a phrase, a paragraph or even an entire section deleted or rewritten between the lines, while other pages were wholly unaltered. The years I had devoted to the study of paleography in numerous hands now paid immediate dividends. I was able to decipher enough of the work right there to suspect strongly that I had very likely stumbled onto a "find." I realized just then that I could distinctly feel my pulse, and was convinced that everyone else must be able to hear it as well. Could my burning face betray my anxiety?

The auctioneer appeared ready to begin the proceedings; so I inquired, in the most casual and detached manner I could muster, if that stack on the credenza were here for auction. I purposely used the subjunctive mood of the verb in an effort to mask my eager anticipation.

The auctioneer indicated that he had not intended to auction the papers because no one had shown an interest in them. Since I had asked about them, he thought it might be just as well to begin with that lot as a sort of warm-up. I was both pleased and dismayed: pleased to have the papers available so soon, dismayed that someone else might outbid me. I had not many spare pounds left for my remaining time in England.

Had the papers not been for auction, I thought I might have been able to buy them directly for a few pounds; or better still, perhaps the gentleman would have been most pleased if I should just take them away. Imagine my consternation when the auctioneer announced that because of a request from a visitor from Canada, the auction would get underway with bidding commencing for that pile of old odd things on that lovely Edwardian credenza at the side; the excellent piece under the papers would come up for bid with other furniture later on.

I nearly panicked. So there was someone else interested in my treasure! The bidding had yet to begin, but already those papers were "my treasure." After all, I could read the writing on those pads. Who else could know? Was this Canadian visitor a man or a woman? I looked about with what I thought was my best devil-may-care expression as I tried to recognize a Canadian who might become an adversary. No one appeared to be the least interested in the papers; no one appeared to be Canadian. While I could not be certain about the ladies, the gentlemen, at any rate, appeared to be non-Canadian. That fellow, if fellow he be, must be very cool indeed. Meanwhile, I thought that I was about to begin to twitch with anxiety.

The auctioneer rapped for attention and invited bids on "that lot of papers" for which he set no minimum bid. As nonchalantly as I could, I bid three pounds forty pence. The auctioneer thanked me -- I suspect half-heartedly, smiled strangely and said he rather hoped that, even with "less desirable items" bidders would refrain from bidding in pence. With my permission, he would record my bid as three pounds. His manner betrayed either a patient resigned acceptance of the ignorance of colonials or an incredulity that anyone at all could be interested in that peculiar stack of oddments.

I waited eagerly, even fearfully, for a countering bid from that mysterious Canadian. I tried to calculate just how much I could afford to offer. Perhaps I could impose on my friend for a loan. Silence. Would that Canadian outbid me? By how much? Again I waited, this time ready to shout, "Five pounds!" Silence still. I opened my mouth and blurted out, "Fi ..." just as the auctioneer rapped to repeat his invitation for bids, indicating that if no one else was interested in the items under consideration, he would accept the bid from the gentleman from Canada and most happily award the papers to him.

Silence bespoke general acquiescence. I hastened to depart with the papers. It was only after we were nearly halfway back to London that I remembered and explained to my friend that, because my English pronunciation and syntax are rather different from the American English spoken on syndicated American television programs heard frequently in the U.K., I have been mistaken fairly often in England for a Canadian.

During the many months that have passed since that memorable June day when I obtained the Pyn manuscript, whatever time I could garner or borrow from my responsibilities at the university or even steal from my work preparing a modern edition of a medieval scientific treatise, I have devoted to transcribing *The Pyn Papers*. This edition of Miss Pyn's story is the result of those labors.

Even though I have studied, arranged, rearranged, and sometimes guessed at the prose of C.C. Ellis for several years, I know virtually nothing more about the author today than I knew that eventful day in Wiltshire. Although I write these words in London, I have had thus far neither the opportunity nor the wherewithal to retrace my journey and conduct a proper scholarly inquiry in the vicinity of Chawton in Wiltshire. I have every expectation that one day I shall qualify for a research grant; perhaps then I shall be able to discover more.

One of the more vexing questions continually nags: Is or was C.C. Ellis an American man or woman who lived in England for a time -- which seems the most likely scenario; or was he or she an English writer who lived long enough in the United States to acquire what appears to be a decidedly American perspective? The manuscript notepads are of no help on this point. Some of the pads were manufactured in the U.S. while others were produced in the U.K., a fact that rather obfuscates the matter of the writer's country of origin.

On the whole, the manuscript does provide some indirect evidence of American authorship. Except for Miss Pyn's unconscious occasional use of British expressions incorporated to reveal the character of the speaker, and except for even fewer examples of such expression in the words of the narrator -- which are invariably present as humorous narrative devices, the manuscript is wholly devoid of British English expression and characteristic British spelling. This could very well be a means of disguise, especially by a knowledgeable English author very much aware of and sensitive to differences in British and American English.

Clearly, the manuscript suggests that the author of *The Pyn Papers* had a good understanding of the language.

The principal American setting of the story, the town called Seven Oaks, in which Miss Pyn lived and worked during her adult life, is not at all helpful in determining the authorship. In all of the midwestern states of the United States of America, stretching from western Pennsylvania to Kansas and from Minnesota and Michigan on the Canadian border to Missouri and Kentucky and to the South, I have not been able to discover a town or village called Seven Oaks. In the county of Kent in England there is an old town known as Sevenoaks. Even if the spelling difference is overlooked, the possibly coincidental association is assuredly too nebulous to afford any credible conclusion. Moreover, the only direct reference in the manuscript connecting a Seven Oaks pioneer with England places old Mr. Thrust in the Cotswold Villages, a considerable distance from Kent.

Although I have examined every word of the text numerous times, I am not at all certain that the creator of Miss Pyn maintains consistently a masculine or a feminine point of view, however meticulously that may be defined. Of course, the author may have, again for his or her own reasons, conscientiously disguised personal attitudes, perspectives, and predilections.

One might conjecture that the author may be, or may have been a second-generation American with strong ties and identity with England. While that is entirely possible, Miss Pyn's incessant awareness of the melancholic bittersweet dimension of the human condition suggests at least a kinship with those who perhaps most consistently express that particular world view in their literature, the people of Eastern Europe. If this conjecture, after further analysis, were to prove tenable, it would be possible to posit that Miss Pyn's author is or was an American with an Eastern European heritage or an Eastern European resident of England who was displaced by the last great war or its aftermath, and who subsequently resided for a time in Mid-America.

Furthermore, the enormous importance of the religious experience in Miss Pyn's world may be seen as additional evidence of the author's Eastern European heritage with its deep religious commitment at the very center of life. However, a similar commitment to religious faith is apparent in a medieval view of existence. One with a close kinship to medieval thought may well develop such a philosophical conviction. The manuscript evidence which suggests the writer's probable knowledge of medieval scribal practice supports the conjecture that the Pyn author had a good knowledge of medieval culture and could well have been influenced by the philosophy of that period.

In summary, it is not yet possible to identify the country of origin, the culture, or the literary heritage of the author. Doubtless, it is entirely injudicious to attempt assessment of the literary artistic merit of the author on the meager evidence that *The Pyn Papers* afford. Further conjecture may well serve to nourish continued speculation more readily than definitive conclusion.

D.G.C.
Cartwright Gardens
London

Miss Pyn's Teatime

C.C. ELLIS

Miss Pyn spent her whole working life in Seven Oaks, in the library. The hours of each day, from nine to five, were taken up by books, mainly those of English writers. At five o'clock sharp, Miss Pyn would promptly collect her umbrella and her little plastic lunch kit -- her one concession to modernity -- and she would step to the cadence of the quick click of the heels of her proper walking pumps along the path leading from the library toward the shops on Main Street. She called the street -- but only to herself, "The High Street," because that was what the main shopping street was always called in the English novels she read: "The High Street." She didn't dare let people know she used those words. They might think that she was -- well, strange. In fact, on most days she worried a little that she might slip one day and say "postman" or "high street" or maybe even "brollie" or "lorry."

She reached the curve in the street with the bakery opposite. She would see if one of her favorite little cakes was left for her tea. She forgot always to ask that one be saved so she could have it at tea. The bell on the door of the bakery jingled.

"Good afternoon, Agnes; it is another warm day, is it not? This April has been unusually warm, would you not say so?"

"Why hello, Miss Pyn! How very good of you to stop today! 'Tis a very warm day, especially so early in the season. You know, I think I just might have a cake left -- a little cake, the kind you like with your tea. I'll get it now."

Each day, Miss Pyn stopped at the bakery. Each day, she had a weather-word for Agnes. Each day, Agnes welcomed her as a friend who had not been by in many days. And even though Miss Pyn always forgot to ask that a cake be saved, each day Agnes saved the little cake -- the kind she knew Miss Pyn would like with her tea.

What Agnes didn't know was that Miss Pyn thought that those little cakes so popular in this Midwestern American town were really like perfect little scones. Miss Pyn had read about scones as she had read of most things British; once she even found a recipe for them in a Scottish cookery book, but she had never tried to make scones. That was years before, when it would have been very difficult baking anything in the tiny old gas oven without a temperature control in the range that came with her first apartment over Jensen's Hardware.

She had suspected then, when she studied the recipe, that the cakes from the bakery were not really like the scones she would like to have had with her tea;

but over the years she forgot the lost recipe. By the time she moved into her present apartment with a proper working oven, she had become convinced that those little bakery cakes were proper scones. Now and then, she remembered that she once had a scone recipe and it might be good to look for one again just in case the bakery would one day have no cake left for her. She could not even imagine that they might stop making them altogether. She never did look for the scones recipe. It was just as well, for she would have been very surprised and a little hurt to discover how different the little cakes which she called scones -- but only to herself -- were from the Scottish cakes.

"Agnes," she said, "I have some news. This is Thursday. On Friday a week I shall take a holiday."

"Oh my," she thought, "I should have said 'vacation.'" To Agnes she continued, "I am going to be away for nearly a month!"

Agnes was puzzled. "Whatever will we do? How will the library survive without you? Why, you've not taken more than two weeks ever in a whole year, and never two weeks together!"

"The library patrons will manage. Beginning next week all books will circulate for six weeks. None, even those already in circulation, will be due before the second week in June. Besides, both school principals,

4

Mayor Johnson, Officer Hicks, and Miss Thrust have their own keys. If things are needed, things can be had. The mail and any new books can await my return. Since I have no one to visit this year, I expect to go where I have planned to go for the past thirty years. I expect to go to the place I have thought about visiting since before I started as a volunteer in the library, opening the mail and unpacking all of those new books from Foyle's bookshop and from Blackwell's. If all goes well, I shall go to Charing Cross Road. I shall go to England, to London -- to Oxford, and to Cambridge."

Agnes was unable to say anything for a full minute. She studied Miss Pyn's smug smile. "You will be traveling across the ocean on an airplane by yourself? Are you daft? As I live and breathe, as m'name is Agnes Marie O'Reilly McGee, I think you're daft. Have you ever been overseas before -- alone by yourself?"

"No, but one must start sometime. And besides, I have planned to take this trip since before you were born."

"But to England, Miss Pyn!" Agnes continued, still amazed. "Those people are so formal. They probably don't like our casual American ways. Why, I think they are polite even when they don't want to be polite. Are you sure you want to do this? Are you sure you want to

5

go? If you must go, why not go to Ireland instead? Now there's the place I'd feel at home."

"No, Agnes. I have made up my mind. My tickets and my renewed passport should arrive tomorrow and on Friday a week I shall leave. Only I would ask that you not say where I am going, until after I have gone." Miss Pyn knew Agnes well.

"Oh, you can trust me, Miss Pyn, not to say a word until next Saturday mornin'! I can be quiet till then, but probably not beyond. Now here's your cake, and I hope t' see you again soon." She said that, knowing full well she could expect to see Miss Pyn on the very next day.

Miss Pyn paused at the door, "Remember, Agnes, not until next Saturday."

By five-thirty, Miss Pyn was ready to prepare her tea. She put the teakettle on to boil and took down her teapot with great care. It was fine, even delicate English china, eggshell white with tiny blue forget-me-nots sprinkled all over it, even including the spout and the handle. As always, she looked at the bottom to see if it was still there -- to see if it was still legible. She read as she did each day: "Stratford-Upon-Avon, Warwickshire."

Miss Pyn's day was not complete until she encountered her early evening cup of tea, and only then was the day most complete. She long ago had met Mr.

Twining in a novel, and she soon learned that Messrs Fortnum and Mason would dispatch Twinings Tea anywhere in the world, even to Seven Oaks. The price with shipping charges was a bit dear, but Miss Pyn had no other indulgence -- just her tea and her teacake. For many years she was unaware that Twinings best tea was available locally, in the city. By the time she learned she could get it in town, she had for so long looked forward so eagerly for the arrival of her semiannual package from Fortnum and Mason, she couldn't bring herself to cancel her standing order. And besides, she never did like going to the city anyway.

It was a very good thing too, for had she purchased her tea in town she would have made a most astonishing discovery. She would have found that although Twinings great teas -- blended since the eighteenth century at the same location on the Strand in London -- could be ordered for shipment anywhere, those purchased in the United States and in Canada were blended in Greensboro, North Carolina.

Miss Pyn poured boiling water into her pot to warm it before putting in the tea. She had learned to do that many years before. Now she tried to remember where: "Was it from Jane Austen?" Elizabeth Bennet was probably her best friend now that her college friend Carole was gone. Certainly, Elizabeth was her closest acquaintance. Was it she who had taught her to warm the pot? Although Miss Pyn read through each of the novels of Jane Austen every three or four years and renewed her acquaintance with Miss Elizabeth Bennet even more often, she could not remember. What she did not remember, too, was that those directions could be found on the tea package as well.

It was time to add the tea: one spoonful for each cup with only one-half teaspoonful for the pot because Messrs Fortnum and Mason charged a frightful price for the tea; and besides, Twinings tea -- it said in an old advertisement -- was rich and full-bodied. A half spoonful would do nicely, thank you.

As she poured in the water to let it steep, she remembered her college days. Miss Pyn's undergraduate college friend and roommate, Carole, was able to study abroad during her junior year, while Miss Pyn had had to stay home. She envied Carole a tiny bit because she herself had also hoped to go abroad, and they had planned to live together in England. When she had learned so long ago that she could not go, she had thought, "One day, perhaps, I shall go to England. For now I have my books – in them I can visit there anytime I choose. Not for just a summer or for only a year; I can go whenever and as often as I wish and stay as long as I please."

Miss Pyn checked her tea. It would be too strong now, but she had extra hot water and sometimes she thought, "I do prefer it white. Oops! I must remember to say 'with milk.'" She would have it with milk today; that seemed so much more proper. So she carefully took the milk pitcher in one hand and the teapot in the other and poured both, simultaneously -- in the proper manner -- as they always did in her beloved books. "They do know how to pour tea," she thought as she looked out of the window on that April afternoon. "How good it is to have, at the end of the day, a fine cup of tea that is properly poured."

Miss Pyn remembered the day the teapot had arrived. Carole had written from France that she and her friend, Brad, would visit in England during the "spring break." Instead of a note, that April, a package came from Stratford-Upon-Avon. It was so exciting to find a real package from England at her door with lovely stamps and a customs declaration. The declaration said that the package was a gift valued at two pounds. A note inside said, "For you -- because I'm so happy. Brad has asked me to marry him next year in England. Love, Carole."

Miss Pyn thought about that now. She did not realize even after all this time that the modest two-pound value was declared in case Miss Pyn would have to pay duty on the package.

Carole had thought aloud as she taped the box, "Maybe the customs agent might not believe that the package was a gift."

Brad was sure that all of the Irish American customs agents in probably every American port were more than likely convinced that all packages from England should require duty -- every penny the law allowed. "If one of those fellows inspects it, she'll have to pay. You'd better write 'one pound' on the declaration tag."

Insisting she still had some scruples left, Carole wrote "two pounds." "And besides, they might not believe it was worth only one pound."

Had Miss Pyn known then the real value of that lovely teapot, she would have been dismayed. Now as she looked out her window still hoping to go to England soon, the thought of the compounded value reflected in the fading forget-me-nots on that little pot evoked a quiet wistfulness. "Am I really going to get there?"

"Surely," Miss Pyn thought, "this April sun must be very eager, maybe even anxious, to get on with the day which already appears to be very nice indeed."

It seemed to her that the sun was up earlier than usual that gentle morning. Miss Pyn started each day in late winter, spring, summer, and fall precisely as the sun climbed above the horizon. There was a lovely bay window in her room; she liked bays very much -- a bay was less of a barrier against the out-of-doors than an ordinary flat window. On bright mornings, when the robin could be heard through the window greeting the day, she could pretend she was engulfed by her beloved nature rather than protected from it. The sense that she was immersed in God's handiwork rather than surrounded by human fabrication brought much more vigor to her whole day. She even placed her bed near the window bay so that the first glimmer of sunlight filtering through trees and window caught her eye. But even on dull days, when the sun disdained to shine, she knew instinctively when the sun would cross the horizon and up she popped.

This morning it was very good of the sun to be early, to be eager. She too was eager to get on with the day, the sooner to get on with the weekend and on with the week to next Friday, that Friday of her expectation. Though she was eager for each hour to rush by as quickly as possible, she knew she was becoming increasingly anxious as each hour flitted by, and she wondered, "Will I be able to endure it? I have wanted to do this for so long. Will I be able to stand the stress and the excitement? What if London is not what I expect?

What if it is not the place I have found on my library shelves and discovered in my dreams? Silly, these thoughts are not for now."

As she did each morning, she reflected for a few moments on the wonder that was life. And as she did each morning, she thought about some of the precious people who had touched and even given direction to her life. Always, even though it was difficult, she thought of Michael -- wonderful, forever happy and forever young Michael, her dear friend of long ago whom she missed so very much. On most mornings she thought of her father; she still missed him as much after all these years. Or she would think of Carole and Brad on one day, or of her mother and sister and her sister's family on another. Sometimes she thought of Joe who brought so much beauty to Seven Oaks, and she even thought of Agnes -- talkative, thoughtful but innocent, loving Agnes. But always on the morning of each day, she thought of Thomas. How she wished nothing but goodness and happiness for her beloved friend who long ago had touched her life so deeply, and who now had been gone so very long. This morning she thought, "How very fortunate I am to be here, and happy too; and how good it is to be able to think that I shall soon, at last, be there -- in England!"

As she dressed, she thought, "It is nice to have a little extra time this morning. Thank you, my friend Mr. Sun. If the morning air is warm enough, I shall take my breakfast tea on the balcony. If I wear my knit sweater from Scotland I shall be warm, for surely it will be warm enough by eight o'clock."

Miss Pyn's small kitchen consisted of a working area most times used for humdrum but sometimes creative cookery -- she loved to be adventuresome in the art of the kitchen, but only when she had a rare guest. Of all her particular creations of the kitchen, she found the greatest pleasure in seeing the surprise and gleeful delight on a guest's face when her baked brie in puffed pastry with just a drop of Cointreau first assaulted then conquered the palate. In the kitchen, too, was a glass-enclosed alcove that served as a breakfast nook, a luncheon nook, and a dinner nook for most days, and for some days a writing nook when the sunlight was there too. Opening out from her multipurpose nook was a tiny balcony.

Today, she would use the balcony for the first time this season. She thought, "Spring is so exciting! It does mean new life and renewed life. No wonder green is the color of hope. Oh, I'd best remember to keep those thoughts to myself, however exhilarating this day becomes. My sophisticated or perhaps jaded patrons

13

might think them trivial or even worse, trite. Thank goodness for children. Often, they see so much better than we. There is very little that is commonplace to them. They would understand."

At her morning tea this morning, Miss Pyn would desert Mister Twining for Major Dashwood; not because she was fickle, but only because this was a very special occasion -- the first balcony tea of the season. Mister Twining could never be replaced. She would remain faithful always. After all, she had known and loved Mister Twining in happy times as well as in sad times nearly all of her adult life. No, he could never go! After so long, it would be like breaking a solemn promise. Besides, it was only recently, in Philadelphia, at the last librarians' conference that she had been introduced to Major Dashwood. A friendly librarian from Baltimore, Harriet Clippings, had suggested that they try some fine Darjeeling at afternoon tea.

For now she sipped her morning Darjeeling. It was probably not the best tea for breakfast, but it was ... special. The balcony was small, with just enough room for a tiny tea table and two chairs. The chairs were large enough, with little enameled arms, to be quite comfortable. Sometimes she thought, "Why do I keep these two chairs? Just one would make the balcony seem a bit bigger. But then, how should I be able to serve my guests properly?"

The truth was that there were very few real guests, despite what Miss Pyn thought. But there were many from her past who would come to tea faithfully and without hesitation every time Miss Pyn invited them.

So she had her little white tea table and her two light-blue chairs. They were difficult to keep clean during the long season, but they were so inviting. Miss Pyn was pleased with her tiny balcony; whenever there were flowers in the garden -- first daffodils and then candy tufts and lavender in the spring;   delphinium and shasta daisies in the summer; and asters, marigold, and chrysanthemum in the fall -- she cut just one for her "outdoor vase" on her lovely tea table. Always, from late spring until killing frost, there were the roses. Imperial and regal, looking as though they enjoyed a patent of divine right, the roses graced her table on very important days -- her birthday, or Carole's anniversary, or the anniversary of that day in the garden with Thomas.

She knew the names of all the roses -- not only those in her garden at home, but those in Joe's magnificent gardens on the grounds of the library. She had two favorite roses, and each May she eagerly awaited their appearance. "If I go to London next week,

I shall not be able to greet the first blossoming of my two good friends. Must there always be a disappointing edge lurking about one's happy time?"

The building in which Miss Pyn's apartment -- a flat really -- was located, was built into a hill on an acre of land not far off the high street -- that is, the main street. Although it was within shouting distance of Adams Road, the main road through town, the noise of the commerce and trade of the small community was seldom audible on the balcony. Now and then the occasional visitor would remark, "How close you are to the city; yet magically when I entered your road, I entered the country."

Neighbors whose backyards abutted her garden for at least one mile did not enclose their backyards. They undoubtedly found the expense of fencing prohibitive. Miss Pyn thought, "Perhaps they too understand that there is something in nature that does not like a wall."

So from her balcony she could look down a valley which had the gentle slope of a dried-up streambed. She could look as far as she could see through an uncluttered fairway of meadowland with bushes and trees punctuated only by odd patches of briar and brush which pheasants and rabbits and quail shared with resident and transient birds of many persuasions --

orthodox and mildly exotic. Squirrels were there too; chipmunks occasionally. An odd snake of the garden variety, and possums, skunks, shrews and tiny voles surely must be there, but seldom if ever seen. Sometimes in the late winter snow or spring mud, Miss Pyn even recognized the footprints of a stealthy raccoon.

The warm sun bade her a joyous welcome when she sat with her morning cup of Major Dashwood's finest tea. She had noticed that the table and the chairs had the dregs of winter all over them. Never mind the dust and grime of winter, "My suit is washable and it needs a good wash-up. These unforeseen moments of peace and warm sunlight are worth a whole month of washings." While she suspected she would very much enjoy walking the world in the sunshine, certainly sitting during such unexpected moments in the warm sunlight was a very grand blessing indeed. "If I were to write an ancient blessing I would include the smallest moments of warm sunlight, especially those that were wholly unexpected."

The balcony had a railing -- "frightfully modern." It consisted of what appeared to Miss Pyn to be timbers two inches by six inches, fastened so that they were set on edge. Numerous balusters, about two inches square and thirty inches high, supported the railing. All had a soft redwood hue, but the wood was undoubtedly treated-and-stained pine or fir. Never mind, real redwood would have been charming even if it was not as exotic as teakwood; as it was, the railing was still a delight and useful too.

The morning was always Miss Pyn's favorite time; this day the morning was very still as if to mark her annual initiation into the season of the out-of-doors with great solemnity. She strained her ears, very carefully, to hear the silence. She felt she would be content and very happy to remain there listening to the silence, always. At such moments, she felt a twinge of her conscience so finely honed by generations of a Puritan heritage. "I should not be here doing nothing. Such self-indulgence surely could not be right. Oh well, I shall have to go to the library soon enough."

She thought she heard -- sensed really, and perhaps felt -- tiny zephyrs darting in and out, over and under and all around the balusters of the balcony railing. "These must be the children of the west wind, the harbingers of a glorious warm season." Miss Pyn remembered her Chaucer and her Shelley.

"Do I really want to leave all this just as the glory is beginning? The season in England is earlier than ours. The Gulf Stream sees to that. Perhaps I should have gone sooner so I would have been back for the reawakening of all the beauty of our land. Why is it that all my expectations – really, all my joys -- have always a side to prompt regret, to give pause and call up misgiving?"

Just then, the resident cardinal, the one Miss Pyn had seen all winter long at one of her bird feeding stations, broke the silence with his spring morning song, strident and melodious. The cardinal was perched high in a nearby ash tree which would bring to the balcony welcome shade from the warm afternoon sun of summer. "Oh! How can I leave now? Maybe my passport will not come. Or better, maybe my travel booking is wrong. I could go some other time." She sipped her tea, remembering she must soon go to the library whatever might happen next week.

In the morning paper, the weather forecast caught her eye. Sunday, it promised, would be a grand day, pleasantly warm with sunshine and very little breeze. "How wonderful!" thought Miss Pyn. "I shall attend early morning service and spend -- or is it invest -- the remaining part of the morning on my balcony listening to the sounds of springtime."

Miss Pyn's resolve was wholly unnecessary. She always attended the earliest worship service because she believed in the proper sacredness of the day of rest. Not that she thought she ought to be pious about the whole day, but rather she believed she should get the earliest start on the day in order to devote as much time as possible to earnest and sustained resting -- the earlier the better. And besides, she liked her peaceful Sunday mornings.

Now with new resolve she found she could look forward to the day after tomorrow. There was, however, all of Friday and work still facing her. "P," she said to herself and to the cardinal who was still in the ash tree, "it is time to go to work."

She did not remember just then that it was Carole who had first called her "P" almost from the moment they met over thirty years before. For now, she gathered her things: her brollie -- that is, her umbrella; her purse; briefcase; and her lunch kit. She closed the door and began her walk in the direction of the library.

"Good morning, Miss Pyn!" The voice greeted Miss Pyn as she was about to push open the wrought-iron gate in the low stone wall that marked the long front of the library grounds. She stepped onto the brick walkway that curved between two formal rose gardens and led up to the front entrance of the library.

Pausing at the rose gardens she responded, "Good morning, Joe! This day surely shows promise of becoming a most delightful day."

"To be sure, Miss Pyn."

"You are here very early this morning. Do you wish to help advance the season?"

"Only the plants, Miss Pyn. There's much to do at this time of the year. Looks like spring will be early. The roses need special attention just now. They look very good -- little winter damage. If this weather continues, they should be particularly brilliant this year and likely early in bloom too."

"Oh my, then I shall surely miss their first flowering. Joe, must every happy expectation have disappointment lurking about it somewhere? You have not told anyone about my plan to travel to England next week, have you?"

"Of course I'll not tell anyone. You asked me not to, remember. I know how much this trip will mean to you. It will be very special and personal. When my lovely lady, Elisabeth, and I first traveled to Europe, our journey to England was very important. It was rather like going home."

"And I," replied Miss Pyn, "have thought of this holiday -- that is, vacation -- as neither a pilgrimage, nor a return. I have thought only of finally confronting an important part of my life that for far too long has not been available to me."

"In the end, it'll be very much like going home, Miss Pyn, for you as it was for us. My work with

21

mathematics brought me much more familiarity with German culture. Even so, when we traveled in England, while much was very new, much was most familiar. I've noticed your life here in the library is permeated with English culture. Why, just now I heard you say 'holiday' for 'vacation.' You will discover that there is always much that is forever new and fresh in another country. It cannot all be captured in even the very best books; you will discover that much over there is familiar, very familiar indeed.

"As for, just as you say, the bittersweet character of your expectation, I've learned that every joy has its price. It's not always apparent, but mark my words, the price is always there."

Miss Pyn pondered those words for some moments, recognizing Joe's insight, and moved by the freshness of its simple wisdom. He then apparently changed the subject. Later she would wonder -- did he really change the subject when he said, "I've opened some windows. I can close them if you like before I leave. Would you like that?"

"Thank you, Joe. I should like the freshness of the air all day long. I shall be able to close them when I leave."

She thought again. This man understands so very much about so much in life, but I fear he cares for everyone but himself.

"You had best not work too long and too hard today. The gardens will, as usual, respond to your care especially if you care for yourself as well. Let the boys do more of the work after school. They learn so well under your direction, your tutelage. Your lifetime of teaching is perfectly apparent in your dealings with the young men. Oh, incidentally, of late more and more young ladies ask their school counselors to recommend them to the library garden project. They have even asked me if they could qualify. We will probably have to accept some, you know. Could you manage?"

"Of course I can. During the years before I retired, I found that more and more young women majored in mathematics. A number of them proved to be among my very best students. One holds a professorship in California and another in Massachusetts. Of course we can manage. If they will put up with me, I shall find delight in their learning -- especially if they are bright and quick-witted as I frequently found the young ladies majoring in math to be. I shall need a few hulks, though, for the very heavy work. Perhaps the library could accommodate a few more places for the work-study program? I could use more help, and you know teaching is my life."

"That, Joe, is an excellent idea. I shall consult with Miss Thrust to see what can be done. I think that she should be asked to approach the school principal. In that way two problems could be remedied -- your workload and our need to set an example by not discriminating among our young people. In the meantime, remember, the gardens need you as we all need you."

Joe only smiled as Miss Pyn continued up the curved walkway toward the library's grand front entrance. She crossed the flagstones of the front terrace, passing without a glance at the building's cornerstone with its carved legend, "Whitewood on the Wold - 1884."

That the library was once a private, though formidable home was readily apparent. It was a great stone building with a red clay tiled roof. The stone was striking; there was none like it for miles and miles around. In fact, Miss Pyn was sure to look for similar stone wherever she traveled to librarian meetings throughout the country. She found none.

It was stone all right. Yet it projected warmth, even softness with its unique hues. At dawn, especially when the air was fiercely clear and the sky crystal-blue, the stone had at first a burnished hue awaiting the touch of sunlight which always transformed it into astonishing gold. Some mornings when the mist was just right and the entire eastern sky, at dawn, was aglow with the soft promise of a precious perfect day, the stone facade shone as a luminous pale copper-and-gold-tinted palette. At evening, delicate rose and pink washes, surely distilled from the dust of ancient gems and rare metals, were splashed over the lingering gold-magic. Like the richness of the lore encased within it, the very stone of the library beckoned the thoughtful spirit.

Miss Pyn pulled open one of the two great front doors. Although the door was enormous, it opened readily; like everything in this grand building it was beautifully maintained. The Thrust Foundation and the inimitable Joe saw to that.

Beyond the oak door, the morning sun reflected off the white and red marble of the foyer floor onto the rose and blue stained glass panels in the top half of the sliding foyer doors. These doors disappeared, at Miss Pyn's touch, into the walls at either side, revealing a substantial entrance hallway paneled in rich red oak with a magnificent staircase fashioned of crosscut oak in superbly blended hues. The staircase, masterfully crafted, towered up above the fifteen-foot-high ceiling of the first floor, and up and up two more levels to the third floor above.

Miss Pyn often thought, "We really should call the floor at the top of the stairs 'the first floor' in the English manner; after all, that is the first level one encounters in negotiating the stairs. On second thought, the library patrons might find that peculiar if not confusing. I shall just regard it in that way myself."

The stair railing was fashioned of beautifully matched wood sections stretching for yards and yards up the gracefully curved staircase with hand-carved balusters, each the work of a master craftsman. The bottom step was fully seven feet wide with a very large carved post marking the step's end and the beginning of the vast railing. The steps rose to three landings, one between each floor. At each landing there was a door leading to the back of the building, which apparently led to quarters designed for servants when the structure was a private home.

Miss Pyn sat at her meticulously arranged desk in the public reception area in what once was a sitting room in the old mansion. The scene might have been a painting by a grand master -- a Rembrandt perhaps, but with only a few deep tones. The warmth of the scene radiated from soft light that was accented by exquisitely delicate shadows. It would have made an astonishing painting, for the setting and its occupant were so perfectly suited one to the other.

Indeed, all her life Miss Pyn had enjoyed a wholesome beauty. Her radiant complexion was flawless, with lively shades of white and pink that bespoke health and vigor. Her eyebrows were naturally arched and required only occasional light trimming. Perfectly placed eyes with their blue irises complemented her every mood and glance. Her mouth of excellent proportion was graced by lips that required only the faintest coloring to accent the wonderful smile few people could ever forget. Though the features of her face were memorable, it was her hair that left lasting impression.

Ever since her college days when she took up tennis-playing seriously, she always had her hair styled in a short feather cut. In those bygone days of chignon and bouffant, her haircut was "noticed." In fact, it was thought quite striking and worthy of radical types. She sought neither to be noticed nor to "make a statement." She thought of it as the perfect hairdo for tennis, and since her hair was naturally curly it afforded her the freedom of speedy movement. Just a "run-through" with comb or brush, and all's well and away she could go.

It was not, however, the style of Miss Pyn's hair that one always remembered -- it was its striking color.

The morning sun highlighted silken gold threads among chestnut hues; at high noon the gold became a rose-gold amid a splendid auburn; in the evening, a rare russet-gold like that of precious metal mirrored the sunset.

Now and then, she could "escape" to another office located in the southeast corner of the building. Its floor-to-ceiling French windows opened onto a stone terrace that stretched across the front and half the side of the house. This room was a most comfortable workplace. At her desk here, she could feel the welcome warmth of the sun and look out across the lawns to the lily pond beyond the old carriageway. Across the room from her desk was the most impressive example of the ten fireplaces in the main rooms of the library building. Each fireplace was in working order; each was made of beautiful marble quarried from a different Italian source. Above the rich red marble of the mantle opposite Miss Pyn's desk hung the imposing though attractive portrait of the designer-builder-owner of this magnificent building, the honorable Mister Benjamin Thrust.

The morning hours would pass rapidly. There were inquiries to answer, bills to pay, and books to order -- all punctuated by requests for assistance or simply warm greetings by the few patrons who visited the library during morning hours.

Miss Thrust was due for a luncheon meeting with Miss Pyn. Miss Henrietta Thrust -- granddaughter of old Ben Thrust, trustee of the Thrust Foundation, and president of the Friends of the Library created by the Thrust Foundation -- was certain to be punctual. She had always been precisely on time each month for many years. When the weather was warm, she packed a box lunch to share in the library garden with Miss Pyn.

"Miss Pyn, I do think that I've packed something that you'll find very special. At least I hope you will enjoy them. I've made some little sandwiches. I found some light cream cheese in the market. Since the package boasted that it was lower in fat, I cheated just a wee bit and I added some olive to the spread. That is not all! Even though I much prefer shopping here in town, I did go out to the mall. You will not be able to guess what I found -- a real English cucumber! I've packed cucumber sandwiches on bread without the crust as you taught me to do. I smile to remember how, when I told you I had discovered a very quaint and funny tea sandwich in the play, *The Importance of Being Ernest*, you quietly assured me that cucumber sandwiches were commonplace if delightful English tea fare. These should be quite nice; the bread is my own."

29

Miss Pyn found Henrietta Thrust a perfect gem, and always amazing. Every ordinary thing she did every day was always special, and her efficiency exceeded conventional human expectation.

At lunchtime, Beth Holms, a volunteer member of the Friends of the Library, came to work at the desk in Miss Pyn's absence. The air out-of-doors was fresh and warm enough to make lunch in the garden very inviting. Miss Thrust and Miss Pyn crossed the carriageway that ran along the side of the library. Even though Miss Pyn knew that a carriageway in England was today a major roadway, she felt that "carriageway" was the appropriate name for the drive that had brought folks in carriages onto the property when the mansion was built. At several intervals along the way, large sandstone platforms carved with steps stood ready to assist travelers to alight from carriages.

The ladies walked in the direction of the garden near the edge of the lake. "The lake" was really an extravagant name for what was rather more like a lovely pond. It was, however, large enough to support a modest fish population. The lake and its garden were surrounded by a low wrought-iron fence with a canopied gate that served as an arbor for climbing roses. Around the outside of the lake fence, Joe had cultivated three rows of vigorous tea roses so that the lake area was quite secure and the library grounds safe for young children who were thus prevented from running near the water unattended.

Miss Pyn chose a lawn table at the west end of the lake. Here the soft west-by-southwest breeze would be behind them and they could look across the lake at an ancient magnolia tree just awakening from the long winter.

"Joseph and his young assistants prepare the outdoor furniture very early," observed Miss Thrust.

"Joe says that he wants to have the furniture used as much as possible over a long season. I think he knows how many people enjoy his garden. As the weather warms, there is someone here reading or just thinking nearly all of the time. And in addition, he tells me, the furniture can be prepared early before the spring garden requires so much of his time. Incidentally, Joe much prefers to be called 'Joe.' He does not wish to have the boys who work with him, or anyone else for that matter, addressing him as 'Mr. Epworth.' He thinks that 'Joe' is just right for his time of life and for the work he does."

Miss Thrust considered that for some minutes, a smile of amusement breaking over her face. "You know, Miss Pyn, I've often wondered why you speak of him and address him as you do. You are always so formal --

no, not formal exactly, but correct. So much so, that whenever I speak in your presence I feel I must be particularly careful not only with the choice of my words but with their precise meaning and exact pronunciation as well."

Miss Pyn took a big bite of a cucumber sandwich just to show that she was perfectly capable of a social impropriety. She added emphasis with a hardy laugh that shocked Miss Thrust. "Why, Henrietta," she said in her well-modulated voice, "you astonish me! I am not overly fastidious in the least. I simply love our language, and I try to use it with all its profound richness, precision, clarity, and wonderfully variegated connotation to the fullest extent without becoming tedious and tiresome. I call Mr. Epworth 'Joe' because he asked that I do so, and I do not address him as Joseph because 'Joseph' is not his name. If you do wish to know, it is Josiah -- Josiah Epworth. Actually, it is Dr. Josiah Epworth, Ph.D. Evidently, in New England as a professor of mathematics with a rather widespread and respected reputation, he felt his full name was most appropriate. When in retirement he moved west with his bride Elizabeth, who believed she was returning home for a long retirement, he wished to become just 'Joe' -- an appropriate name for a new life in a Midwestern town. I sometimes wish that he had kept his formal name, but he wanted a fresh beginning and he wanted to become a much more casual person."

"I'd forgotten that Elizabeth grew up in Seven Oaks," Miss Thrust admitted. "She must have been off to college about the time I became conscious of her family."

"Joe told me," Miss Pyn continued, "Elizabeth became his bride upon their being graduated. The wedding was here in Seven Oaks some years before I came here. They promptly returned to New England -- she to work for their sustenance; he to encounter graduate school. They prospered, and he achieved recognition eventually as a full professor of mathematics. They had no children, and by retirement time most of his New England relatives had died or moved away. They then looked forward to a long quiet life in retirement in Seven Oaks."

"Elizabeth didn't live many years after they settled here," Miss Thrust remembered.

"Yes, though it was truly sad, Joe had said then and he says often even now that they enjoyed a wonderfully loving life together. 'It is a special blessing to love the very same person for over forty-five years,' he tells me. Then he adds, 'not really the same person; for while the union remained -- the same individuals were forever fresh, forever new, changing each year, each week really.'"

"What a marvelous thought from an extraordinary man -- beautiful really! You must find him a true treasure."

"I do," murmured Miss Pyn thoughtfully. "I wonder how we shall ever get on when Joe is no longer with us. You know, he uses nearly all of the small stipend the library can afford to pay him to buy supplies for the gardens. He says so typically that he really does not need the money and besides the supplies make his job easier. Speaking of making the job easier, there is something the library fund could do to solve two problems. Joe could certainly use more help, and I hear that some of the girls at the high school are asking to get assigned to work-study under Joe. Our cost for work-study is minimal; perhaps you could approach the Board and the Principal with a proposal to include some young ladies in the program."

Miss Thrust frowned, "Yes of course. I'll do that." After some moments, she added, "I too have wondered, what will the library do when we no longer have Joe's help?"

"Perhaps we could establish a garden fund."

"Who would contribute to Joe's Garden Fund, especially after some time?"

"School children would," Miss Pyn answered. "Perhaps after a few years -- I should say many years -- it could be called a 'memorial fund?' Could it not?"

"I should think so. But even that seems not quite as inspiring as one would hope."

"When he is no longer with us, you could use his full name and title."

"Yes! That's much better: 'The Doctor Josiah Epworth Memorial Garden Fund.' I like that. Too bad we couldn't add 'Reverend' to the title. 'The Reverend Doctor Josiah Epworth Ph.D. Memorial Garden Fund' would work wonders."

"It is probably best not to wish for wonders, especially by -- shall I say -- 'shading' the truth, even in a good cause. I realize that Joe brings substantial spiritual refreshment through his beautiful garden to all of us in Seven Oaks, but adding 'reverend' to his name now or later is, I am afraid, entirely unwarranted."

"Once again, Miss Pyn, I must admit you are right."

Miss Pyn only smiled. She and Miss Thrust continued their conversation for nearly an hour. The subject largely dealt with routine and generally mundane library matters with only occasional departures that permitted comment upon either local news or the distinctive character of cucumber sandwiches. In the end, Miss Thrust agreed to propose to the Library Board two new places in the internship program for high-school young ladies to assist Joe with the gardens. She was certain that the Board members would agree, as they usually did, as long as she could find the funds. She would also propose, while she was at it, that they make provision for another place inside the library so that a young man might take advantage of Miss Pyn's direction, thus ensuring that the new program would be clearly politically correct. Miss Pyn was delighted, and was pleased that Miss Thrust would consult with the high-school authorities as well.

As she was leaving, Miss Thrust apparently just then remembered that she had heard from Ann Harris's mother that Ann would return to Seven Oaks several weeks earlier than expected. "Ann has completed her library study and has excellent references. Her mother says that although she could go many places with her recommendations, she is pleased that Ann will be home at least for a while.

"You really did wonderful work with Ann, Miss Pyn. Her mother agrees that until Ann came into your care she seemed to have no sense of purpose in life. Mother and daughter concur that your patient direction and concern transformed Ann from a mediocre student to the honor student she is."

"Oh my!" sighed Miss Pyn. "Ann only needed some time to grow. She did the growing. While others may have helped, her potentiality was there all along."

"But you recognized it when no one else did."

"I am as pleased with Ann's success as anyone, including Ann. But I insist, Ann is the one responsible."

"Many of us think otherwise -- that you as well as Ann are responsible. Be that as it may, I mentioned Ann because she knows the library well -- she learned much serving as your assistant during her senior year. We planned on welcoming her back in the library as your full-time assistant in June. It was to be a surprise that we knew you would enthusiastically welcome. I know I have to get your agreement sometime, so with your concurrence we would like her to join the library staff a bit early so you needn't be concerned about your vacation hampering the work of the library."

"For once in my life, I am speechless, utterly unable to say anything -- anything at all. What does Ann have to say about this? Will she be willing to work in our modest library? I am unable to believe it."

"Ann feels that she should begin her professional career here. She wrote that she would like nothing better. Not only is Seven Oaks her home, she feels a great debt to Miss Pyn. The Board and I agree whole-heartedly.

"So goodbye, Miss Pyn, and have a safe, delightful journey. At the risk of sounding like you, I wish you a grand holiday. I shall miss our meeting next month. Perhaps we could meet twice in June? Rest assured, Ann needs no orientation. Your good direction has already seen to that. So you needn't give a thought to us. I shall welcome Ann; and she is, as you might say, a 'serendipitous Godsend.' I trust today's tidings were truly glad. God speed!" And Miss Thrust was gone before Miss Pyn could reply.

Miss Pyn remained in the garden for some time pondering the "glad tidings." She remembered nearly every one of the young students who had come, over the years, to assist her in the library. At first, they came as high-school juniors; later, some really fortunate students came as sophomores who continued with Miss Pyn for three years.

Many of the library "alumnae" hoped to stay on in the library, but there were no funds then. Some moved away with their parents. Several went on to higher study.

She remembered their names, especially the names of two who went to Vietnam after completing their professional preparation. She would never forget the young nurse who did not return; she thought of Christa Fulton every time she said grace at mealtime and every time she prayed in church "for those who have died."

Other students had remained in Seven Oaks and begun their life's work, eventually marrying. Some of those who had gone off to university eventually returned. There was one who had already asked that the name of her prospective high-school-freshman daughter be put on the list of those students who would be considered for Miss Pyn's library program.

There were so many students who had served the library over the years. They all tended to be good students; Ann Harris was outstanding.

Now she would be coming back. Miss Pyn thought a moment, "I hope Miss Thrust can find the funds. Silly, she would not have said anything if she had not made the necessary budgetary adjustment. That is her job; yours is the library. Oh my, so it is! I have forgotten about Beth. She surely has other things to do away from the library."

Miss Pyn hurried toward the library, still pondering the "glad tidings."

Much later, her week's work completed, Miss Pyn stopped at the bakery on her way home. "Good afternoon, Agnes. It is Friday, and the weather forecast leads one to believe that we shall enjoy a glorious sun-filled weekend."

"Why, good afternoon, Miss Pyn! How good of you to stop, and your weather tidings are very welcome and truly glad. Weekends should always be sunny. 'Tis Friday for sure, and we have our little special two-for-one sale on your favorite little cakes today."

"How very nice, Agnes. I shall be able to have one with my tea on Sunday morning after church. It is good of you to have saved them for me. Thank you."

If Miss Pyn suspected that the special sale on the little cakes was exclusively for her each Friday, she never admitted it even to herself.

"Agnes, I have even gladder tidings. Do you remember Ann Harris?"

"Of course I do, Miss Pyn. She was such a darlin' girl when she lived in Seven Oaks. She helped you in the library, did she not? She must be a grand young woman by now."

"She is indeed, and she will be given appointment as my assistant next month. So you need not worry about the library in my absence. Now you must keep two secrets -- my destination and Ann's appointment. At least until I am gone and Ann is here -- promise?"

"Glorybe, Ann as your assistant! What a blessing for us, for you, and mostly for Ann. Workin' with you she's bound to grow into a generous refined lady much like you. I surely will not say a word, not even to Ann's mum, though 'twill be hard, you know! I do like sayin' things to folks."

"Keeping a secret can be rewarding too. Do enjoy this weekend, Agnes!"

"Goodbye, Miss Pyn and I'll be enjoyin' it, to be sure."

At teatime, Miss Pyn remembered that she had deserted Mr. Twining at breakfast. At the risk of feeling only a trifle guilty, she thought she might continue her daring abandon, and again sample Major Dashwood's Darjeeling Tea to see if it was truly better at afternoon tea than at morning tea.

As she sipped her properly poured cup of Darjeeling, she remembered the time she had discovered Major Dashwood. It was in Philadelphia at the library conference. She remembered her friend Harriet Clippings expostulating at teatime.

"It is my carefully considered opinion," Miss Clippings went on with the studied precision of one of her characteristically extended sentences, "predicated on years of wide and consistent experience, that Major Dashwood's Particular Teas of Superior Quality afford the very best Darjeeling Tea."

Miss Pyn had truly enjoyed her tea and the teacakes as well with Miss Clippings, but the cakes were not nearly as good as those Agnes saved for her.

Later, when she took an afternoon away from the Philadelphia Conference and rambled about the shops in the fine old suburb of Jenkintown, she found Major Dashwood in the tiny British Specialty Shop located on an equally tiny street that resembled a back alleyway for shops in an ancient city. Miss Pyn could imagine that she was in a medieval town, maybe the old city of London where some streets, she had read, were too narrow to accommodate even medium-sized trucks, or "lorries." This street was not quite that narrow, but it was so irregular that it seemed very narrow. The large American automobiles crowding onto the street that zigged and zagged and then zigged again gave her all the impression she needed to be able to pretend she was in a very old and revered place.

The shop's tiny door and the single step down into its interior served only to heighten Miss Pyn's feeling of reverence. "Surely," she thought, "I must be a latter-day Alice entering a land of promise and new wonder."

In truth, the shop was at once a gastronomic delight and a veritable archetype of culinary chaos. There were packages everywhere: on shelves and on tables, on counters and on stools, even on the floor under tables and stools. Packages abounded on windowsills and on the floor, pushing each other to the outer edges of the room, pressing hard against the walls.

Boxes and tins atop boxes and tins littered the shopscape. Shelves against walls, and on tables as well, were stacked high with little tins and with big tins -- some red, some green, and some in several hues of blue. There were tiny boxes, and big boxes, and even medium-sized boxes of every color and every shape.

There were jars and crocks and pots and glasses of various and peculiar design filled to the very tops brimful with jams and jellies and cheeses; some jars even had cakes -- sweet, moist, and liqueur-laced -- baked inside them. Packets of tea-bag samplers and ten-pound tins of tea with exotic if familiar names -- Eastern teas blended according to the oldest, most secret, long treasured, and scrupulously guarded ancient English formulae -- stood in formation like colonial lancers ready to assault formidable citadels of taste.

Simultaneously, aroma and appearance alerted Miss Pyn to the refrigerated cheese tables which were strewn with the very best European cheeses from Greece and Albania, Ireland and Italy, England, France,

Norway and Germany, Switzerland, The Netherlands, Austria, Denmark and Luxembourg, Sweden, Spain, Hungary and Montenegro crowded together hugging each other, vying for space.

Miss Pyn observed a distinguished French Brie, elegant and rich, an aristocrat of pre-revolutionary lineage. "Ah! I see I shall have to make my puff pastry. Perhaps Harriet could be persuaded to visit me one day soon and I should serve her some. No ... on second thought, Miss Harriet Clippings is not at all the puff pastry type, definitely not. I suspect for a starter -- oh my, for an appetizer -- she would like an asparagus tip, tiny and blanched pure white, and marinated in a fine though low caloric French-Italian marinade with just the subtlest suggestion of tarragon or perhaps a light raspberry served on leaf lettuce edged with crisp delicate tiny spinach leaves -- but definitely not puff pastry. For that, I shall have to think of someone else, someone less committed to a healthful and virtuous diet.

"Now there," thought Miss Pyn, "just there, alongside that pert and superior Danish Blue cheese is a grand-looking Bavarian Blue -- majestic even, solid but creamy yet sturdy, an excellent triple-cream specimen exuding that celebrated German self-sufficiency. My word, it is rather like an *Oktoberfest* and a *Fasching* in a single five-kilo round. I should have to devise something extraordinary for such a truly impressive cheese."

There were so many cheeses that Miss Pyn easily could have devoted the entire afternoon to their examination. As always, there were old *Parmesans* and hard *Romanos;* a true Blarney; a piquant *Asiago*, a very worthy *Jarlsberg* of the first order -- ten pounds of nutlike flavor in just one round; unmistakable red-wax-covered *Edams* and *Goudas*; a blue-veined *Gorgonzola;* a smoky *Caciocavallo;* a fully aromatic Limburger rivaled by a robust *Liederkranz* and a memorable *Port Salute* from a renowned Trappist monastery; a sharp crumbly Cheshire; two soft salty *Fetas*; a genuine French *Roquefort* speckled with distinctive blue-green veins; a marvelously pungent *Tilsiter* requiring careful wrapping for public transport; and an equally pungent and wonderfully flavored *Sapsago.*

"The inviting light green color of that *Sapsago*," Miss Pyn thought, "is absolutely correct for a perfect pasta salad with minced shallot, red sweet bell peppers, and just a sprinkle of chervil."

There were others too, even an unexpected Wensleydale and real English Cheddars from Somerset. "Oh how very nice!"

Near the authentic Cheddars was a cheese Miss Pyn found puzzling – a white sharp New York Cheddar from Wisconsin. "How very odd."

Tucked in a corner was a surprise: a veritable cadenza of cream of the finest, richest, and sweetest triple cream from deep in the remote clover-dusted hills of Piedmont and Lombardy -- a magnificent *Dolce Latta* waiting to be scooped up by an avid aficionado to be tasted and savored bit by bit for days and days. "How on earth could such a delicate cheese get here? Silly, there have been daily flights from Italy for years. And look, there is a notice promising the arrival of the best winter *Mascherponre* directly from Lombardy. Air Italia is going to be very busy this season."

It was then she saw it, the crowning glory of the cheese horde, a beautiful genuine Stilton prominently displayed with regal dignity worthy of the special treasure Miss Pyn knew it was. She decided that this shop was one she liked ... very much. Then just near the Stilton cheese she noticed a sign, small and hand-lettered, quietly proclaiming that Devon clotted cream could be had by special order air-shipped directly from Devonshire for the holidays.

"How nice it would be to live close by here and be able to order real clotted cream for the holidays. How very nice it would be to be able to share such goodness with someone at Christmas."

Miss Pyn smiled a greeting to the shopkeeper, a handsome woman -- striking even, tall and very trim with just a touch of gray in her hair -- a woman who would be noticed always, and who looked especially at ease and at home in the shop. She seemed to Miss Pyn to be so much a part of the shop that there would have been a dreadful emptiness here if this woman were not present. There was no doubt she belonged here and brought order to the shop, perhaps precisely because her very presence created an indisputable and evident contrast to the chaos of the place.

As she continued to study the cheese, Miss Pyn noticed that the shopkeeper was serving another patron, a young woman selecting a few teas and jellies and looking for "a gift. It will have to be very special because it's for my ... er ... friend."

"No, no, my dear!" the shopkeeper exclaimed. "You don't want that one. It's far too expensive and rather sweet as well. It is for a young man, I take it. If it isn't, it ought to be -- it ought to be for your young man."

The young woman blushed her answer.

"Well then, let me recommend this collection of miniature Liqueur Cakes. I have these in for the holidays. They are one of few domestic items I stock because they are every bit as good as my finest imported delicacies. I will guarantee that he will be pleased and then you will be pleased because he will be pleased; and furthermore, the price is ever so much better. Let me see now, I shall total your purchases."

Miss Pyn, pretending to study the cheese, looked about for a cash register or a calculator or even an old adding machine. None was in sight; she was delighted. She found here a kindred spirit, one who would let no mechanism addle the brain.

The shopkeeper found a writing tablet, the kind that Miss Pyn remembered from her school days. Pulling a pencil from her hair, the shopkeeper began to list each purchase and each price separately one by one on a page of the writing tablet. This lady was all that Miss Pyn could hope for. She was her ideal of a shopkeeper, nothing frightfully modern about her. She undoubtedly knew her arithmetic and clearly delighted in serving her young customer.

She finished her calculations and then handed the tablet to the young patron. "You had best check my sums to be sure they are correct. You've been to school ever so much more recently than I have, my dear."

The young woman, surprised but pleased, reviewed the figures, nodding agreement. Then the shopkeeper reviewed them yet another time.

"That's right, twenty-one dollars and eighteen cents. Never mind the eighteen cents, my dear. You can remember to add them to the reckoning the next time you are in. Do come again soon. And bring that young man with you, do you hear? You know, I would very much like to meet a fellow who has the extraordinary luck and good fortune to have such a lovely and pretty young friend as you are. He must be very handsome as well as very lucky. Cheers, my dear."

The pink of the young woman's prim suit was indistinguishable from that of her face as she quickly slipped out of the shop, earnestly if unsuccessfully trying to hide a grand satisfied smile.

Miss Pyn thought of that young woman often. She wondered if it was possible for such a young person to know and understand or even to grasp the degree of happiness she radiated just then. Could her happiness endure? Did her "friend" continue to be her friend, perhaps even for life? Would it be, or has it been their happiness, always?

"Oh my, I must not let these thoughts delay my preparations, however intriguing they are. Though I may not learn their answers they are interesting --more interesting, surely, than tidying the tea things. Tomorrow and next week will be here soon enough -- perhaps not soon enough to please me, but too soon to do all that I must do before I leave."

Saturday morning as she gathered her wardrobe for her journey, Miss Pyn so vividly remembered the lovely young purchaser all in pink in the tea shop in Jenkintown that she thought she herself could have been there once more exploring the shop. She recalled that she had asked the lady in the shop, "How many varieties of cheese are there?"

The shopkeeper replied cheerfully, "There are many. I try to have at least fifty varieties on hand. There are even varieties within kinds of cheese. Take for example, the Cheddars. There is the original Cheddar from England. There are also Cheddars from Canada, Vermont, New York, and Wisconsin. All of those places produce mild, medium, and sharp varieties."

Miss Pyn turned from the cheese. There were biscuits and sweets galore. Digestive biscuits and tea biscuits and English water biscuits of various persuasions were stacked in a kind of wall defending the sweets as if they in turn needed protection. High up on a shelf, as though overseeing the logistics of a military field, original Irish oat cakes stood like sentinels from an expeditionary peace-keeping force from County Wicklow.

The sweets were legion -- jams, jellies, and marmalades made with real Seville oranges, Dundee Marmalade from Scotland and Classic Oxford Coarse Cut right from the High Street at number 84 in Oxford, Oxfordshire. Miss Pyn imagined that she could taste the tingling bite of the bittersweet orange just by studying the labels on the colorful jars. "That taste," she thought, "is so much more like life than anything sweet."

There were other sweets too, proper sweets -- Roundtree Christmas candies from the candy makers in Yorkshire next to taffies, fudges, and marzipans. Best of all, there was Kendal Mint Cake fresh and pure white with perhaps only an imagined hint of very light and delicate green suggesting its mint flavor -- a cake so wonderful and so absolutely delicious that without a doubt it could not be other than at least sinful, no matter which theological persuasion the indulgent eater held.

On a preserves shelf, Miss Pyn found a treasure, a gem, a sparkling red gem from Tiptree. Messers Wilkin and Sons Limited produced this gem -- Little Scarlet Strawberry Preserves, made in England since 1885 under appointment to Her Majesty the Queen and made with none other than tiny luscious scarlet strawberries grown only on The Tiptree Farms. "Why, these must be Alpine berries," she thought. "These tiny berries produce at least as much patience in the grower as fruit for the harvest. What a wonderful discovery! I suspect Harriet would be jealous ... very."

However hard she tried, she could not resist the purchase. Besides, "Harriet will be jealous. She will be so envious when she remembers that she stayed at the conference in order to listen to that professional paper on 'Current and Contemporary, Computerized and Innovative Cataloging' instead of coming with me. I could, of course, buy a jar of the preserves for Miss Clippings -- she is very fond of strawberries. No! That would diminish my triumph. I will just show her my purchase in secret glee and say with a most superior air, 'After all, Harriet, I did invite you to join me.' Then, I will send a jar to her at Christmas."

Miss Pyn turned her attention once more to the tea section. It was a wonder-world. She could not believe, certainly could not even imagine that there were so many different teas. The Twinings Tea section alone was enormous -- Twinings Tea in a myriad of blends. An entire wall of the shop was reserved for Twinings finest teas, row upon row stacked all the way to the high ceiling. There were English Breakfast and Orange Pekoe Teas, Darjeeling and Lemon-Scented Teas, and the great favorite blended especially for the second Earl Grey by Thomas Twining himself and now universally acclaimed with the name of His Lordship.

Irish Breakfast Teas were flanked by Black China on one side and China Oolong on the other; Gunpowder Black came next pursued by Gentle Jasmine in a teashop version of *War and Peace*.

"Why, it would take months and months to sample all these teas properly. I should have to be very earnest in such a project. Of course, tea drinking is important and very special. I could plan carefully. I suppose it could be managed if one persevered."

A bright yellow box attracted Miss Pyn -- a bright yellow square box -- no, rectangular and yellow ... a package of decaffeinated tea stuffed in a yellow box and labeled Earl Grey.

"How could this be? Would Lord Grey, could Lord Grey even in a most unguarded moment approve of tampered tea ... in a yellow box to boot; and, with his picture on it?"

She noticed that the tea came from Italy. "Oh well, I am certain that Lord Grey would be relieved to learn that the tea came from Italy, for most probably he and his ancestors would have been accustomed to expect such oddity from Italy. I suspect they would be not at all surprised that something so strange originated in the land of the *Borgias* and City States. They would be relieved to discover that it had not come from the shop in London's Strand where Twinings Teas have been blended and sold since the eighteenth century."

Miss Pyn, however, did not share what she imagined would have been Lord Grey's attitude toward Italy and things Italian. She had long wished, even planned to buy an Italian automobile, "very soon." For many years now it had always been -- very soon.

It was then she saw it! She saw what she did not expect to see, what she did not even hope to see, ever. Tucked in an unobtrusive corner of an unobtrusive shelf was an unobtrusive stack of Harriet's favorite -- Major Dashwood's Darjeeling Tea.

"Oh my!" As soon as she spotted Major Dashwood on the shelf, Miss Pyn looked about, furtively -- much like an apprentice shoplifter might look intent on seeing that no one was watching -- and, with the calculated and quick move of a lithe and splendid carnivore striking its prey, she pounced on a packet of tea. She felt her ears burning ... her forehead, her cheeks, her chin, even her nose burning as she purchased the tea, fully convinced that she must look every bit like a very nervous would-be felon must look because her two-tiered guilt just had to be obvious all over her face -- two-tiered for having abandoned, however temporarily, both Mister Twining and the librarians' conference.

"Oh my!" thought Miss Pyn when she realized she was not in the tea shop in Jenkintown, but in Seven Oaks supposedly packing for her journey. "How can I choose and pack all that I shall need for nearly a whole month in England?"

Then she remembered that her friend Carole long ago had sent her serious advice about travel to Europe. "Remember, P, travel in Europe is not as easy as it is at home. I've learned through sad experience. Believe me. Gather up the things you think you'll need during your stay. Be sure you limit your things to those that you know are most essential. Pack your bags several days before you leave and walk at least one mile with bags in hand. That way you'll learn how much stamina you'll need, and you'll probably decide that you'll be able to do without some of your 'essentials.' As for money for your travel, collect all that you possibly can gather and expect to need more, for you will."

Later at tea, her packing nearly complete, Miss Pyn thought, "Oh, how I would dearly love to be able to meet Carole and Brad in Stratford when I arrive there. They were so genuinely happy when they sent that precious teapot from England. I do wonder how happy the lives of these two fine artists might have been ... I wonder too about the young woman in pink in the shop, exuding such spirited happiness. Did I, or ... could I ever have appeared so very happy?"

Sunday morning was glorious! "The sun," mused Miss Pyn, "should always shine on Sunday, even in dreary winter. After all, the day is named for the sun." Miss Pyn was on her way home from an early liturgical celebration. Everything was quiet. Except for the members of an uncommonly small congregation, few folks had stirred. There was just a hint of a cool breeze to temper the warmth of the bright sun. Here and there jubilant birds were serenading each other from treetops.

"This day," thought Miss Pyn, "is certainly worth singing about. No wonder Francis of Assisi was so fond of birds. Birds proclaim the glory of the world. In truth, they sound much more joyous and spirited in their praise of creation in song than did the members of our congregation this morning -- especially after that dismal homily denouncing human frailty. Surely, the homily of the birds touches much more deeply those who will only listen."

When she returned to her flat, she remembered that it was the last Sunday she would be able to enjoy her wonderful balcony before she left for England. On such an occasion, there could be little doubt whose tea she would prepare. First the hot water to warm the forget-me-not pot, then Mister Twining's best tea, then the tea water and then, the *piece de resistance* -- the cake -- and all was in readiness for an excellent morning tea respite.

Comfortably situated in her chair next to the tea table, Miss Pyn wondered again, "Am I really going to get to England? But I shall miss these quiet Sundays. They are so peaceful, so restorative."

She turned on her little radio. The Sunday morning programs tended to feature semi-classical music -- serious music to be sure, but music written for musical show productions and lighter operas. She tested her tea gingerly as she heard a favorite melody. It was "Memories," from the show, *CATS*, suggested by the work of the poet T. S. Eliot.

"Ah me, what beauty we are privileged to meet over and over again, and often in unexpected circumstances. That music contains the beauty of the word and the beauty of melody woven together."

The song continued, and at the place Miss Pyn found most familiar, she even recalled the words: "I remember the time I knew what happiness was ..."

She remembered that time very well, even though it was so very many years before. Her roommate, Carole, had just returned from her life-drawing class ...

"Carole! Michael has invited me to the prom!"

"It's about time. You two have been engaging each other in intellectual, sometimes esoteric discussions all term long. You'd think the two of you were preparing to go to an Institute for Advanced Medieval Philosophical Study as soon as you graduate, and you haven't even finished your first year here. I say it's about time you got real."

"Do you think I can go? Should I accept?"

"Are you nutty? Of course you should go. You must. Haven't you hoped for this all term? I'd say it's an answer to prayer ... mine if not yours."

"'Hoping and praying' are rather extravagant terms, but I must admit I thought that an invitation to the prom would be most pleasing and, I confess, I rather looked forward to the possibility even though I thought it rather remote. We are, after all, only freshmen; and he is a junior. Do you think I could be sophisticated enough for his friends?"

"Oh my dear, you'll run circles around his friends. Why, you have forgotten more than most of them will ever know. How many languages do you know already?"

"Never mind that. How will I fit in socially? I do not wish to be 'the resident intellectual.' On second thought,

58

I can dance and sing and laugh and enjoy the world and every moment to the fullest dimension. So there!"

"I know that, and I suspect Michael knows that; and as for the others, do they really matter?"

"You are probably correct, but what shall I wear?"

"Of course I'm right. So now the real woman emerges from behind her philosophical conundrums! I'm supposed to be the impractical artist, but you with your run-on speculations make me look like the most down-to-earth practical pragmatist that ever lived. 'What shall I wear,' she says. I know just the thing. You'll need a prom gown. First we begin with the color."

"With a color? I do not have an appropriate dress, let alone a gown."

"Yes, with the color. Remember, I'm the artist. Color is most important. I see you in cerulean. Yes, that's it -- a bright yet soft cerulean."

"I think that you are showing off your superior artistic knowledge. Pray tell, what is cerulean?"

"Well, I ought to get some benefit from all the tuition and fees I pay at this institution. Cerulean is blue. It's a splendid blue like the morning sky on a clear day. Believe me, P, it's your color. It's bright but it's subdued. Just like you ... sometimes."

"I shall overlook your smart remark. Color cannot exist by itself. It must either adhere to or be inherent in something."

"There you go again! Must you always pursue metaphysical implications? Of course the color will adhere to or be part of your dress. You idiot!"

"That may be well and good, but I have no suitable dress nor the means with which to secure one."

"Do you have any money at all? I know just the place that should have what you call 'a suitable dress' for you."

"I have only ten dollars. I cannot ask for more help from home, especially so near the end of term. I certainly cannot purchase a dress, suitable or not, for ten dollars."

"Of course not, but I have a plan. Remember Brad Stockwell, who is at architectural school in the East? Brad has hinted that he will invite me to his junior prom; it's a week later than our prom. So we could both invest in the same dress and no one would be the wiser. We're close enough in size so that only an expert could tell that the dress was not tailored especially for each of us."

"How could we do so? Surely we cannot purchase a correct prom gown for even twenty dollars."

"True, but I have my own twenty dollars. I've seen a dress in your color that should do nicely for thirty dollars. You could buy one third of the dress and I could own two thirds for the time being. Later, when you find five extra dollars, we could both have a half interest in a prom gown. Isn't that a good plan? Neither one of us could own a whole gown at the moment."

"That is certainly a practical pragmatic solution. But what of the color? You have said color is the primary consideration. Is cerulean your color too?"

"Sometimes it is. At other times my best color is cerise, but I'm certainly not going to Brad's prom as the scarlet woman from the Midwest. The blue will go very well -- so well that I wouldn't be surprised if someone might think either one of us could've inspired 'Alice Blue Gown.'"

Miss Pyn, once again on her balcony, smiled to remember the "corporation" those two first-year college students created, engaged as they were in an investment scheme to acquire a single prom dress. They would each attend their respective proms in glamorous raiments. No one would be the wiser!

The peaceful quiet on this bright Sunday afternoon in Seven Oaks was remarkable. The peaceful quiet at Miss Pyn's balcony was, if possible, even more remarkable. The old Puritan responsibility-conditioning once again made its appearance. "With so much to do in preparation for my journey before week's end, I really should not just sit here enjoying this beautiful afternoon. But Sunday was made for restful reflection. There will be time enough for mundane things. Besides, my bags are already packed. Oh, but I have not walked the mile Carole advised in her letter. I know -- I shall carry my luggage to the library one morning. The walk is not quite a mile, but it is generally uphill. That should serve the conditioning purpose.

"So I can remain here enjoying the beauty of the day and my colorful birds as they fly to and from the feeding station, and I shall remember beautiful times as well. Later on, I shall have high tea. That should be excellent and delightful preparation for my journey."

So she relaxed, remembering that beautiful prom night ... "Carole, our dress seems to fit well. Is the color just right? It seems so strange that I am concerned about my appearance, but I do wish to please Michael."

"As I've told you again and again, the color is perfect. Michael will be pleased -- very. If he isn't, I'd say he must be blind."

"I feel so inept, especially with his sophisticated classmates."

"I've told you before, they don't matter. Besides, if you think that you're socially inept, you two are a perfect couple. No one would say that the brilliant Michael is remarkable for his social 'eptness'. You'll do well together. Maybe one day I'll succeed in convincing you that you are a beautiful lady. It's no sin to recognize that you are beautiful when you are. That's true humility. It might be false pride to pretend you're beautiful when you're not. Now there I go! You'd think I was trying to outdo both you and Michael with my homemade ethical distinctions.

"Just remember tonight and every night that you are a beautiful lady. Be sure to take good care of our dress! Remember that I'll be wearing it next week. And I have another reason for taking special care of our joint investment."

Carole's eyes sparkled with glee. Her satisfied facial expression bespoke other plans -- perhaps mysterious other plans.

"Of course," Miss Pyn assured her, "I shall be very careful with our investment. By the way, when Michael comes he might call me 'Needles.' He says, I think playfully, that 'Needles' best befits me because my mind is much more incisive than an ordinary pin suggests. Never mind that 'Pyn' is not ordinary! Nonetheless, we ought to humor him. One thing more. What exactly do you have in mind as future plans for our dress?"

"I want to paint you in our dress. Maybe then, every few years, I hope to paint you again and again in this and perhaps other costumes. I see the paintings as a study in maturing beauty. Why, my series of studies of 'The Mysterious Beautiful Lady in Blue' will eventually make us both famous."

"I wish to be neither famous nor infamous. I wish only that Michael and I have an enjoyable evening."

"You both will if you remember that you are beautiful and that he will be very proud of his date. Now let's do a final check. Turn around… Nice! Next, your hair…You are blessed. It never needs anything. It's naturally curly and its color is wonderful. Your shoes… face… nails… All in order! Now take a deep breath; he will be here soon."

The birds on Miss Pyn's balcony were not only colorful, just then they were feisty and noisy as they vied for places on the feeding stations. "Such pretty birds ought to be polite and considerate, since I always see that there is enough for all of them. I suppose they must act on instinct."

The interruption of her reminiscences was not unwelcome. She thought she should see if teatime was approaching. "Though it is rather early, and I am not really hungry." She listened to the music that came from her radio. "How perfect – Strauss ... the perfect reminder of all one's dances."

Michael had arrived punctually, a corsage of yellow roses in hand. He was more than a dream in summer formal wear, a handsome young gentleman. He explained, "Some of my classmates had a formal induction last night into the honor society. Most of them are going to the prom. But since my buddy, Stash, has no date, he loaned me his rented tux."

Carole had to step on Miss Pyn's toe to prevent her from explaining her borrowed dress when she began, "What a coincidence! My costume is also ..."

"... perfect for summer wear, as is your tuxedo," Carole finished.

They went off to the prom. It was not a formal ball, but for those young college students it might just as well have been. The music was well played. It was their music -- not exactly music that would have pleased their parents, but it was melodious. Mixed among a number of informal contemporary dances were a number of traditional musical selections that all of their elders would have recognized and that, in the end, helped

65

make the dance "formal," and justified the formal attire that all of the ladies and many of the gentlemen wore.

The evening was short, and Miss Pyn demonstrated that she certainly could participate in and thoroughly enjoy the excitement of the moment. They danced every dance, contemporary as well as traditional. Michael's twin, Michelle, had taught him to waltz. When Michael and Miss Pyn began to waltz they became an exquisite pair, dancing so beautifully that others stopped to watch them. They were so stunning that orchestra members joined in applauding their dance and added more waltzes to the program.

Later, Miss Pyn even showed Michael how to dance a polka. And she promised, if the orchestra obliged, she would demonstrate a mazurka as well. Michael was the envy of his classmates.

"Goodnight Sweetheart" came all too soon.

Still full of youthful energy, the jubilant couples led by Michael and Miss Pyn trooped to The Village Restaurant, a Cantonese establishment serving enormous meals at that early morning hour. They all partook, amid riotous laughter, of food that could only be described as delectable, and they ate ravenously. Then it was time to say farewell.

Michael and Miss Pyn walked along the river-walk in the direction of the residence halls. Miss Pyn was the first to speak: "Is it not a beautiful night? Has it not been a marvelous evening?"

Michael agreed. "I couldn't imagine that we could ever have so much joyous fun together. I thank you for being my perfect date."

If she blushed, it was not apparent, even though the bright moonlight shone on their faces and on the stones of the path they followed.

Suddenly, Michael hesitated. "Like everything else this evening, the moonlight on the river is flawless. Could we sit on the bench over there to rest a few moments and contemplate the moving water -- and maybe its significance for us as well? I wish this perfect evening wouldn't have to end so soon."

Miss Pyn was not entirely certain that Michael had only philosophical inquiry in mind, but she agreed because she too was reluctant to see the evening come to a close. "Of course, a brief respite would be most welcome. We will be able to implant in our memories the wonder of this evening and the grandeur of this night."

They sat watching the moonlight on the river water for some minutes. Then Michael observed, "The gentle movement of water, the source of much life, is endless, calling to mind immutable rhythms."

"Yes," Miss Pyn murmured. "The soft light from the moon imparts an eerie celestial aura to the eternal movement."

"You know, Needles, I'm indebted both to you and to my friend, Stash Nowicki, for the marvelous success of this evening."

"Why is that?"

"To you, of course, for all your grace on the dance floor. And you are, after all, a beautiful lady. Many of the women looked downright jealous of you! And Stash, as you know, has so much experience and social grace that he is apparently at ease in every situation. He not only loaned me this formal evening outfit, he coached me with pointers of behavior so that I wouldn't be socially inept this evening."

"First of all," replied Miss Pyn with a smile, "the other girls must have been jealous of me because of my handsome escort. On the other hand, why are you so indebted to Stash? You say he coached you. As if you needed any coaching! How did he 'coach' you?"

Michael moved just a little closer. "Well, he said to me, 'After you've danced through a grand evening and settled in soft moonlight, you should offer your girl a gentle invitation by saying *Daj mi buzi*.[1] She won't know what you mean. She'll look puzzled, and she might even

---

[1] Give me a kiss.

force a smile -- that's your cue to demonstrate the meaning of your invitation.' You see?" Michael's eager explanation faded. "Only you don't look puzzled at all, and you're frowning as well."

"Of course I am frowning!" Miss Pyn rose abruptly. "And of course I am not puzzled! I know the meaning of your 'invitation'! Did you not know that I have studied Eastern European culture and languages? Why do you suppose I know all of those Polish dances?" She shook a scolding finger at the subdued Michael. "Furthermore, you should tell your friend that his Polish expression is not a gentle invitation at all. It is a demand! A country girl might find such a demand inviting -- especially if she, as might be said, 'had an eye' for the lad. But a university student -- even a first-year university student -- might very well be offended by your 'invitation,' and expect something much more refined."

"Are you unhappy with me, Needles?" Michael grasped Miss Pyn's hand and gently pulled her down on the bench beside him.

Miss Pyn tried, without success, to look completely unflustered. "Of course not! However, if your friend is going to give you social conduct advice, it at least ought to be accurate. Otherwise, you might run the not inconsiderable risk of getting your handsome Celtic face slapped."

"I'm sorry. What can I do?"

"First, do not rush." Miss Pyn avoided Michael's pleading eyes and assumed a professorial manner. "If you wish to use a romance language, then French, Italian or Spanish would be very good, but Polish would do nicely. For example, *Ja cie kocham*.[2] That expression of your feeling delivered gently will usually be most effective. It means ... it means, 'I ... I love you.'" Though her voice had softened as she almost whispered that translation, she resumed her instruction. "If ... If that expression is happily received, then you could request a kiss in a refined gentlemanly manner, and definitely not in a manner that a director might use in calling for a boisterous line in a farce. You could say instead, *Ja cie kocham*."

"I see, Needles," replied the penitent. "*Ja cie ko* ... what did you say?"

"There you are -- rushing again!" Once more Miss Pyn rose abruptly, and with her back to Michael, continued, perhaps only to convince herself: "All of this romantic talk is utterly premature. It is talk that is best left to people who are convinced or at least nearly convinced that they want to live the rest of their lives

---

[2] I love you.

70

together -- people willing to accept solemnly a vow -- to promise their troth forever." She turned to Michael with her own solemn but wistful look. "We are not ready for that, Michael, not yet at any rate."

"Can't you give me some hope, Needles?"

"Oh, Michael, we must not confuse hope with presumption! We must wait for some time yet. I have at least three years of undergraduate study to complete before I shall be able to consider my life's path. I need to grow, and all of that should come before I, and possibly you as well, could even begin to decide which direction to pursue."

"I know that, Needles! I also know that I'm willing right now to pledge a lifetime commitment to you because, *Ja cie* ... oh nuts! I think I love you deeply."

The only response was the sound of the rippling waters of the moonlit river, and then a sigh. Finally, Miss Pyn spoke with resolve, "Michael, I trust that our lifetimes will be very long, and so we will have to be sure -- very sure -- before making a pledge that will oblige us for a very long time. I do believe that I will one day join in a commitment with you for life -- for all eternity!" She grasped his hand, almost pleading, "I am not able to be certain yet, nor can you be sure. Three years, no matter how we feel tonight, is a very long time. I do hope, and I shall pray, that we will feel the same hope for happiness then as we feel tonight."

"My dear Needles, once again, you are probably right -- except for one thing." He turned his head slowly to gaze at the river water flowing, it seemed endlessly, into the moonlit distance. "It will not be for only three years. It will be at least four years. I have volunteered for military service. I leave on Wednesday."

Miss Pyn was clearly stunned. After some minutes she whispered, "Why, Michael? Why?"

"There are many reasons, my dear. Perhaps the first is that I'm a coward, I guess. I couldn't shoot at or kill anyone or anything. Why, I can't even kill a spider if I have any way of pushing it outside."

Miss Pyn smiled at this confession. "Michael, do you not have a college deferment for military service?"

"Yes, I do. I wrote the national placement test and, if I may say so, I did very well on it."

"Of course you would do so!" He laughed to hear the pride in her voice. "So why must you interrupt your study at this time?"

"There are other reasons. It's really time I should begin paying my own way. In our family, there was never any question that I, rather than my twin Michelle, should be the first to go to college, even though she is ten minutes older than I! She wants to be a teacher; I know that she will be a very fine teacher. God alone knows how often and how well she taught me -- particularly during our early years when I had difficulty understanding my lessons, especially English and arithmetic.

"Michelle took a job as a receptionist for our dentist. We knew our folks couldn't support both of us at the university. I can now earn enough, and possibly get G.I. assistance to finish my study when I come home from Korea."

The frown on Miss Pyn's face betrayed her anxiety. "Can you not complete your study here?"

"I might be able to finish my study here, but there still would be the question of my year of internship." Michael's voice took on a new urgency as he took both her hands in his. "I could be drafted next year. Even if my deferment were to continue, I'd still face the draft. Some of my classmates have talked of leaving the country for the duration of the war. I have neither relatives overseas nor other means to leave. Besides, I'm not sure I could abandon my country."

"Is there nothing you can do?"

"The recruiting officer tells me that if I were to volunteer now, I'd have a good chance of choosing the job I'd like to have in service. That way I could avoid deadly combat -- combat I could never engage in."

"Michael, are you certain? I fear for you -- for us!"

"I see no other way." They both gazed silently for some minutes at the soft moonlit waves. Then Michael turned to her with a brisk smile. "So, my dear Needles, I'd like to ask you for a date. In just two years, you'll have your junior prom and, God willing, I shall return -- not the conquering hero -- but at least, I hope, your hero. Would you consider attending your junior prom in your wonderful blue gown with me as your dancing partner?"

"There is no way I could attend the dance with anyone but you, Michael, and under no circumstances could I ever wear any other gown to that ball."

"It's a date then?"

"What a beautiful smile my Irish Michael has," thought Miss Pyn. Then, almost to reprimand herself for such presumption, she urged, "Oh, Michael, let us not waste this beautiful evening worrying about the days that have yet to come. Since we have only a little time left, could we think about things that are most likely to endure? Where shall we begin?"

Michael was as eager as she to share delight in the beauty around them. "How about this river? Tonight it's very special, with the moon shining on the water. We might say that it is a moon-river."

And Miss Pyn, always the serious student, replied, "Your name for the river is very lovely, but I suspect that it is not really precise English usage. 'River of moonlight' is probably more precisely correct, but I think your expression touches the ear more readily even though it leaves something to be desired in the realm of syntax and usage."

"I too thought it a very fine description," replied Michael with a bemused grin, "but you're probably quite right."

Miss Pyn was ready to explore other possibilities. "I have a question for you, dear friend. Could there exist a moon rainbow?"

"Do you mean," was Michael's earnest response, "that the light of the moon passing through water droplets could produce refractive light in colors on an object opposite the source of the light?"

"Yes, I think that is what I mean."

"Why, Needles, I think that's quite possible if the water mist caught the light rays and refracted them."

"Then," Miss Pyn pronounced triumphantly, " We would have a rainbow-river!"

But Michael, eager to continue the debate, cautioned, "Perhaps. But wait a minute. You just dismissed the term 'moon-river' as unacceptable. Why would you allow 'rainbow-river'?"

Miss Pyn retaliated, "The moonlight on the river is not caused by the river, but the rainbow is, at least in part, caused by the river mist rising through the moonlight. It is simply a matter of causality -- not so?"

And Michael, delighting in their repartee, declared, "Maybe we'd have to say it's a 'rainbow-moon-river.' In Ireland, at Tralee there's said to be a pure crystal fountain shining in moonlight. This light on the river is crystal-like. Could it be our 'crystal-river'?"

Miss Pyn contemplated this for a few moments, and then with a triumphant smile, replied, "Yes! We could call it whatever we liked!"

"I agree. But listen to us, Needles! Here we are in awesome moonlight on a wonderfully romantic after-the-ball delightful evening on a superbly beautiful river walk, and what do we do? We discuss philosophical causality and linguistics. What a funny pair we are!"

They started to laugh, with vigorous boisterous laughter -- the very hardy, hilarious and explosive jubilant laughter usually associated with more youthful practitioners of mirth. And each secretly hoped that their laughter would be adequate antidote for the mounting anxiety each felt for the future.

They began to walk hand-in-hand along the walkway -- sometimes skipping, sometimes running, occasionally dancing in the bright moonlight – still, always laughing. They might have gone on that way, walking and skipping and dancing and laughing for a very long time, had not an inconsiderate cloud wiped away their moonlight ...

Once again on her balcony, Miss Pyn became aware of the lengthening evening shadows and the approaching darkness. A very familiar song came from her radio, once again recalling that night in the moonlight when she debated with Michael about a title for their special river.

"That night was," she thought, "fully ten years before that lovely young actress named Hepburn first sang 'Moon River' in the film, *Breakfast at Tiffany's*."

The song continued, and Miss Pyn again remembered -- this time aloud. "I remember, Michael, that night in the moonlight. You told me of your love in so many ways! I remember you said, 'Tis a darlin' evening, a darlin' evening, *mavourneen*.'

"And I replied, 'Yes! So hurry home to me, my dear one.' Oh, Michael, how I wish I had added, *Ja cie kocham, moja droga. Dai mi buzi*![3]"

The evening star was already visible in the eastern sky when Miss Pyn realized where she was, and how rapidly time had passed. She thought, "Even

---

[3] I love you, my dearest Kiss me!

77

though it is too late for high tea, I must eat something, for tomorrow is a library day."

As always, Miss Pyn was up with the sun on Monday morning. "What a glorious day for the first day of the last week before I leave for England!"

She knew she would have to hurry this morning because there remained so very much to do before she could feel comfortable leaving the library. She hurried through her morning reflections and prayers, feeling a bit guilty. She assuaged her guilt by adding, "And bless Ann Harris coming early to her first assignment. Ann will do well at the library in my absence, and she will do well elsewhere too."

This morning, Miss Pyn would follow Carole's instructions and carry fully packed luggage for a mile in preparation for the journey. She thought, "It is not exactly one mile, but it is uphill most of the way."

She gathered her lunch-case and her brollie, and only then remembered that she had two fully loaded suitcases. "What shall I do? Am I able to carry all of this through my door, yet alone to the library? Perhaps I should ask Beth to stay a little longer at lunchtime so I could return home for lunch and carry the luggage back with me."

Dismissing that plan with a sigh, she set off, suitcases in hand, in the direction of the library. As the incline up library hill began, her walking became trudging. Miss Pyn, usually extraordinarily fit, began to show signs of fatigue. She even debated with herself: "Should I sit on the suitcases for a brief rest? I should think the cases would offer a much too precarious perch, and my sitting there would be entirely too unladylike."

So she carried on! Just inside the library grounds near the rose garden, she heard, "Good morning, Miss Pyn! 'Tis a fine day."

"Good morning, Joe. Do you always begin the workday so early?"

"I do in the springtime, especially on fine days. And this day is among the finest -- just perfect for the first day of your last week with us. I see you have your suitcases with you. You're not leaving us early, are you?"

"Oh no, Joe, I could not leave before week's end even if I wanted to leave. There is so very much to get ready both here and at home. I am just following instructions to practice with fully loaded luggage before traveling overseas."

"That's an excellent idea! I'd've suggested it had I not thought you'd think I was a worrywart about something you probably already knew about travel. May I help you with those bags? They look heavy."

Miss Pyn stopped with a sigh of relief, and put the two cases down on the walk. "I must confess, they are formidable. I am not entirely certain that I will be able to travel with so much luggage. I do, however, think I should take two bags. Even though I am not inclined to make many purchases in England, I know I shall make some purchases, especially books. I already have in mind a few for the library."

"Well, Miss Pyn, there are two things I've learned that you might find helpful." Joe continued to cultivate the garden beds as he advised, "One, use what the English call 'the post.' You can mail books especially. For books that need not arrive here very soon, surface mail is quite reasonably priced, and there is no duty on books. Surface mail by ship will take seven or eight weeks, but the savings are well worth the wait."

"Oh Joe, that is a very good suggestion! I suspect that airmail is considerably more expensive."

"It is." Joe continued his advice as he worked the soil. "Except for light air letters and urgently needed small packages, the five-to-seven-day delivery time is just fine and usually reliable. Although I once had a disappointing experience. One summer, when I had agreed to co-direct a seminar at The University of

London, I airmailed a copy of my text to the English co-director of our seminar two full months before my departure for England. A week before my flight the book was returned, even though it was correctly addressed. No one in a post office either here or in England could figure out why the book arrived in London within a week of its mailing, was postmarked on both sides of the Atlantic, and returned to sender. Even though it remains a mystery to this day, I wouldn't hesitate to use the service again."

"Really?" responded Miss Pyn. "Why yes, books are sent by air and by sea probably every day. I shall have the books I select at Oxford and Cambridge sent directly to the library. There may be, however, some other purchases I shall want to make, and I should be prepared to transport them personally -- hence my two suitcases."

"I have a second suggestion for you as well, Miss Pyn. My sister's niece, Pamela, who traveled for some years for the British Broadcasting Company, sent us, before Elizabeth and I traveled to Europe, a marvelous travel case. It is a lightweight device about the size of a medium-size purse or a small attaché case that will fit nicely in one suitcase with all else you will really need. If you find you'll need more luggage room, the device will unfold into a case the size of your other case. I'll bring it for you tomorrow."

"That will be wonderful! But you really should not be so generous. May I purchase the case, or at least lease it?"

With an amused smile, Joe replied, "I'll tell you what. You may purchase part-interest in the case by taking it out of my house for however long you are gone and for however long you'll be willing to store it. Then, we can both own it, and whoever needs it can use it."

"You are entirely too generous, Joe. I shall be grateful."

"I'm not generous at all. I'll get extra room in my closet, and a little bit of me in the form of my travel case will go to London."

Joe took the cases into the library and placed them at her desk in the inner office. Miss Pyn thanked him and thought, "But for Joe I could not have arrived safely at the library. I shall, as usual, follow his advice."

The morning hours passed quickly this Monday. There was little mail, no books to be accessioned, and patrons were few. Mrs. Montgomery needed help locating a medical book on tropical ailments. She said, "I hope there are enough different kinds of ailments to enable me to write a twenty-five-hundred-word term paper. I need twenty-five hundred words to finish the assignment."

"You need not worry about your subject providing enough words. I suspect you will find entirely too much material for an adequate study. I will show you a number of references with which you may begin your research."

"Thank you very much, Miss Pyn, but do you think I would do well to include semi-tropical ailments in my study to be certain of enough material?"

To Miss Pyn's relief, just then, Beth Holms arrived in plenty of time to manage the library during Miss Pyn's lunchtime. "Beth, I believe you are an experienced nurse. Perhaps you could assist Mrs. Montgomery in her research project, and may I ask you to stay a short time longer today? I am practicing carrying suitcases for my journey. I should like to take this luggage home. That should convince me not to plan on taking so much overseas when I go."

Beth was all too eager to please. "Of course, Miss Pyn, I have no other commitment until the children arrive home from school; and even then my neighbor, Jennifer, will see to them. You know I enjoy coming here to help out. Please take all the time you'd like."

Miss Pyn struggled home with her cases, which seemed to get larger and heavier with each step.

"Carole was so wise to have sent her advice as she did. Otherwise I might not have practiced, and I would have taken too much luggage. I shall also follow Joe's advice, and travel with confidence and ease."

Having resolved all this, she returned to her library work with a much lighter step and a less anxious heart. Thus the afternoon afforded her ample carefree opportunity to accomplish tasks that she had thought would either have to be left for her return from England or -- she hoped not, and heaven forbid -- left for Ann Harris to face. She was most pleased with her afternoon.

The high-school senior participants in the Library Experience Program arrived, as they were always expected to do, at precisely their assigned time. Yvonne and Christie were not only accomplished well-disciplined honor students, they were mature and experienced enough to be able to manage the library well until the nine-o'clock closing hour. Miss Pyn was free to leave, but she thought it best to stay for a few minutes and converse with "her ladies" about the library during her absence.

"I am very pleased that you two are scheduled together this evening, for I have some news. On Friday, I shall begin a holiday. I shall be traveling to England for the better part of a month."

Christie and Yvonne were surprised and delighted by Miss Pyn's news, but also a bit dismayed. "What will we do while you're away? Will the library remain open during regular hours?"

Miss Pyn reassured them: "At first we thought that the library would be open on a limited schedule, staffed mainly by you and your colleagues from school. However, we have learned that a former member of the library program has completed her graduate school library training course. She hoped to begin her professional work here, where she knows the collection; and the Library Board has offered her a position as assistant librarian. Ann Harris will begin in my absence next week, and so the library will be open on a full schedule."

Yvonne beamed, "That's wonderful news! My mother and Mrs. Harris were classmates and I know Ann slightly; she's been away at school about six years, but I remember her well. You'll like her, Christie."

"I know I will if you say so! I'm pleased, and I'm sure Yvonne is too, to discover that you are going to travel to England, Miss Pyn. We are happy for you, but we are just a little jealous. We'd like to go too!"

"Your time will come. I dare say you will not have to wait nearly as long as I have waited. I am grateful and pleased that you two will be here and will be most helpful to Ann. Until I return, goodbye, and God bless."

Miss Pyn stepped with sharper than usual cadence along the library walkway. Quite aware that the day of her departure was rapidly approaching, she planned on making only the briefest stop at the bakery.

As she opened the door, she was greeted by a myriad of festive aromas. The sweet smells of cookies and cakes abounded, but it was the aroma of newly baked bread that was deliciously unmistakable. She called out her usual greeting, "Good afternoon, Agnes." But Agnes was not there. In her place was a young woman with a strikingly white complexion, eyes that were a legendary green, and long dark hair sparkling with hints of vibrant red.

"Good afternoon! You'd, now, be Miss Pyn of the library. It's just gone five o'clock and m' cousin Mary Agnes said I should be keepin' a watchful eye out for you about this time; and she said as well I should be sure t'listen for your weather word, and then say we've saved the little cake you'll be wantin'."

"The weather is very pleasant," Miss Pyn reported. "However, I am at a loss, for I do not know with whom I have the pleasure of speaking. You could not have been in Seven Oaks very long, for surely I should have seen you. But where is Agnes?"

While she added to the display of tempting cookies, the young stranger hastily explained, "I arrived just last evenin' from m' home in Boston for a fortnight's holiday. As Mary Agnes had an errand t' run and as I've m' own bakery in the East, I said I'd manage the shop; and she said I should expect you and say what I've said, so there. She said I could expect t' have a lovely chat with you about the new books you've been addin' to the library collection."

Miss Pyn groaned inwardly. "I am on my way home for tea. So I have come for a little cake. There are many preparations for my holiday that I must complete this evening. But I am still at a loss. I do not know your name."

"I'm Mary Kathleen -- Mary Kathleen McGuinn, Mary Agnes' second cousin. I'm usually called 'Mary Kate.' Our families both lived in Cork where we've many relatives livin' still. This is my first visit to the west country -- that is, west of the Appalachians. It's such a grand lovely country you have here with so much space in between places! Oh, I should say 'we have,' for I've come t'stay! And this is such a darlin' place -- but don't you be tellin' Mary Agnes, I think Boston is just a trifle more excitin'."

Mary Kate's cheerful banter was astonishing. Words tumbled out of her as though she were sharing her secret self with a very old and treasured friend: "Wouldn't you be knowin' now! I've no holiday of even a single day, not even a holyday to honor a saint, mind you, since I left m' home in Cork. And what is it do you s'pose I do on m' very first day away? I work in m' cousin's bakery! I ask you, is that not the way of it?"

Miss Pyn began to suspect that this visit was not likely to be the brief stop at the bakery she had intended, and she wondered if her dismay was apparent as Mary Kate chattered on.

"Cousin Mary Agnes says that yu're plannin' t' travel back across the sea to the old country. I think that's a lovely idea. I've been thinkin' about that all day, and I've a scheme that'd let you visit Ireland. It's on the way, you know."

Startled by this sudden proposal, Miss Pyn hastened to reply. "Even though Ireland must be a very beautiful country, I have not thought of visiting there. I have planned for many years to visit England, primarily literary London."

Mary Kate leaned across the counter and responded earnestly, "Don't you see, it might be yer only opportunity. So take the advantage of it! You could just land at Shannon and hire a motorcar. You've an operator's license, do you?"

Miss Pyn tried to reply in the affirmative but Mary Kate's words rushed on: "You must be most alert motorin', you know. People over here think that people over there travel on the wrong side of the road, just as people over there think that people over here travel on the wrong side of the road. When I first came to Boston, I thought all people operating motor cars had gone daft!"

Miss Pyn was beginning to feel flustered. "Were I to travel to Ireland, I think I should be most reluctant to drive an automobile. Certainly not in a large city."

"Ah, but you could travel t' Galway, a comfor'ble small city in the west of Ireland. 'Tis a darlin' city and only a short journey along a good road, a car-riageway, north from the air terminal at Shannon. Galway is really lovely, and there m' very prosperous brother, Sean, the solicitor, would welcome you for a night or two. After that you could go south again t' Killarney; m' sister, Mary Rose, would be very happy t' see you!"

"A visit to Ireland must surely be wonderful," Miss Pyn replied wistfully. "However, I have not had the good fortune of knowing your family. Why would they welcome me, a complete stranger?"

Mary Kate laughed. "Never mind, they'd be very happy t' meet you, and I know Mary Rose would be more than happy t' accompany you 'round the Ring of

Kerry. If the mists aren't too thick on the windscreen, she'll show you 'round the rugged Dingle Peninsula as well."

Miss Pyn was not quite certain what she should do. Should she make an excuse and leave hurriedly and risk offending this gracious lady, or should she stay and risk looking too preoccupied, worrying about all that she must do before Friday.

"Ye're not in a frightful hurry are you, now, like all the women who come in t' m' shop in Boston? Some of 'em act like very proper New England ladies, but they always seem to be late for somethin' or other. I wouldn't want t' spend m' whole life always thinkin' I was just a bit too late for everythin'. In Ireland, a soul couldn't survive a fortnight with that attitude! The awful frustration of it would be yer undoin' in no time a-tall! In Ireland, 'specially in the country, nothin' ever is on time because nothin' is ever expected to be on time. You might even say, for that reason, that nothin' is ever late! So there's never a disappointment."

Though Miss Pyn found this logic puzzling, she said nothing, and continued to grow more anxious about all she had yet to do before her holiday could begin. But Mary Kate talked on of Ireland, enthusiastically offering Miss Pyn a sample of each kind of cookie as she replenished the cookie trays. Miss Pyn tried to refuse each offering with a polite "No, thank you"; but she could only shake her head in wonder as Mary Kate's river of words rushed on.

"Though we've got relatives galore in Cork, I wouldn't stop there. I'd go directly t' Waterford t' the crystal production. M' cousin, Mary Margaret, has a lovely home just outside Waterford on the main road t' Dublin. Her oldest daughter, Delia, has a 'position,' mind you, in the office at the glass works. And her younger daughter is a student at the university. Why, she'd welcome a ride in t' Dublin! She'd even assist you very ably with operatin' the vehicle so that the road journey t' Dublin wouldn't be over-taxin' none. Are you sure you won't have one of these delicious cookies? They're uncommonly good, I can attest t' that m'self, y' know. In Dublin -- actually in Drumcundra at the north side of the city close by the air terminal -- m' lovely Aunt Mary Frances'll welcome you handsomely.

"Oh, I know everybody in Ireland has a lovely Aunt Mary -- includin' this Aunt Mary! But m' Aunt Mary Frances is the loveliest of 'em all. She's positively enthralled with American accents and gossip from the States."

Miss Pyn could only stare in disbelief as Mary Kate, polishing the counter top vigorously, continued without taking a single breath. "Now then, there's the complete itinerary: a day or two with Aunt Mary Frances which you'll not soon forget; then return the motor car at Dublin Airport, and in less than two hours you'll be through Heathrow in t' London. In a very few days you'll have seen enough of Ireland t' want t' return again and again. With this scheme you'll be havin' what I should call the dream of a grand visit -- a grand visitation worthy of Eamon De Valera himself!"

"Grand!" exclaimed Miss Pyn. "It would be, without doubt; but I insist, I would be an utter stranger to your family."

Mary Kate would have none of it: "Ah, but you must take advantage of this possibility. Surely, the only way for most of us t' travel is t' visit relatives and friends and save the costs."

Miss Pyn was astonished. She was speechless for many minutes -- a most unusual predicament! She could not decide whether she was amazed that Mary Kate had at last finished her persuasive invitation to the homes of her Irish relatives, or whether she was astonished that anyone could tender such an invitation to a stranger.

"I am utterly overwhelmed, Mary Kate. Surely, you do not even know me."

"Ah, but Mary Agnes knows you well and she says that you're a fine, generous, perfect lady. I think, and Mary Agnes agrees with me wholeheartedly, all my family would like t' know you."

Miss Pyn had made up her mind. "Your proposal is entirely too generous. I could not possibly accept it. Besides, while it may be prudent, even wise to take advantage of one's relatives in travel, it is quite another matter to take advantage of the generosity of the relatives of an acquaintance. I thank you very much. Even if I could accept your kindness, the booking is already fixed and it cannot be changed without substantial penalty. Thank you again, and thank Mary Agnes too. I see her deft hand at work here as well."

"Yes, we'll both be very sorry that you'll not be goin' t' Ireland," Mary Kate sighed. "And we wish you a safe journey." Her bright smile reappeared. "Oh yes, I nearly forgot! I've got the special cake for you. It'll take but a moment t' wrap it."

"Thank you so much. I trust I shall see Mary Agnes beforc I leave. Goodbye, and I hope you will enjoy your stay here."

"Thank you too, Miss Pyn, and God bless."

Miss Pyn hurried home, thinking there was still much to do, but she really did need her tea after such a full day. Yet as she walked along, she felt a very strange apprehension, a feeling she had not known for a very long time.

Later, after she warmed the teapot and added the tea to steep, she put on her comfortable sweater, tuned the radio to "The Afternoon Classics," and settled into her balcony chair. The music played softly. Sipping her tea, she thought about Mary Kate's "scheme" over and over again. It might be very nice to stop in Ireland on her way to London, but that would delay her.

She was very eager to get to England at long last; what she said about not being able to change the itinerary was true. Then why was she so perplexed by the Irish plan? Why did her mind keep returning to the thought of it, especially when she needed to consider so much else about England and about the library while she would be away.

The thought of Ireland would not leave her, no matter how hard she tried to put it out of mind. She could hear Mary Kate's voice like the soft rhythms of an ancient harp urging her to travel to that land called Erin and enjoy a "grand visitation." That was surely an unusual use of the word "visitation." "Visitation" meant something quite different in Miss Pyn's memory -- not a joyous visit and tour, but a difficult parting -- perhaps a final farewell at a wake. She contemplated her tea, quietly remembering ....

The long afternoon in the funeral home crept slowly through many hours -- through many more hours than an afternoon ought to have had. Outside, the sun brightened the land and warmed fresh gentle breezes. Inside, the air, saturated with the perfume of funereal flowers and the scent of half-burnt candles, was very still in a heavy silence that enveloped the room and inspired whispered condolences.

The place was called a "chapel." And it did resemble a place for worship -- the quiet, the subdued light, the flickering candles. Even the chairs were arranged in rows like pews. The only thing missing was an altar; in its place was the catafalque flanked by candles and flowers. At the head of the casket, a single tall taper cast soft light on the image in an ebony frame.

Miss Pyn had urged her sister to take their mother home for rest and nourishment: "Please go. I shall remain here. I can greet whoever might come. You can return about half six in time for evening visitation." Alone now, she found the faded Wedgwood blue walls of the viewing parlor oppressive. The windows were covered with heavy draperies, curtains, and Venetian blinds so that little light entered from outside. Indirect lighting and flickering candles produced a strange glow, an aura of relaxed and comfortable death that the director of funerals continually referred to as "passing" or "crossing." If she heard "passing" one more time, Miss Pyn knew she could not nor would not endure it.

"Father is dead," she thought. "'Dead' is the only correct word, the only word that could signify this dreadful emptiness." Though she felt that she wanted to cry, that she should, that she must cry, she could not. That served only to extend the emptiness.

She studied the furniture; it was eclectic. Some pieces appeared to be genuinely Victorian. These were chiefly tables and cases and chests scattered about the room. The rest of the furnishing would be best described as "Contemporary Funereal."

Again she thought of her father. She thought of the joy of her childhood with him, of all that he taught her ever so patiently -- so kind, so loving, so very much always and in all ways interested in her learning to do everything as carefully and as well as she possibly could; whatever was done must be done right. She heard him say again, "Whatever is worth doing is worth doing well."

Again she tried to cry, to weep for herself if for no one else. And again she could not.

She heard – rather, sensed really -- a presence in the room. In the dim light, she turned to see what appeared to be a vision at the door signing the registry of callers. She wondered, "Could this beautiful young woman be real? Might she be 'a visitor' from another place?"

The young woman was slender and tall with golden red hair. She wore no cosmetic except a subtle lip rouge. As she moved across the room, her step was firm, her movement lithesome. "Hello. You are Miss Pyn, are you not? I am so very sorry we should meet only now on this occasion."

"You must forgive me," Miss Pyn stammered. "My father's accident has left me so muddle-headed. You look so very familiar, yet I am unable to remember you."

"I'm Michelle Hughes, Mickey's -- that is Michael's -- twin. When I read of your father's accident, I knew I must come because I felt deeply that you must be Michael's friend. Am I not right?"

"Yes, of course, forgive me." Miss Pyn smiled warmly. "I should have known. But while your brother is very handsome, you are ever so much handsomer than he. I do scc the resemblance, though I have not seen Michael in over a year. Yet I am at such a loss; my thoughts seem all ajumble. We must talk about your handsome brother, but first I shall tell you about my father."

Michelle looked away from Miss Pyn and noticeably shivered.

"You must be chilled. Had you a long drive? I think the proprietor must keep the temperature low and the humidity high in this chapel because of the flowers."

Michelle shook her head. "It's nothing. I'll get used to it. The drive was a little over an hour. I didn't know we lived so near to one another until I saw your dad's story in the paper, and I suspected that you'd be here."

"Are you certain you are not chilled? I have a sweater on that chair. May I get it for you?"

Michelle merely shook her head and looked toward the flowers, the candles, and the casket.

"Come then, I will tell you about the most wonderful father that could ever have been. The casket is closed not because of my father's injuries but rather because my mother and my sister and I agreed that we wished to remember him as he was in life, not as he looked in death. So here at the head of the casket is his most recent formal picture, taken within the last year. Was he not a handsome man -- with a kindly face?"

There was clear resemblance between father and daughter: the same silken wavy hair, the prominent cheekbones framing a small nose below those thoughtful gray-green eyes. A most handsome man.

Michelle knelt at the priedieu. She prayed for the Pyn family -- the father whom she would never meet and who had left his family so early; and the mother and daughters who would always know a void, an emptiness that could never be filled. She prayed as well for her own family, for herself and for her other self -- her twin, the brother she so dearly loved. Then with another little shiver, that Miss Pyn did not see, she rose, noticing a single golden-throated, rose-hued calla in a silver vase inscribed simply, "A Most Wondrous Father." Then she saw another little silver vase with no inscription -- a single perfect, deeply red rose in it.

"Over here," Miss Pyn said. "I would like you to..."

"But may I ask about these two magnificent flowers?"

"Of course! Father was very fond of callas. He grew them, taking them in each fall and repotting them each spring. His callas were quite special; they were a dwarf variety with unusual soft colors."

"How beautiful this one is, sort of rose gold. What of the vase?"

"We had ordered the vase for Father's Day, next week. It was to be a little gift from his girls. We argued over the inscription. I thought it was too extravagant, and I insisted that Father would think so too. Now, of course, I feel that it was not extravagant at all, and it seems an understatement."

"So very sad and yet so beautiful. What of the rose? It is perfectly beautiful too. There is no inscription."

"People who live in town and especially the people from our church would understand the significance of that rose. Everyone knew Father's fondness for roses. Father believed that the proper place for peaceful meditation was out-of-doors amid God's grandeur. He thought our church should have a quiet outdoor place for thought. Father Jim was not only our pastor, he was Dad's friend. Sometimes they were able to go fishing together. So after Father planned and planted and tended his rose garden at our church, everyone -- including Father Jim -- was pleased, and we all called it 'The Saint Francis Garden.'"

Michele was amazed. "Where could such a perfect rose come from?"

"From his garden; it is an older variety named Crimson Glory. Most of the roses in the garden are Crimson Glories. There are others too, but the Glories predominate amid pathways of cedar chips, and places to sit for contemplation. This rose was found in bloom yesterday by a member of the parish -- on it a single drop of dew glistening like a jewel in the early morning sunlight. She said she knew exactly where it belonged."

"What a marvelous, extraordinary person your father surely was! You all must feel his loss deeply."

Miss Pyn appeared not to hear Michelle's last remark or notice a slight tremor in her voice. Instead she said, "Come -- over here. My sister and I made a collage of our father's life. We gathered all of Mother's pictures of him and some of ours as well, and my clever sister made this board."

It was a simple board, perhaps three by four feet in size, covered in pale blue felt, with pictures chronicling a lifetime. Michelle studied the pictures carefully. "These are truly a treasure. What a beautiful remembrance!"

"Oh yes," agreed Miss Pyn. "Here is Father at aged three with his maternal grandmother. Then came his First Communion, his Confirmation, and his first grown-up double-breasted suit! His military service photograph. Then the wedding pictures. They were a lovely couple, were they not?"

Michele studied the photographs and agreed, as Miss Pyn pointed to the next: "Soon I came along. Here is Dad holding me at my Baptism, holding my hand at my First Communion, and offering me his arm at my high school graduation. We have pictures of other less formal activities as well. Here we are repairing the roof, digging the garden, fixing the downspouts -- some of my most precious memories! We played too. Here we are camping, canoeing, and fishing. Father was a fisherman; here he is with a picnic table stacked with a catch of trout, and here he rests on a little waterfall in the middle of a trout stream. I shall be forever grateful for this picture. It is most like him. Oh, there are working pictures that we treasure as well. Here is my father in his tree-climbing gear. He loved trees. He began by studying horticulture at the university. He had to come home when his father died."

Miss Pyn's voice softened and slowed. She seemed unaware that Michele had grasped her hand.

"And then there was military service – limited, because Grandmother was a widow. Upon his return, he took a job with the power company trimming his beloved trees. Soon he met Mother, and then my sister and I were born. I am sure it was to better support his daughters that he accepted a promotion to a desk job.

"He never gave us the slightest hint, but I shall always believe that he deeply missed his work out-of-doors. Then, he died suddenly, with his tree-surgeon's gear on, helping a neighbor take down a tree."

Many moments passed before Miss Pyn looked up. "There it is, the life in pictures of a good and wonderful man. It is nearly all there, yet almost none of it is there. He became a hero in death; he turned to push Mr. Stoner out of the path of the falling tree and in doing so he was crushed by it. We did not need to learn that he was a hero in death, Michelle! We always knew he was a hero in life."

"How sad, how very sad! What else can I say? It is so overwhelming," whispered Michelle with tears streaming down her face as she hugged Miss Pyn.

"Life must continue, however sad," Miss Pyn declared resolutely, with her arms still around Michelle. "But now you have come, and there is so much to talk about. We must get to know each other and share stories about your wonderful brother."

At these words Michelle blanched and shook with a fierce shiver, tears continuing down her cheeks.

"My dear heart!" exclaimed Miss Pyn. "You are ice-cold and trembling too. You must have my sweater. I know what we can do. We can leave this cold place of death; no one will come to visit just now, and my mother and sister will return soon. You surely do not wish to meet them as you are. I have a secret place just over the road. It is warm and peaceful there. Here, take this sweater and come into the warm sunshine. The chill will pass."

Miss Pyn led the way out into the sunshine and around the corner. Eight hundred yards along the road was an old stone bridge spanning a little river. On the near side was a brick walkway with benches every several hundred feet facing the river. On the far side was a woodland.

"This is an enchanted place. When we were youngsters, we would come here after school and pretend it was our 'Wonderland.'" They walked on toward the stone bridge. "We thought old farmer Schmidt, who owned the land on both sides of the river, was a nasty grump, because he would chase us away from his land -- especially the land across the river. After he died, we learned that he devoted his last years to building a preserve that he gave to all the people of our town along with a fund to maintain the preserve and build this little park on this side of the river. It is a very special place.

"Come, we'll sit and study the river and the forest beyond, and find refreshment in this most amazing time of day. It is my favorite time -- just as the early edge of evening greets the waning afternoon, when shadows begin to stretch ever so imperceptibly and the breeze begins to subside into mischievous little zephyrs that skitter in every direction across the water's surface, rippling silently through the river music."

Michelle, still looking very pale, moved as she was directed, without a word. Miss Pyn continued, "If we are very quiet, perhaps we shall see the great blue heron hunting its prey. I observed him just yesterday. Yes! Look just there in the shadows where the river bends into the deep woods! We can see the bird if we look carefully and move softly."

Near the opposite bank where the river turned, the heron stood motionless, searching the murky waters looking for signs of life. "The bird is so still and so camouflaged," Michelle said in a faint shaky voice. "I have not seen such a large bird ever before. It hasn't moved at all."

"The bird," Miss Pyn whispered, "will remain so for a very long time until it finds its prey or it is startled. Have you ever heard the call of the heron as it flies? Its long neck produces a very deep sound. Some years ago, I sat on this same place when old Mr. McCormick came along studying the river. He lived here all his life, and he knew the river better than anyone. There was a bird at the river's edge just like that one. The bird was startled by Mr. McCormick, and it flew up the river into the deep forest calling mournfully.

"Mr. McCormick turned to me with only the faintest laughter in his voice and just a hint of a smile on his face. 'Did ya hear that, lass? That bird hears what we can't hear. I tell ya. It's a response, 'tis, to what he hears. That special rare low murmur of the bird as it flies to its home in the deep woods is an echo. It is just like the piteous groan of a banshee at the sound of a death knell. As sure as m'name is Sean McCormick, I'm certain that it is so.' He walked on without another word."

The two young women sat silently on the bench facing the river. They gazed at the forest across the river and watched the heron for some time. Then Miss Pyn continued, "I did not think about what Mr. McCormick said until yesterday. After I spent hours in the funeral home chapel, I sat here in sorrow and thought the heron's call was a perfect lamentation -- a dirge proclaimed for all who would listen."

The sunlight and the rhythm of the river and the beauty of the heron revived Michelle. Slowly her color returned and she no longer shivered.

Miss Pyn advised her: "Let us sit here for a while enjoying the stillness of the evening. Now then, is not the quiet here truly astonishing? In school we hear of 'silence and slow time.' Our silence may not be the 'silence' of which the poet sang, nor is his 'slow time' our slow time, but this perfect peacefulness is surely heir to both, wherever they may be found. Tell me now all about your handsome brother."

The silence that followed was long. Michelle was a statue -- immobile, quiet, slowly drained of all color. She trembled, then sobbed. "Then you don't know! Oh

Miss Pyn, I'm so very sorry -- so very, very sorry." Shaking, she could say no more.

"Is Michael in trouble? He has always been outspoken. His Irish wit can offend. Has he been arrested?"

"No." She shuddered.

"Is he missing?"

"No," she whispered.

"Please tell me. Has he been wounded? Can he walk? Can he see? Please, please!"

Michelle gazed across the river, tears now streaming down her cheeks. Trembling, she moaned, "Mickey is dead. I'm so sorry. I thought you knew."

Miss Pyn said nothing. She looked ahead at the river and the forest beyond without moving a muscle, without moving a nerve.

"Oh, Needles!" cried Michelle. "May I call you that, as Mickey did? We should have known when we received the Chaplain's letter with a note in it for you! Yet Mom and Dad thought you must have been told by someone. We didn't know where you lived. We were not sure of your name. When I saw the account of your father's accident in the paper, I thought I should come just ... in case ... just ...

"I didn't bring the chaplain's note addressed to you. It is safe at home, unopened. I was not sure that

107

you were the right person. Mickey always called you 'Needles,' never 'Pyn.' When I saw you there in the chapel I knew immediately that you had to be the beautiful friend Mickey so often described. I did bring a copy of the letter the chaplain wrote to all of us. It relates things about Mickey that even I did not know. I would read it to you if I could, but forgive me ... I can't."

Miss Pyn had not moved. She stared at the river. Michelle took the letter from her bag, unfolded it and placed it in Miss Pyn's hand. For many minutes, Miss Pyn remained transfixed. Presently, from across the river high in a tree a tiny wren filled the air with its evening song, and Miss Pyn grasped the letter.

To: The family and friends of Warrant Officer Michael F. Hughes

I write not in my official capacity as a military officer, but as a friend of a man I grew to respect and cherish. Although we are on opposite sides of the world and we might not meet until after final judgment, I take the liberty of writing to you because we share a kinship in having known Mickey -- an extraordinary young man. No doubt you have been notified officially of Michael's sacrifice for his country. I should like to share my thoughts and my memories with you who knew him well.

Mickey came to our base hospital less than one year ago. I can't forget our meeting, nor would I ever want to forget it. He sauntered into my little office with his grand Irish grin, his unmistakable red hair, and his engaging eyes. 'Father,' he said, 'Can I help you with anything?'

And I replied, 'Helping is my job. How can I help you?' I confess I suspected that here was a young man hoping to find a nice soft job as the chaplain's assistant. I was wrong. Michael's words and later his actions showed me how very wrong I was. I remember what he said that day:

'Padre, I drive the Whirly Bird that brings in the casualties. Actually, I'm the co-jockey, and I see that some of these guys need a lot of help from somebody they can feel comfortable with -- you know, a guy away from home like they are and scared sometimes too.' Without another word, he had shown me what I had suspected -- that many wounded, exhausted men were too frightened to see the chaplain.

For months after that first meeting, Mickey spent his work-time helping to collect the wounded and his off-time ministering to them, just 'shooting the breeze' with them. Men who had in no way wished to see a chaplain -- let alone a priest -- asked for me after Mickey 'jawed' with them.

Of course you know that Michael preferred to be called 'Mickey.' He told me that when Michelle and he were young they both loved to be called 'Mickey' and so confuse nearly everybody, much to their great delight.

But as an adult, he had an adult reason that I believe he shared with no one, not even Michelle or the wonderful young friend he called Needles. I'd like to share it with you now.

After a day when casualties were particularly heavy and we both had worked at least seventeen hours straight, we sat over a late-night drink. It was then that he confessed, 'You know the real reason I'd rather be called 'Mickey' is that I don't feel worthy to be 'Michael.' Michael the Archangel was a fighter, a warrior. He had valor, and strength, and prowess in battle. I'm no fighter. I've got none of those things. I volunteered for service early because I hoped to serve without engaging anyone in combat -- I couldn't kill anyone, ever. I've been lucky not to have to prove that I could kill another human being.'

I said nothing. But I kept those thoughts in my heart, and I pondered them often. It's natural to assume that someone who wants to avoid combat is afraid of danger. Well, Mickey rescued the wounded in one of the most dangerous jobs in a dangerous war. He was honest -- astonishingly honest, and was not afraid as a coward is afraid.

Not long after that, Mickey reminded me that during World War II, resistance fighters in France -- laymen -- were permitted to carry the Eucharist to administer to wounded and dying fighters. Then he made his unusual request: 'Could I carry the sacrament in a pyx for the wounded guys who might not make it to the hospital?' I knew that he had helped many a man to reconciliation, so I didn't hesitate to engage him as a special minister of the Eucharist. God alone knows to how many men Mickey brought relief for physical and often spiritual distress.

One evening, after a very long day, we again talked of St. Michael and young Michael's feelings. I told him that the popular image of Michael the Archangel was well founded in both tradition and scripture, but it was woefully inadequate. Yes, St. Michael was a fighter and a defender, but that was not all. The name 'Michael' means 'like unto God.' God is just: the rebellious angels had to be driven from heaven. God is also mercy and, above all, God is love! I told him that these were the characteristics he could seek to cultivate in the name of his patron. I thought to myself he'd rather done so already!

Michael said he would think about that, but he wasn't sure. I had no way of knowing it was the last time we would speak.

You need to know what happened in the end. On that last day, he proved to many what I knew all along -- he was a hero. The appropriate authorities have recommended that he be awarded his country's highest award: The Medal of Honor that only Congress can bestow. This great honor will come in due course, but he has enjoyed, I am convinced, the ultimate Medal of Honor ever since he gave his life in service to his comrades.

The corpsman, Andrew Zeff, related the events to me. I relay his words as I remember them: 'We flew in under heavy fire; the Gooks were ready for us. We touched down at the edge of the woods, quickly collected four seriously wounded men, and lifted off into a volley of automatic ground fire. Our pilot, Jeffrey Barr, was hit and knocked unconscious. I saw that our copilot Mick was well in control as I dragged Jeff away from the cockpit.

'The firing continued heavy, but Mickey got us out of there. I yelled that all these guys including Jeff were in bad shape. I knew that the Mash unit had wounded stacked up. So I shouted at Mick, 'Could we make the base hospital? It's about twenty-five minutes further on, and they could take better care of these guys there.' Mickey only nodded. Had I only known!

'I was very busy helping all those guys, and the flight seemed to take a long time. I thought two of them might not make it. One of them prayed aloud; the other said nothing through his clenched teeth. At last, the hospital was in sight and Mickey brought down the bird with the gentle touch of genius.

'The hospital staff and I rushed the five wounded men into surgery in time to save them all. I turned to congratulate Mickey, but he wasn't there. I found him in his seat in the chopper, unconscious. He must have been hit along with Jeff when we took off. During those extra twenty-five minutes that he flew without a murmur, he lost too much blood. He never regained consciousness. He died after saving five buddies. Padre, Mickey was a gentle guy, and he hated fighting.'

Corpsman Zeff's words are eloquent epitaph for a very brave man. It's superfluous to record here that Mickey had within him all those characteristics he believed he lacked, and so felt unworthy to be called Michael. He was courageous, loyal, and dedicated far beyond any expectation.

I know it's small comfort for us to realize that Michael -- for Michael he will always be -- is a hero recognized by his country for his valor. Even though we believe in perfect reward for all eternity, even though we know that Our Blessed Savior told us personally that there is no greater love than to sacrifice one's life for another, and even though we can know certainly that Michael has already achieved what we each hope to achieve, I know the sad, sad emptiness will remain as long as we live.

Perhaps it's little comfort to realize that we personally know a saint in heaven. However, I pray that you can find some strength in that knowledge to help you endure your sorrow. There is little more I can say except to end with the prayer of Thomas More that I alter only slightly: Please 'pray for me as I will for you so that we may merrily meet each other and Michael in Heaven.' For surely he awaits our coming!

Yours most sincerely in Christ Jesus Our Lord and Savior,

Fredrick M. Hart, O.S.B.

P.S. I enclose a note for Michael's friend whom he called Needles. If you know her name or where to find her, please see that she gets that note. If not, you may destroy it.

Both women sat motionless for a long time. When at last the sun began to decline, Michelle, who had quietly sobbed from time to time, whispered, "You are so very brave -- not a tear."

"No, Michelle, not brave. I am not brave at all. I have only a deep bitterness of spirit. At school last term we studied poetry. We heard the English poet speak of 'thoughts too deep for tears.' What I could not understand then, I now know. Oh, how I know it! But while the poet's thoughts were thoughts of awe, wonder, even joy, my thoughts are of the bitterest gall."

Miss Pyn stood up, staring at the murky river water. She moved toward the river's edge. With each step, she uttered a phrase. With each phrase, her voice grew in intensity to the cadence of plainchant.

"No, Michelle, no! It is not fair. I say, it is not fair! I have loved but two men -- both have died within weeks. Their lives violently ended much too soon saving the life of another. No! Again I say no! I cannot weep today. No, I shall not weep tomorrow. Nor will I weep for them or for me ... ever. No, never!"

Alarmed, Michelle jumped up, throwing her arms around her new friend to console -- or was it to save her.

The sudden sound and movement alarmed the watchful heron. Unfolding its great wings, it lifted itself but inches above the water, and flew into the deep woods. The mournful cry of the bird rolled along the surface of the river, echoing among the trees of the dark forest.

The sun now declined in the west, etching a few puffy clouds in the eastern sky with rose-golden accents. Miss Pyn sat motionless in deep reverie. The tea in her cup, only half consumed, was cold; the little cake untouched. Still she sat unmoving. Ever since she had sat down with her steaming cup of tea, her radio played recordings of soft classical tone poems selected by the radio host for a peaceful afternoon. She heard none of it even now.

The chickadee that greeted her most afternoons with a cheery "hello" and an occasional gentle admonishment to refill the bird feeding station, had been perched on the railing of the balcony for some minutes looking rather like a *maitre d'*, formally dressed, beckoning patrons, with a flutter, to enjoy a superb repast. Its familiar chirp, chirp did nothing to arouse Miss Pyn from deep thought and far-off gaze.

The bird continued its call in full song, now looking as though it suspected something must be wrong; its gentle human friend failed to respond to its cheerful greeting. Alarmed, it continued to chirp.

Meanwhile, on the radio, the tone poems for a peaceful afternoon were replaced by a new and familiar sound -- a sound and spirit that could rouse Miss Pyn from a memory that, even after so many years, was so overwhelming that little else could restore her consciousness.

The selection was from Aaron Copeland's ballet suite, *Appalachian Spring* -- the variations on the Shaker melody, "A Gift to be Simple." Miss Pyn treasured that simple song.

As the orchestra played the last variation and moved toward the final crescendo, she listened; she slowly recovered and, with a smile, reluctantly recognized the little bird on the railing.

On Tuesday morning, Miss Pyn was again aware that little time remained before her departure date. Today she would arrive at the library even before Joe and open the windows to her great satisfaction.

Moments later, Joe hurried through the front door. "Why, Miss Pyn, you've beaten me to it and done my job as well. You must be careful opening all those windows. Some of them need attention. You could sprain something and have to put off your trip."

"Good morning, Joe! It is good to see you this fine morning. I appreciate your concern, but a reasonable amount of stretching is good exercise in the morning."

Joe smiled at this sage advice, anticipating his own exercise all day in the garden. "I've learned that Ann Harris will be joining us. That's good to hear. You do need professional help, and Ann was certainly your best student assistant when she was here."

"Yes, I am so pleased that she will be here. Her presence will be especially welcome during my absence." But Miss Pyn suddenly frowned. "It is difficult to believe how rapidly the days of this week are passing. I came to the library early to complete tasks that should not await my return and to initiate some of the things I would ordinarily accomplish during the time I shall be away. I feel I should not burden Ann with too much minutiae during the early days of her first truly professional position."

"You're too kind, Miss Pyn." Joe had absentmindedly begun sorting books on the cart. "Not many supervisors would be as considerate as you are. I'm sure Ann will be able to handle everything that will need doing. I can help as well. While I'm not professionally trained, I did work part-time at my university library as the head page and later as an assistant to the reference librarian. And if the two of us can't solve something we could always ask Miss Thrust for help."

"Thank you, Joe. I shall not give the library a second thought while I am away -- except to purchase some books. I realize that the ease of mind I shall enjoy will be possible because you and Ann and Miss Thrust will be here. I did not know of your experience with the university library. I certainly should have surmised why you are always so much at home in the library. Now I know that the library will be in very competent hands. Again I thank you, Joe, and the others as well."

"Not at all, Miss Pyn, not at all. I will be very pleased to help."

Miss Pyn turned to her unusually cluttered desk. The task of addressing all that needed attention would take up the greater part of the morning before she could feel that she could leave the library for Ann to assume the position as assistant to the librarian.

The afternoon passed even more rapidly than the morning. There were few patrons, but there were some books to be accessioned. The accessioning process was interrupted several times. Mr. O'Mara, who usually arrived early Tuesday morning, came in apologetically after lunch to check *The Irish Times*. For some years, Sean O'Mara had his personal subscription of the *Times* sent to the Seven Oaks library. He had learned that the library had a limited newspaper budget that allowed for few domestic newspapers and only *The Toronto Star* and *The London Times*. He was convinced that his neighbors should have available an Irish point of view as an antidote to the British view from London.

Ida West needed help with *Books in Print* and the periodical indexes in compiling a bibliography on classical and modern dances. Ida, who had danced professionally for a number of years, thought she could offer a course in The Dance at The Seven Oaks Senior Center.

"While I know how to dance, Miss Pyn, I feel I should know more dance history and other more academic bits. Then maybe I could offer the course at community college or high-school level. You don't think I'm too old for such ambition, do you?"

"Of course not! You have more vigor than many women half your age and, I might say, a more attractive personality and figure than most people -- your dancing has kept you young at heart!"

Ida West was pleased with Miss Pyn's encouragement, as many other patrons of the library had been over the years.

Miss Pyn had just begun to accession the last book for the day, when Christie appeared for late afternoon duty. She, along with her friend Yvonne, had been in the library program for some time. Both had merited the title, "Student Assistant Librarian." Christie was especially good at detailed work and could accession very well.

"Good afternoon, Christie! Is it that late already?" Miss Pyn looked at the clock in disbelief. "My, how quickly time does pass! You will learn as you grow older that time passes faster and faster. There is reason why time appears to grow shorter and shorter. Our perception of time is measured against our cumulative sense of time. When we have experienced only a few years, a single year is a rather large part of our memory, of our cumulative sense of time. However, when our experience consists of -- let us say -- twenty years of time, a year is a twentieth part of our cumulative sense. After our experience consists of forty years, our sense of a year is only a fortieth part -- at sixty a sixtieth part, at eighty an eightieth part, and so on. So each year seems shorter than the preceding year. That is why time flies."

Christie looked rather puzzled. "I haven't thought of time in those terms, Miss Pyn; but I think I see your point. Is there anything special you would like me to do this evening?"

"Yes, my dear, would you finish accessioning this book? I have saved it to the end of this lot because it needs to be carefully checked. It has an ambiguous title: *The Last War*. You will need to determine which last war is the subject of the book and accession it accordingly, and then add it and these others that I have finished to the collection. After that, you can see to the regular activities for the evening. Is your co-conspirator going to join you this evening? I prefer that you work in pairs rather than alone."

"Yvonne will be a little late because she has a dental appointment. Oh, don't worry, Miss Pyn, it's only a checkup! And besides, we'll be quite safe. Fred Casey and Bill Fleming from school are working in the garden this evening. They won't leave before we close the library. And if Yvonne isn't able to come, I can call Jennifer Cooper. She'd like more time on duty."

"That is just fine, Christie. I know that I can depend on all of you. Good afternoon!"

Miss Pyn hurried along the walkway toward the bakery as quickly as she dared without jeopardizing her reputation for refined, ladylike deportment.

At the bakery she began her usual greeting. "Good ... Oh, Agnes, you have returned! Good afternoon, Agnes! How nice to see you in your familiar place, although I did thoroughly enjoy meeting and conversing with your cousin from Cork. She seems to be a lovely person. I suspect it is a family characteristic."

"Good afternoon, and thank you, Miss Pyn! Mary Kate will be pleased to learn of your nice words. She did come from Cork as did I, but she's very proud to be able to say she's from Boston now. I suspect she might think that Seven Oaks is a bit rustic compared to her sophisticated Boston cosmopolitan neighborhood. She probably thinks that Seven Oaks is more like Cork than Boston." With a mischievous grin, Agnes added: "She, of course, won't admit that to me.

"I've saved your favorite cake today. And I haven't told a soul about your pending holiday, Miss Pyn -- that is, of course, not a soul except Mary Kate so she could help you decide to go to Ireland. She told me you have very definite immovable ideas about your travel. 'A shame 'tis too!' she said to me. 'Our family in Galway, Waterford, and Dublin would be very happy to meet her.'"

"You understand, Agnes, that it is not possible to do so during this holiday," Miss Pyn said with some regret. "I would enjoy meeting Mary Kate again even if she would persist in trying to change my mind about the trip."

"She will probably try tomorrow if you stop by," Agnes warned. "She'll be here in my place again. I've just learned, this very day, I must attend the wake of my husband's brother tonight and the funeral tomorrow morning. Life's too complicated, Miss Pyn!"

"Oh, Agnes, I trust the circumstances of your brother-in-law's death have not been too trying for you and his family. I hope to see you before I leave for England. And thank you for the warning about Mary Kate."

Miss Pyn hurried along her "high street." She would have been pleased to chat with Agnes a bit longer, but each day now she became even more acutely aware that there was still much to do before Friday. First, however, she must have her tea. She rationalized that, after her tea, she could approach whatever task she had chosen to complete with much more vigor. And besides, even if a few things remained undone, would they really matter? Tea Time must not be missed at any cost.

In the afternoon sun, the balcony was most comfortable. It occurred to her that if the weather was not good on the next afternoon, this could be her last opportunity to enjoy the balcony tea properly until she would return from England. While the tea brewed, she remembered that Agnes would be away again. She was going to attend a funeral. How very sad.

There was one funeral she could not forget, ever; she remembered every detail, even her every thought …

The day was gray. The sun had not yet pierced the morning mists. Miss Pyn had come with her mother and sister to the funeral home early in anticipation of a very large gathering. It seemed that the entire community knew and cared for Tom Pyn. Those who knew him only slightly had enjoyed or at least knew about the Saint Francis Garden on the grounds of Saint Clare's Church. Everyone learned of his untimely death.

A crowd was already waiting outside the funeral home in respectful silence. No one would enter before the family. Quietly, they expressed condolences. The Pyn family together and separately thanked everyone. Suddenly, Miss Pyn burst out, " Oh, why could the sun not shine today of all days!"

Michelle Hughes, Michael's sister, came forth from the gathering and hugged her friend. "Dearest sister, the sun will shine for both of us this day, but it needs some time to find us. May I call you 'sister'?"

"Michele! You came! How thoughtful you are. Of course you must call me 'sister.' I would not have it any other way. But why should the sun not shine today?"

"It will shine, dear heart. Look there -- the mist is starting to lift. The day, however sad it may be, will be good. Shall we enter the chapel?"

"First, may I present my family? My mother, and my sister, Mary Jo. I should like you two to meet Michelle, Michael's twin. If Michael had come home, I should most probably be introducing Michelle as my soon-to-be sister-in-law."

As Miss Pyn drew her closer, Michelle smiled. "This is not the best time to meet you, Mrs. Pyn and Mary Jo, but, at long last, I' m very happy to know you."

They walked into the chapel, with Michelle a slight distance behind the Pyn ladies.

People came. There were many, some completely unknown to the family. They offered condolences. They signed the registry and waited for the ceremony to begin.

The funeral director, Mr. Howard, began: "In a few moments, Father Jim will begin the rites with special prayers for Mr. Pyn. After the initial prayers, we ask that you pay your final respects by filing in front of the casket beginning with the last row so the family will have the final farewell. We ask that you line up in our foyer and hallway. The family has asked that we walk in solemn procession the three blocks to the church. We will see that those who are unable to walk will be driven there. And now, Father Jim."

Father Jim stepped forward. He was tall, vigorous, quite young-looking for a pastor of a large parish. He was the same age as Thomas Pyn. They had attended grade school together and had renewed their friendship when Father Jim came to St. Clare's. He spoke in full voice, but haltingly.

"Good morning! Before we begin there are some thoughts I'd like to share. While the service this morning will be a regular Requiem Mass and Burial Service, it will also be ecumenical -- because every congregation in town, represented by clergy and by church members, will participate in this celebration. Though we mourn Tom Pyn's death, we celebrate the entrance of our friend and brother, husband and father into the glory of everlasting life. After the Holy Mass and the Rites of Christian Burial, we are all invited to return to our gathering room at St. Clare's and enjoy an ecumenical meal that is being prepared for us by ladies from every congregation in town. Truly, this is a marvelous testimony of esteem for our dear beloved Tom Pyn!

"Many in our community will remember that it was just five years ago that Bishop Lynch presided at the dedication of Tom's gift to all of us of the Saint Francis Garden. When the Bishop learned of Tom's untimely death, he was most dismayed by the news of his early departure from this life. When I asked, with the family's concurrence, that we be permitted to set aside a plot, within the garden, as a burial site dedicated to the Pyn family, the Bishop was most enthusiastic. He promised to bless the site on his return from Rome, where he will be for the next week. He also approved wholeheartedly of our special liturgy this morning and wished, with all his heart, that he could be with us instead of answering the call to the Vatican. So I am pleased to announce that Tom's remains will be placed in his beloved garden this morning.

"One thing more. At the church entrance, you will be given a pamphlet containing the readings and the service. On the first page are the words to our entrance song -- as yet unpublished, but we have permission to use them. The melody is a traditional Celtic melody that you will hear along the way to the church. We invite you to join in the singing of it as we enter.

"Now let us begin. In the name of the Father ..."

Miss Pyn had been seated that funeral morning between her mother and sister on one side and Michelle on the other. She remembered that she had thought: "How very considerate of Father Jim, but my father never sought recognition. He really shunned approbation, even acknowledgment. He often said he wanted only to love his family and his work -- which he did -- and little else mattered. Now he is dead, and nothing else matters. Why? Why should two such very good men have their lives so abruptly ended? I cannot accept it. I will not believe that it is just! How can it be just?"

"... and may his soul and all the souls of The Faithful Departed rest in Perpetual Light and Everlasting Peace."

The congregation responded, "Amen."

The assembled friends, neighbors, fellow-workers, and distant relatives passed by the casket. Some paused at Tom's picture. Others felt a need to touch the casket. All could see the single rose in one vase and the single calla in the other vase flanking the casket. The family came last, and paused for just a moment -- Mary Jo Pyn supporting her mother, and Miss Pyn clutching the arm of Michelle. Mary Jo, her mother, and Michelle had tears in their sad eyes. But Miss Pyn looked grim, with clenched teeth and with fiercely penetrating eyes searching a place beyond the casket as she thought, "I must not weep for Father nor for Michael. I will not weep for them nor for me. Not now, not ever!"

The women walked out toward the foyer to head the procession as Mr. Howard came forward to direct the pallbearers. "Good morning, gentlemen. Everyone here this morning appreciates your assistance. The task is rather more demanding because we will walk to church and to the place of burial. As you have heard, Father Jim has received permission to inter Tom's remains in the part of the St. Francis Garden that abuts the church cemetery. The burial plot will be consecrated next week. The burial site cannot be seen from the roadway, so it won't be apparent to anyone even though we plan a brief pause in the procession at the garden on the way to church.

"Several of you have asked if you could lift the casket on your shoulders in the European manner as a special tribute for your superintendent and friend. Even though you are all obviously fit and strong, we cannot recommend it. Unlike many European caskets, our caskets are too heavy. Along most of the way, the casket will rest on our portable bier with sturdy wheels. Your assistance will be required at stairways, at doorways, and at the burial site.

"One last word. The pause at the Saint Francis Garden is a tribute to Tom. At that point you could raise the casket a bit as your own tribute while Tom's lifelong friend, Matt McGregor, joins the procession to pipe his friend along the way into the church. If you have no questions, we can begin."

The procession with the casket on the bier moved slowly and silently along the roadway toward the church. As the cortege approached the Saint Francis Garden just outside the church cemetery, people lined the sidewalk in respectful silence. The procession continued on and then paused, as planned, opposite the Saint Francis Garden. The eight stout pallbearers raised the casket nearly to their shoulders and lowered it down again. Mr. McGregor began to play the Celtic melody as only mournful pipes could play it, and the procession walked on.

The melancholic yet joyful melody was played several times until the cortege arrived at the church door. Tom Pyn's eight strong friends lifted his casket into the church vestibule and onto the bier. The celebrant offered a brief blessing. Then the piper and the organist took up the melody again and began the entrance hymn in unison with the choir and congregation:

Morning has broken.. .... Like the first morning.
Blackbird has spoken .... Like the first bird.
Praise for the singing!......... Praise for the morning!
Praise for them springing.... Fresh from the Word!

The singing continued with Mr. McGregor playing at the rear of the church as Father Jim led the procession up the long aisle toward the altar:

Sweet the rain's new fall .... Sunlit from heaven,
Like the first dewfall.. .... On the first grass.
Praise for the sweetness .... Of the wet garden,
Sprung in completeness. .... Where His feet pass.

The casket was moved up the aisle, the pallbearers close behind. The Pyn family and Michelle followed. Miss Pyn's expression, still grim, was now beginning to look almost defiant.

At the altar, the pall was spread over the casket as the congregation entered the pews singing the final verse:

Mine is the sunlight,.. .... Mine is the morning
Born of the one light . ... Eden saw play!
Praise with elation, ... Praise ev'ry morning
God's re-creation .... Of the new Day!

Father Jim spoke: "Before we begin our liturgy, I should like to welcome all of you -- Tom Pyn's family, and his friends and associates from here and elsewhere. Perhaps many of you have come to our church for the first time. You are most welcome! It's a marvelous tribute to Tom that we are all here.

"This morning, members of the clergy from other congregations are here honoring Tom. They will join me in proclaiming the Word in our liturgy.

"We are delighted to welcome Rabbi David Weiss and his associate, Cantor Howard Small, of Temple Beth El; The Reverend Christopher Eriksen, pastor of Christ The King Lutheran Church; and The Reverend Malcolm Fenwick of St. Paul's Episcopal Cathedral.

"Let us begin. *In nominae Pater*...."

Miss Pyn whispered to Michelle, "This is all very thoughtful and kindly done, but I am not sure that I can endure it. Father is dead and Michael is dead. God may be in His heaven, but all is not right with our world. We must not pretend that it is."

Michelle's whispered response was vehement. "You must! We must endure it -- for your mother's sake, for your sister's, for my sake and your sake, and for Michael's as well as your father's sake. For all our sakes. You must! We must, no matter how difficult."

Miss Pyn remained motionless, even rigid, as the Rabbi began the first reading:

From *The Book of Wisdom:*
    ... the souls of the virtuous are

133

in the hands of God, no
torment shall ever touch them.
In the eyes of the unwise,
they did appear to die,
their going looked like a disaster,
their leaving us, like annihilation;
but they are in peace.   The Word of the Lord.

Michelle, who shivered at those words, held on to Miss Pyn, who remained fixed in apparent dismay. Cantor Small intoned "The Ninety-first Psalm" in remarkable *Old Testament* tone and cadence.

If you live in the shelter of the Most High
and make your home in the shadow of the God of
    heaven
you can say to the Almighty, 'My refuge, my fortress,
my God in whom I trust!'

He rescues you from the snares
of fowlers hoping to destroy you;
He covers you with his feathers,
and you find shelter under his wings.

You need not fear the terrors of night,
Or the arrow that flies in the daytime,

the plague that stalks in the dark,
the scourge that wreaks havoc in broad daylight.

... No disaster can overtake you,
no plagues come near your tent:
He will put you in His angels' charge
to guard you wherever you go. ...

"Michelle, I beg you -- tell me, how can I endure this! What must I do? Father is dead. Michael is dead. Where were the angels to guard them? I want to scream out, 'What had they done to offend their God?' Tell me if you can! Tell me now. How can I believe in justice, how can we believe in a just God when we know those two saints gave their lives for others, and there were no angels to protect them?"

"Again I say," Michelle whispered vehemently, "we must forget our own deep sorrow and try to salve the hurt of others all around us who did not know and love, and were not loved as long and as deeply by our two saints as we have been. Think too, of your mother and sister and my parents and their great sorrow."

Miss Pyn could not utter anything. Only a low murmur came through clenched teeth. Michelle felt a shiver from her brother's friend beside her, and she too responded as though a sudden chill had enveloped them both.

Reverend Eriksen began the next reading.

A reading from "The First Letter of John":
    Beloved! Let us love one another
    since love comes from God
    and everyone who loves is begotten of God
    and has a knowledge of God.
    The man without love knows nothing of God,
    because God is love!
    My dear people, since God has loved us so much,
    we too should love one another.
    ... God is love and anyone who lives in love lives in
        God,
    and God lives in him. The Word of the Lord.

"Michelle, I say again: they are both dead! They loved. We both know how deeply they loved. Jesus himself said, 'There is no greater love ...' If God lived in them and they are both dead, why is not God dead as well? Can you answer me?"

"I can't, dear friend. I do not know enough to explain the ways of God to you or to me. But I do know that you must stay. We must both remain, no matter how painful, if only to honor our loved ones as they loved us. Listen to the Gospel."

As Father Jim continued to pray in Latin, saying *Dominus vobiscum*, Reverend Fenwick proclaimed the Word in English.

A reading from "The Holy Gospel According to John":
"As the father has loved me,
I have loved you.
Live on in my love.
You will live on in my love
If you keep my commandments.

This is my commandment:
Love one another
as I have loved you!

There is no greater love than this:
to lay down one's life for one's friends.
You are my friends
If you do what I command you.
The command I give you is this:
love one another.   The word of the Lord.

The congregation responded, "Thanks be to God."

Some moments of silent reflection followed. Miss Pyn, with a face like stone, only gazed ahead.

"In the name of the Father..." Father Jim began his homily ...

"How can he explain all of this to us?" Miss Pyn whispered to Michelle. "How can he? I say he cannot,"

"We must listen!" Michelle replied. "We must."

"Sisters, brothers, friends -- Our Blessed Lord Himself commanded us to love one another, but we are to do so in a very special way. In the passage from scripture we have just heard, He pointedly said that we are to 'love one another as I have loved you.' That is, in the same way that He loved. What was that way? His love was the love of sacrifice -- that is, the giving of self. In His case, sacrifice included the ultimate sacrifice.

"We are undoubtedly not all called to give the ultimate, but if we give of ourselves faithfully we can expect the limitless reward of perfect happiness, of endless beatitude in an afterlife.

"The enormous number of us gathered here this morning, filling our church well beyond its capacity, is surely most persuasive evidence of Tom Pyn's service to those whose lives he touched -- to the very moment of his death. There can be little doubt that Tom's exemplary life will be rewarded.

"So why are we not jubilant? We should be celebrating the great victory that Saint Paul reminds us is the end of a good life. The liturgy and burial service today really are celebrations, sacred celebrations. Yet even though we believe in another life -- a life of happiness, we mourn and are sad, mostly for ourselves, because we have been deprived of a generous good man who loved all of us.

"Nonetheless, we wonder: Why should this be? How could such a wonderful man, who would undoubtedly help so many others and do so much more good, be called long before his 'three score and ten' expected years of life had been achieved? After all, the Psalmist wrote that the good who seek the protection of the Most High will be protected. Should not Tom have enjoyed the Lord's favor? In our way of thinking and seeing and knowing, these questions are understandable and they present legitimate puzzles.

"There are times, and surely this is one of the most difficult of such times, when I feel utterly incapable of even attempting to 'justify the ways of God to man.' And we find little comfort in knowing that our vision of the Divine Will and Plan is inadequate and that we can see only, as it were, 'through the glass darkly.'

"We are told, by even the earliest religious writers -- including those who knew Our Lord and Savior

Himself -- that we must have faith and trust in the Lord. Is that a satisfactory answer, especially for those among us who are enduring deeply disturbing sorrow? And is it enough to say 'this too will pass' or that suffering can result in a renewal of faith -- especially when it is endured in consideration of the redemptive process initiated by the sacrifice of Our Blessed Lord? Unfortunately, these are not satisfactory answers for everyone. And so, we must pray that all of us will be able to find peace of soul and mind in our hearts even in our mourning. Then perhaps we may be able to learn how to know and understand with the human heart.

"You notice I say that 'we' mourn. Some of you know that Tom and I were at school together and we were close buddies. After our school years, we had little contact until I came here as an inexperienced pastor and was welcomed by Tom, who organized all the landscaping of the grounds that our new church needed. He did much of the work himself. 'After all, Jim,' he insisted, 'it's my field.' Then, he designed and built the St. Francis Garden for everyone in our community.

"So I ask you to pray for all of us and especially for Tom's family who, like all of us, will know a great void, an emptiness that can never be filled in this life; but theirs will be greater and deeper. Say a special prayer too for Tom's elder daughter, who learned only last night that her dear friend, Warrant Officer Michael Hughes, died rescuing his comrades just two weeks ago in Korea.

"Grant them, Oh Lord, eternal rest and peace. We pray."

The entire congregation collectively gasped before answering, "And let perpetual light shine upon them."

The Eucharistic service continued until the time for Communion, when Miss Pyn whispered to Michelle, "I cannot do this! If I take Communion, I would feel like a hypocrite pretending to believe something I can no longer accept."

"Dear friend, do you know what? I think you're presuming that you are the most important person here. Have you no humility? Even if you doubt, you could be mistaken. I'll follow just behind you, and we will both receive Communion."

Although the sun was already in the western sky, the lawn beneath Miss Pyn's balcony was still a striking emerald. Two bluebirds alighting from nearby trees produced a brilliant contrast on the lovely green. Their foraging prompted Miss Pyn to realize she had not tasted the "scone" that Agnes had saved for her. Finding her tea cold, she thought, "A proper scone must have fresh warm tea as accompaniment. I must make another pot." She did so, even though she felt a trifle guilty since it was not Sunday.

She finished the cake and drank deeply. Contemplating the warm tea and listening to a program of traditional music, her mind returned again to that unforgettable funeral service.

It would be many years before Miss Pyn would realize that she should not have resented so deeply Michelle's commanding insistence that morning, and many years before she would understand how truly selfless and generous Michelle must have been in sublimating her own great sorrow and then guiding her dead brother's friend.

The funeral service continued to the final blessing. Father Jim blessed Tom Pyn's remains and then he blessed the congregation. The casket was moved slowly down the aisle to the church door as the congregation sang "How Great Thou Art."

The cortege moved around the outside of the church toward the Saint Francis Garden. Mr. McGregor, at the head of the procession, played "Amazing Grace." Along the way, Miss Pyn whispered to her mother, "Would it be all right if I miss the reception and see Michelle to her car? Will people understand?"

"Of course, dear. Everyone will know that you need some quiet time. Only, try not to grieve too much. Be careful."

They walked on toward the Saint Francis Garden. At the gravesite many eyes glistened, Miss Pyn's not among them. The floral arrangements from the funeral home would be distributed to churches and other places that would welcome them. There was no need to have them at the gravesite, for everywhere in the Saint Francis Garden there were roses in abundant spectacular bloom. Only the two single flowers -- the rose and the calla -- were placed on the casket -- a gesture of enduring esteem and gratitude from all who loved Tom.

Father Jim began the Rite of Burial... "Let us pray.

Oh God,
by whose mercy the faithful departed rest,
bless this grave,
and send Your holy angel to watch over it.

In sure and certain hope of the resurrection to
    eternal life
through our Lord Jesus Christ,
we commend to You, Almighty God,
our brother, Tom

and we commit his body to the ground
earth to earth, ashes to ashes, dust to dust.

The Lord bless him and keep him,
the Lord make His face to shine upon him
and be gracious to him
and give him peace.

"We'll conclude by praying our traditional final prayers. Those of you who know these prayers please join me. The rest, we know, will pray with us in your hearts. Our Father ... Hail Mary ... Glory be ... May Tom's soul and all the souls of the faithful departed through the mercy of God rest in peace."

Nearly everyone present responded, "Amen." Miss Pyn wanted to do so, but she could not. Instead, as Mr. Howard again invited everyone to the funeral reception, she and Michelle slipped away toward the funeral home. Both young women felt that they could not endure the expressions of condolence that many people were obviously eager to say to them; both hoped that they would not be thought rude; both hoped, in vain, that they would not be missed.

When they approached the cars parked near the funeral home, Michelle noticed the bridge over the stream and asked, "Could we stop a few minutes at the place we sat just yesterday? Even though I have an hour's drive home, I'd like to rest there for a few minutes."

"Of course we may. Resting there would be very peaceful, and refreshing too."

The two young women walked along the bank of the stream, and sat down where they had been sitting on the previous evening. Michelle was the first to see the blue heron ever so still like a regal statue.

"The bird is here again looking for his prey, but he might be watching us as well," Michelle whispered. "If we remain very quiet, do you think he'll stay?"

"I think he will. It is so peaceful here. He seems to like it, and so do I.

I could not have endured another moment at the funeral. It was entirely too painful. It was not the sorrow so much as it was the pretense. As well-meaning as everyone was, it was just more than I could bear."

"I think I know how you feel, but we must not let our grief overwhelm us. What are you going to do now?"

"Of course I shall not travel to England now, and I shall not be able to return to the university next term. I must find employment. I think Mary Jo should be the one to start school. She is the talented one among us. Besides, I have had two years of study. I shall be able to study in the evenings. Later on, I think I would like to

145

study Library Science. I should think I would fit nicely in a library. What do you think?"

"I think you'd make an excellent librarian, providing you don't use that as a means of running away from your life and your distress."

"You need not worry. What will you do?"

"Oh, I'll go back to school. My first year was all right, but I sometimes wonder if it is worth all that time and effort. I'll have three more long years of study before I can begin to do something serious. I can't let Michael down though. He didn't ever say so, but I suspect he had more reasons for his volunteering than he ever admitted even to me."

"You are quite right, Michelle, both in your resolve to do well in school and in your suspicions. Michael did want you to start school because he feared that if you did not do so last year, you might begin to think that it was too late. He also admitted to me that he did have more than one reason for enlisting. He believed that in that way he would be able to earn enough in service to complete his education later on; and you would be able to begin your study, since your parents would then be able afford your tuition."

"I knew it! Oh how very sad!" Michelle sobbed. "I knew it all along, because during our lives, we often thought exactly alike -- often knew each other's thoughts. That is exactly what Michael would do! It couldn't be any other way, could it?"

"Your brother was very precious to both of us. Without him, our lives will not be quite complete."

"I know -- and I find comfort in knowing that you loved him dearly, as I did. And I wish to apologize for my conduct in church this morning. There is no way I could wish to hurt you. If you found my bold insistence about what you should do offensive, I'm very sorry. I was only trying to do what I thought Michael would have wanted me to do. Again, I'm sorry!"

"You need not apologize, dear sister. I was not offended, but I was rather surprised -- so much so, that had I not been surprised, you would have had a more difficult time moving me to the altar. However, I shall accept your apology, even if I am no longer able to accept your theology. I simply cannot understand the idea of a just Deity allowing us both to live incomplete lives when we have no evidence of our offensive behavior."

"What can I say that will help either of us find peace? I can only pray, as Father Jim urged, that one day we will be able to see within our hearts that which we are now unable to understand. I will pray for us often. I truly will.

"But I must leave now so that my parents will not worry; I do have a long drive. No, don't get up. Stay here in the quiet that I know you need. Goodbye, farewell 'til next time. God bless." With that, Michelle slipped away.

Miss Pyn remained in silence for some time. She didn't even notice that the great blue heron moved slowly and silently, stepping nimbly along the river's edge toward the deepening shadows of the darkening woods. After a while, she said clearly to the lowering sky, "Michael! Why? Why did you have to leave us?"

On her balcony, the evening shadows also lengthened. From her little radio, she heard a traditional Welsh melody, "All Through the Night." She wondered: were her thoughts only about that particular night so long ago, or were they also of a longer, much darker night that she would come to know?

Thursday morning was bright. Miss Pyn was delighted to discover a cloudless sky, especially since she had expected a dismal Thursday ever since she had read the weekly weather report on Sunday which promised a rainy Thursday. On the previous day, Wednesday, she had spent a full day and evening at the library readying things for her departure. Each time, throughout the day and evening when she thought that she could leave, she discovered still another detail that she had to address. With each discovery, she thought wistfully that she would most likely have no time to spend on her balcony, especially if the weather forecast for Thursday proved to be true.

Fortunately, the five-day prediction was not accurate; her last full day in Seven Oaks promised to be delightful. Since she had worked so very long on Wednesday evening, nearly everything that needed to be completed was done; so that all was in readiness. She could even enjoy her balcony for a few minutes this morning, " -- which I had better do," she thought, "just in case the weather should change. Joe will not mind if I am a bit late. He delights in starting the day before I arrive at the library."

She relaxed, remembering she had made arrangements with her neighbor whose daughter would look in periodically, water the plants and see that the bird-feeding stations were filled. Then she thought, "Am I really going to be away for nearly a month? I find it difficult to believe that I have never been away or even thought of being away for that long. Oh yes, Carole and I planned, long ago, on being away in England for at least three months. Strange that I should remember Carole and our great plan the day before I am really going to get to England at last. Well, I had best get to the library soon."

At the library door, Joe, dressed in a business suit, greeted her. "Good morning, Miss Pyn. Are you beginning to feel excited about your trip? 'Tis your last day here, you know."

"I do know, Joe, and I have mixed feelings too. After all the years of waiting, I am still not entirely certain that I am really going to be there sometime tomorrow. There are times that I am apprehensive about going, and there are times that I am apprehensive about leaving. Should I really be doing this when there is so much I could do here?"

"Of course you should go, Miss Pyn! You'll be a whole new person when you return -- ready to tackle anything. Take it from me."

"Thank you, Joe. I trust you are correct. However, Joe, I notice that you are not dressed for work this morning. Have you a special reason for not wearing your working clothes today?"

Joe looked quickly toward the roses with a knowing expression and smile that Miss Pyn failed to notice. "When I worked at the university, these were my regular working clothes. In fact, during my last semester, before I accepted my emeritus appointment, I gave several lectures in this very suit. You see, faculty members of my generation were rather more formal than today's lecturers. We always wore business suits in the classroom. We thought that the more informal dress one might see on the campus today was appropriate for gardening or fishing or physical labor. No jeans and sneakers and sweatshirts for us! Now mind you, we were never as formal as some of our European colleagues who wear academic robes to class. On the other hand, in Europe, I felt it necessary, even in summer, to carry a necktie with me in case I wanted to study in a library. This was especially true in England."

"You know, Joe, that you need not wear a tie in our library even if you choose to wear a suit coat. However, you have not told me why you are so formal today. Is it a secret?"

For a moment, Joe looked panic-stricken. Again Miss Pyn failed to notice his expression. Relieved, Joe confessed, "I have an appointment later on this afternoon. Since I have no heavy work to do today, I thought it would be all right to dress this way and not have to return home to dress for the appointment."

"Of course it is! You work so efficiently that you could have taken the whole afternoon off -- or the whole day, for that matter -- to keep your appointment. I do not have very much to do today either. The students worked so well with me yesterday that there is not much left for me to do. I thought that I would clear off my desk and perhaps leave a bit early too."

Joe looked troubled. "But if I'm not here because of my appointment, who will greet the students when they come, Miss Pyn?"

"I had not thought of that, Joe. I suppose I can stay until the girls arrive after school. I should still have enough time to relax on my balcony this evening."

Again relieved, Joe continued, "I think, too, that the girls would like to say goodbye to you, Miss Pyn."

"Perhaps you are right, Joe. I shall not disappoint them. Even though I thanked them and said goodbye last night, I could thank them once again."

The work of the day moved along nicely. For a while, Joe helped re-shelve some books, and then said he needed to inventory supplies in the gardening shed. Miss Pyn began organizing her desk. If she suspected anything in Joe's unusual manner that morning, it was not at all apparent.

By two o'clock, Miss Pyn looked eager to leave for home. Joe came in from the shed. Miss Pyn wondered, "Are you going to be on time for your appointment, Joe? You said you would not be here when the girls arrive."

"Oh! I'd forgotten that they can come so early. Anyway, my appointment is quite close by."

Joe was much relieved to see Miss Thrust's car turn into the library drive just then. "Looks like someone else has come to say goodbye to you."

"Why, Miss Thrust! What an unexpected pleasure! What brings you here today?"

Looking a bit preoccupied, Miss Thrust explained, "I have some things in my trunk that we can use at the next meeting of the Library Board. Besides, I couldn't let you escape to England without saying goodbye. Joe, would you mind putting those things in the back room? They're in two boxes in the trunk. Here are the keys. We'll miss you, Miss Pyn, at the Board meeting. But I think we'll survive, despite missing your wonderful wit and your excellent tea."

"I shall miss the meeting as well, but I am confident that I shall not be needed, for both the meeting and the library will be under your excellent leadership."

"Thank you. I thought that you might have left the library by now. You must be facing a very busy day tomorrow. I am so pleased that I haven't missed you. You needn't leave just now?"

"No. I promised Joe that I would stay to greet the girls, because he said that he has an appointment this afternoon. I am beginning to wonder just where and when he will be having that appointment."

"I'm sure Joe would never mislead you, Miss Pyn. You needn't worry about things here. It's time you thought of yourself and your trip. It sounds absolutely wonderful! Many of us here wish we could be going with you. ... Look who's coming up the walk! I believe that is Ida West, probably coming to say goodbye too -- though I don't know how she found out about your trip. I didn't even tell the members of the Library Board."

Miss Thrust greeted Ida West hurriedly. "Why, good afternoon, Ida. I see you've brought supplies for our next Board meeting."

Ida, carrying a box that looked suspiciously like a cake box, appeared puzzled. "The Board meeting? Er ... oh yes, the Board meeting! I thought the meeting was next week. Am I too late or too early?"

"The meeting is next week," Miss Thrust reassured her. "But you have come at the right time, because I, too, just now brought material for the meeting."

Miss Pyn began to look a little suspicious, especially when Ida West said, "Miss Pyn, I heard that you are going to be away for a while, so I wanted to say goodbye and thank you for the help you gave me in compiling the bibliography on dance. I discovered facts about things I've been doing all along, and now I know the proper names for them. I feel that I will be able to give a course now. Thank you so much!"

"I am pleased that you are going to offer a class," Miss Pyn replied. "I might consider enrolling in it myself." Then she added with a mischievous smile, "I see Mrs. Harris coming up the carriageway. Is she also carrying 'materials' for your next meeting in what is clearly a cake box?"

Miss Thrust looked a little uneasy. "I suppose that we may as well confess. I, of course, knew about your plans for travel. Some of the ladies heard about your trip -- but not from me, I assure you. We thought it would be a delightful surprise to have a proper English tea for you as a *bon voyage* party."

"How did they learn of my destination? I told no one else -- except, perhaps, Agnes at the bakery. I shall have a word with her."

"You needn't, Miss Pyn. As far as I know, Agnes spoke to no one about your holiday, as you call it. She did call me, hoping to be included in the celebration."

Ida West added support to Miss Thrust's assurances. "No one needed to say anything at all! A number of us knew you planned to be away, and you had Linda Livingston take new passport pictures of you at her studio. We all knew that there was only one place you'd think of going overseas. It had to be to England."

Mrs. Harris helped by changing the conversation a bit as she entered.

"Miss Pyn, I wanted to see you before you leave and before Ann comes home so I could thank you for all you've done, not only for Ann but for many others too. I've brought this little English walnut cake for you. It's made from my grandmother's favorite recipe. I hope you'll enjoy your trip."

"I thank you, Jane. As I have surely said before, I have had little to do with the maturing of our students. I simply insisted that the library would always be a library in every respect, and the atmosphere and the students themselves did the rest. You are so kind to think that I did make a difference."

"Well, Miss Pyn, now that you know why we are here," Miss Thrust said with relief, "we'd best be about setting up for the party before the others arrive. Joe brought in the traditional sterling silver tea service that my grandfather had sent over from England. It's been in our house ever since. In my grandmother's day the house boasted of an excellent household staff to care for such things as polishing all that was needed for a proper party. Nowadays, I am the entire staff, so the tea service is brought out only for very special occasions. I am delighted we can use the set today."

Livinia Grimsby came bustling up the driveway just then. She had so wanted to bring her very special punch to the *bon voyage* fest. She had planned on presenting it with a flourish. She even planned the words she would use in her presentation: "This punch is most appropriate for such an important time. In my family it was always known as the 'departure punch.'"

After the planners of the tea party had learned of Livinia's ingredients for the punch -- which included, in Livinia's own words, "an excellent bottle of imported Burgundy, a superb cognac, and a dram or two of a wonderful special Jamaican rum that has been our family treasure for some years" -- they had had some difficulty convincing Livinia that, while the punch might be most appropriate for a departure, it was not at all appropriate for a party in a public library, even if the library once had been a great private house. On the other hand, Joe wondered, mostly to himself, just exactly what kind of departure would a punch containing so many spirits be best suited for -- a wake, perhaps?

Livinia entered the library carrying a large plastic bag. "Good afternoon, Miss Pyn! I'm so glad to be part of this celebration of your departure for England! I wanted to bring a generous sample of a punch that our family treasures. We call it 'departure punch.' But the planners of this fete convinced me that it would not be appropriate in the library. So I brought this token of appreciation instead. My daughter and her husband and I are most grateful for the magic you employed to transform our dear Vinny! We all thought that my granddaughter would not be able to qualify for college, or even to finish high school. She so resented having to devote time to study! Your work with the library high-school program changed her completely! She suddenly discovered the joy of learning, went on to college, graduated with honors, and has been accepted in the Graduate School of Education at Columbia University! She plans to concentrate in Educational Psychology. She says, 'I intend to be an educational guidance counselor, because if anyone understands reluctant learners, I certainly do!' It's all your doing, Miss Pyn! We thank you."

"As I have said before," Miss Pyn protested, "students come to the library just when they are ready to grow, and they do. The Student Library Program has had some marvelous successes that have been a joy for all of us. It is the students who change. The librarian does very little to accomplish that development."

"You are too modest, Miss Pyn! We know better!" Livinia insisted. "So I brought along an English dessert.

It's only a trifle. In fact, it's sometimes called a 'trifle.' Some of our relatives call it 'graveyard pudding,' or even 'tombstone pudding,' because the pudding is topped with slivered almonds that are set on end so they look like grave markers in a churchyard! It's really quite light. It's made with an angel food cake at the base flavored with a bit of our family treasure, Jamaican rum, topped with a light pudding, and the almonds. I hope you'll enjoy it!"

Joe, standing nearby, only smiled, shaking his head in amusement.

Just then, Ida West brought forth her treasure -- a wonderful confection from her kitchen, in a large box overflowing with beautifully baked, delicate brandy snaps. "For this special occasion, Miss Pyn, I brought my rare specialty -- one I bake for only a most precious celebration. These snaps are very rich, and we ladies know what rich confections can do! They are rare not only because they are rich, but also because they require patient preparation and dexterous fingers. They must be baked to perfection on a cookie sheet and then, while still warm, nimbly shaped, using a wooden spoon handle, then carefully and precisely set to cool to await the cream filling. I've brought them from home at what I think is exactly the right temperature for the filling. I can add the whipped cream I've already prepared in about ten minutes, and then they'll be ready to be served."

"Well then," Miss Thrust observed a bit impatiently, "we are just about ready to begin. Henrietta Smithfield will be along shortly with warm crumpets and the butter and jam for topping. While Ida adds the filling to her marvelous snaps, would you help me, Livinia, bring in some other treats? I've brought, Miss Pyn, some of the little sandwiches you showed me how to make -- including, of course, the English cucumber ones. We even managed to get something we all thought you'd like -- Twinings Tea."

The party was just underway, when Henrietta arrived quite breathless. "I was so afraid that I would be late! The crumpets took a longer time to bake than I expected, and we might not have had any at all! We just couldn't have had a proper party without crumpets! Fortunately, I checked my old crumpet rings as soon as I learned I could bring the crumpets, and I found they were no longer usable. I didn't quite know what to do! My daughter-in-law, however, knows of a shop in Toronto that was willing to send them express, and so we have the crumpets! I hope you will enjoy them, Miss Pyn."

With a grateful smile Miss Pyn declared, "What a delightful surprise all of this is, and what a perfect introduction to my holiday journey! Even when I say thank you, you all know I am unable to thank you enough. Of course, Henrietta, we will all enjoy your crumpets -- very much indeed."

Joe announced, "The teapot has been pre-warmed with boiling water, and the tea has just been added to fresh hot water and will be ready in just a few moments."

Just then, Agnes entered eagerly. "Good afternoon, Miss Pyn, how nice to see you! 'Tis a fine day t'day, as we all hoped. I learned that there'd be a gathering here, so, thought I, I'll join in and bring your favorite little cake -- in fact, I thought to bring two! Since you'll not be comin' into the shop tomorrow, your usual Friday two-for-one special had to be t'day. With my compliments, Miss Pyn -- have a safe and enjoyable journey, even if you won't be stoppin' in Ireland. I hope ya know that I kept my promise not to say anythin' about yer travel to England. I so wanted to share yer grand news, but now I see 'twas wholly unnecessary. Seems most people know about it already."

"Thank you, Agnes. I did not think that you would inform everyone in the village about my plan for travel, even though it is tempting to share a secret, especially when it is good news. I must say that this table setting on such fine linen with silver and delicate china is simply delightful! And with all the scrumptious English tea fare, this celebration should be in honor of a royal personage instead of the village librarian. It is beautiful!"

Joe quietly interrupted, "Of course, it is set for a very important personage. It's for you, Miss Pyn! We all thank you very much for all that you do at our library!"

At that moment the two student assistant librarians, Christie and Yvonne, came to work for the after-school shift. Both were taken aback by the number of patrons in the library, and the beautiful tea setting. "Christie, have you ever seen such a cool -- or should I say, such an attractive tea setting?"

"I haven't, Yvonne, except maybe in a movie about England. It's really very beautiful, Miss Pyn, and perfect for your going-away party."

"Why, thank you, and good afternoon, Christie, and you too, Yvonne. This has been quite a surprise. Did either of you know about this?"

"We did and we didn't, Miss Pyn. Right Christie?"

"Yes. We were told to wear clothes suitable for a party. So we thought that something must have been planned. Of course we usually wear outfits suited to our job here. Agree, Yvonne?"

"Yes. I, for one, thought that for today we could be a little less professional. So you see our outfits are a lighter color, and we both have worn brightly colored neck scarves. Do you approve, Miss Pyn?"

"Of course I do, ladies. Come, you must sample everything on the tea table before any other library patrons come to be served. There are crumpets, which every proper tea requires, and tea sandwiches -- even a special sweet called a 'trifle.'"

"Girls," Miss Thrust interrupted, "you're just on time. At the risk of breaking an important social rule, I was about to invite Miss Pyn, our guest of honor, to demonstrate how to pour tea properly. Then I'll do the others. Would you, Miss Pyn?"

"Oh my, yes. I have learned how it is done only through reading . Perhaps others here have had firsthand experience. You are not breaking a social custom by inviting me to pour. I am even more honored by the invitation to pour on this occasion which I must insist honors everyone who contributes to the efficient running of our Seven Oaks library -- you, Miss Thrust, and the Board, the volunteers, the students in the library program, even the patrons, and especially Joe, without whom we could not even open."

"Miss Pyn," Joe responded, "you are entirely too self-effacing. Everyone knows you are the library! If you insist that we are all honored by your party, I can think of no one who could better exemplify the generosity of our community than you!"

"Joe, with all these compliments, I think I should pour while I am still able to do so." As she did so, she assumed the role of instructor. "I should like my tea white -- that is, with milk and not with cream. Cream tea is quite a different matter. I take the teapot in one hand and the milk jug in the other and I pour both simultaneously to ensure a good blend." Miss Pyn looked very pleased with the results of her expertise. "Other than this, pouring is quite straightforward. Sugar and lemon may be added as desired. May I turn the teapot over to you, Miss Thrust?"

"By all means. Ladies, be sure to sample everything on the tea table -- especially you young ladies who needn't be concerned about weight yet."

The young ladies were impressed. "Look, Christie, these must be the crumpets -- how cool! And look, here is jam to put on them. Have you ever seen butter served like that before?"

"I haven't -- in such cute little balls. I wonder how that's done. Miss Thrust, did you prepare the crumpets and the butter?"

"No, Christie. Henrietta Smithfield brought the crumpets and the jam and butter. Don't they complement the tea table beautifully?"

"Yes they do, but how did you do that, Mrs. Smithfield?"

Mrs. Smithfield was delighted to reply: "My former Danish neighbor, Grethe Hansen, showed me how to do that. It's fun, and really very easy with a melon-ball cutter."

The going-away tea party continued for some time with continuous talk and occasional laughter. The tea was warm and good and best of all, thought Miss Pyn, it was Twinings Tea.

The time for evening departure was nearing when Joe announced, "There is one thing more. A proper *Bon Voyage* requires a proper toast. I found some 'free champagne,' which is better suited to a party in our library than any other because 'free' does not refer to the cost, but to the alcoholic content. So even you young ladies can join our toast."

The corks were popped, and the glasses Joe had smuggled in were passed around and filled. Joe proposed the toast: "To a safe and refreshingly good journey, Miss Pyn! Cheers and All the Best!"

"To good health!" exclaimed Miss Thrust.

Agnes joined in, "*Slainte*, as we say in Cork."

"*Salute*," said Ida West.

"As my Danish neighbors always said, '*Skol!*'" Mrs. Smithfield added. The toasting might have gone on for some time had not other library patrons begun to arrive. It was time for final goodbyes.

Exhausted, but very happy and pleased with her grand send-off, Miss Pyn relaxed on her balcony with her tea. The evening was cool yet perfectly still, and an excellent balm for weariness. Miss Pyn thought of lines from an English poem, "'Tis a beauteous evening calm and free. The holy time a solemn stillness holds." She decided, "Oh, perhaps those lines come from two different poems. Nonetheless, they provide a perfect description of this evening. The English poets surely knew how to write! Tomorrow I shall be in England."

She sipped her tea as she recalled, "Carole and I were so excited when we expected to travel there. We were so close, and we planned more than our trip. We agreed that if and when we married, we would be each other's maid of honor."

The evening breeze cooled the night air even more. Miss Pyn welcomed the warmth of the tea as she huddled near the precious forget-me-not teapot Carole had sent so many years before from Stratford. Another package had arrived from Stratford a year later, just before Brad and Carole's wedding. The package contained a little pin of silver and rhinestones in an abstract design, suggesting a bird or a butterfly. There was a note too. Carole had written: "Brad and I purchased little gifts for the members of our wedding party. Please accept this token as your gift. Nancy, our new friend over here, was delighted to be your stand-in at our wedding. After she learned of our pledge to each other, she said with typical English wit that she was honored to serve as your proxy at the wedding."

Miss Pyn thought wistfully for a moment and then went in to her desk. She took out a very special box, which held precious keepsakes. She saw Carole's first note about the teapot from Stratford. She put it aside and took out the little pin, holding it up in the evening light before returning it to the box. Then she took out a letter, returned to her balcony, settled into her chair, turned on her reading light, and began to read:

My dear Miss Pyn: I write in answer to your inquiry. You wrote that you wondered why you hadn't heard from Carole and Brad for some time. There is an important reason for their lack of communication.

You remember that the young people were married in England after having studied in France. Carole's mother and I were not able to be at the wedding. Instead, we planned with Brad's parents to surprise our children with a celebration in England during the holidays after the wedding.

That was not to be. The kids had a joyous honeymoon in Italy. They wrote how happy they were in Italy and indeed in all of Europe. They felt that they belonged there. In Florence, they wrote that they as artists came alive again. They sent a card saying that, happily, they had just enough time and money to drive to Salzburg and Vienna. Then nothing. Over a week later, we learned from authorities that our children were killed instantly on a highway when an automobile slipped off a truck hauling vehicles and landed on top of their car.

So we joined Brad's parents on a trip much earlier than we had expected. Instead of going to a celebration, we traveled to claim our children's remains. On the way there, we all agreed that our son and daughter truly did belong in Europe, and we arranged for a burial site on a hill in a little village churchyard in the south of France, where they could rest in peace.

I'm very sorry to have to tell you all of this, and to do so long afterward. While we did know that you had planned to study with Carole in England, we didn't know your whereabouts until you wrote. Our grief is slowly passing, and we hope that this news is not too distressing to you. We console ourselves in knowing that Carole and Brad found each other, and that they found their artistic souls in Europe. We hope that you will be able to find some solace in that knowledge as well.

Carole was truly grateful for your friendship, and we remain so too.

Sincerely,

Harold and Virginia Martin

Miss Pyn remembered her determination, held long ago, not to weep for her father or for Michael. She remembered, too, that when the Martins' letter arrived she still held on to that determination. But many years had passed, and she began to understand that her determination was only the result of her deep-seated bitterness. Then slowly she had learned how to meet her sorrow. Now, she recalled Carole's intention to paint her portrait in their blue gown every few years, and she wept quietly. Then she remembered that she must start her journey to England early the next morning.

The morning was cool, but the early sun gave promise of a comfortable travel day. Miss Pyn was ready earlier than necessary, and eager to ride the shuttle to the airport. Joe had offered to drive her to the airport: "After all, Miss Pyn, the drive will be a pleasant diversion for me amid the routine of the day."

Miss Pyn insisted, "While a good chat on the way to the airport would be a most enjoyable *bon voyage*, I think that the two-hour round trip to the airport is entirely too generous and thoughtful, Joe. You certainly have more than enough to do here at this time of year. I have taken the shuttle many times for domestic flights to library meetings. The shuttle will deliver me right to the door of the international terminal. I shall be most comfortable, safe, and right on time. You are needed here to help the volunteers; and besides, when the students arrive, they will need your direction. So, no thank you, Joe! I truly value your solicitude. I will not be away for very long because I know I shall miss Seven Oaks, the library, the patrons, and your special concern for the students."

"Of course we'll miss you too, Miss Pyn. So don't stay away too long."

Miss Pyn found that the shuttle was right on time. She had followed Carole's advice, and was traveling with little luggage and Joe's fold-up travel bag. There were few other passengers. Those already on board all seemed to be serious business travelers, so Miss Pyn found much time for comfortable quiet reflection as the vehicle continued on the way toward the airport.

"At long last," she thought, "I am on my way! It seems that this marks a definite break with what has gone on in my life so far. I remember so well the last time I had such a definitive leave-taking. Mother had moved to California to be near my sister, and Carole had gone to Europe. I had just finished my Library Science program and learned of a position opening in the Village of Seven Oaks. The journey there seemed to take a very long time before I finally arrived ..."

"Good morning! I have come in response to the request for a librarian that Miss Thrust sent to our school placement office." The woman at the desk seemed to Miss Pyn to be rather formidable for a receptionist.

"Oh yes, good morning! You must be Miss Pyn. I'm most pleased to welcome you! I'm Henrietta Thrust, and I hope you will find our little library satisfactory. Judging from your excellent recommendations, we will be fortunate to have you join us."

"Why, thank you!" responded Miss Pyn, quite surprised by this enthusiastic greeting. "Seven Oaks is a charming village. The library grounds are just lovely. The building itself is most impressive. I have not ever seen a building made with such colorful and warm stone. It is stone, is it not? It seems almost soft."

"It's stone, but it's unique in this country. My grandfather grew up in the Cotswold district in England, and he had the stone imported. This building was the home he built for his family. As you might suspect, the

171

stone gets its name from the district. So it's Cotswold stone."

"It is very beautiful."

"Thank you. I'm pleased that you noticed the character of this building, and I hope you will enjoy working in it. We all think it's very special, and beautiful too. Since the house is too much for me to occupy, care for, and maintain, I've invited my neighbors to use it as our village library. The building will need very little alteration to be suitable to become our library. Grandfather had an excellent collection of books. The English Literature and History holdings are almost complete, except for only some recent publications that I'm sure you can readily identify. That is, if you agree to be our librarian. At the moment, the stipend for the librarian is rather modest, but I think the Friends of the Library will be willing and able to improve the financial picture here. The building is in Trust with ample funds for maintenance. So we are confident that our library will become a village gem as soon as we succeed in attracting the right person for our new endeavor. I think we've discovered that person. I hope you'll agree."

Miss Pyn found Miss Thrust overwhelming. She could hardly believe that the position of librarian for this very special library was being offered to her -- a new graduate from the school of Library Science. She was not sure what to say. She was not sure she could say anything. The building was lovely, the village inviting, the opportunity enviable but also challenging -- very! Miss Thrust and her limitless optimism made the prospect even more formidable. Yet she could not pass up this opportunity despite the ominous "modest stipend." Should she accept? At last she said, "I shall need a place to stay."

"Wonderful! Most wonderful! Your lodging is already arranged. Harold Jensen owns the Village Hardware Store, and has an apartment above the store. As a member of the Friends, he has offered that apartment, except for the cost of the utilities, to the library for use of our new librarian. I'm sure the new Library Board will be able to provide for reasonable utilities. All of that should make your modest stipend a little less modest."

"Yes, that surely makes the position even more attractive. It seems most generous."

"We're pleased that you will join us! We've even planned alternative lodging. If the Jensen apartment is unsatisfactory, we'll be able to arrange temporary living quarters here in the library building. After all, it was once a home. In fact, about one third of the back part of each floor was once devoted to living quarters for resident servants. But most of us nowadays feel that after spending long days at work here it would be better to leave the premises for the night."

"Oh yes, I think that very wise."

At that moment, the shuttle coach driver picked up the last commuter bound for the airport, and asked passengers to name their airlines. Miss Pyn was pleased to say, "British Airways."

The coach continued on its way.

As the shuttle progressed along the highway toward the airport, Miss Pyn reflected on those early years at Seven Oaks. Her life had been constantly busy, filled with sometimes-delightful work and often as not less satisfying, even monotonous activities that often left her exhausted. Yet she found that Miss Thrust's assessment of her grandfather's library of English literature was accurate. English poets from Chaucer to T.S. Eliot were well represented. There were even several collections of Shakespeare's plays and poems: one three-volume set with iron-cut illustrations from the nineteenth century, a facsimile copy of *The First Folio*, and several modern editions of collected works, as well as individual publications of the plays with extensive notes and illustrations. This was a horde worthy of a scholar. There were many other volumes of fiction and non-fiction literature, which included works from *Moll*

Flanders and *Gulliver's Travels* to *The Forsythe Saga* and *A Passage to India*.

The works of Dickens, Scott, Thackeray, and even Collins were well represented. The Brontes were there, and best of all, the complete novels of Jane Austen. Miss Pyn found all that she could have hoped for in a personal library. There was more: English and Irish dramatic literature, Irish poetry, an excellent selection of World Literature both ancient and modern, and a rather complete collection of American authors filled the literature collection. Miss Thrust was quite right. Miss Pyn would have little to do to improve that part of the holdings.

Over many years, she grew to know that literature very well. The work in the library and the richness of the life she lived - vicariously as well as actually -cultivated a depth of spirit in her inner life. Yet she was never quite comfortable reading those authors who might be called "religious." Even though she was very fond of the poetry of Gerard Manley Hopkins, and felt a special kinship with his mastery of language, she often avoided his deeply religious poems. She did not at first realize that something was missing in her life.

The airport shuttle moved along the freeway, passing on the way a country church with a lovely garden. The church, and especially the garden once again prompted Miss Pyn to recall her first meeting with Tom.

She had ridden her bicycle out of Seven Oaks into the countryside north of town. She paused to rest at a beautiful garden across the road from a church. She gazed around her admiring the flowers, and did not see the figure kneeling in front of the roses until he moved.

"Oh! Good morning! I did not see you there, caring for the roses. They are very beautiful. I suspect you must be the gardener. My name is Pyn. I am the librarian in Seven Oaks."

"How do you do. My name is Tom, and people say I'm the gardener here. I do go to your library rather regularly." Tom stood up, and took off his gloves. He was tall and fit, and he had brown hair with a few hints of gray in it. "I usually get to Seven Oaks in the evening when most of my work is done. I don't remember seeing you there. It's quite an impressive library."

"Thank you! You do not see me there because my responsibility fills the entire day. I'm usually not there in the evening. It has been only a few years now since I have had students in the library program who are capable enough to keep the library open during evening hours."

"Well, your assistants are most capable and thoughtful. One or the other and sometimes both students have helped me find things quite often. I thank you!"

"I am pleased to hear that. Our students are always eager to help the library patrons."

Miss Pyn once again admired the roses. She was surrounded by fragrant blossoms. "Your garden is very pleasant. You must find great satisfaction in caring for it."

"I do. In fact, I feel very privileged to be able to care for this garden. You're certainly welcome to rest here whenever you like. The church is open most hours. The atmosphere there is even better suited to refreshment. You're certainly most welcome to stop there."

"I thank you, but I find that the garden with its aura of nature is most conducive to spiritual refreshment. So I shall surely come again."

Miss Pyn smiled to herself, remembering, as the shuttle coach continued on the way, that Thomas had been away working in Italy for some time now and perhaps she should have written that she was going to visit England. Then she thought that it was just as well she did not write, because he might have tried to persuade her to visit him in Italy and she certainly could not have afforded the time for that. She remembered, too, that after that first meeting with Tom she had looked forward to riding out into the countryside to rest in his garden.

One afternoon, Tom was again working in the garden. She greeted him: "As is always the case, the garden is lovely, and I have had several opportunities to enjoy its beauty. I thank you!"

"I'm sorry I missed you, but unfortunately I can't be here all the time. In fact, I'm not here most of the time." Tom rose with a welcoming smile. "But it is very pleasant here, and I come to work whenever I can. Oh dear!" Tom looked up at gathering clouds. "The weather has suddenly become rather threatening! I think we're in for a shower. I suspect it'll be brief, but we'd better find shelter in the church."

"Thank you, but I am weatherproof!" Miss Pyn reached into the bicycle basket and took out a small package. "I seldom ride anywhere without my rainwear. You see, I have my poncho, and I even enjoy a light rain in the garden as long as there is no lightning."

"As you wish. But you're most welcome to seek shelter -- or is it sanctuary -- in the church. Listen! I hear thunder in the west. Where there is thunder there is at least the possibility of lightning. We'd better go in!"

"Again, you are most generous and again I thank you. I must be off!" With that, Miss Pyn mounted her bicycle and started toward Seven Oaks. She paused long enough to explain, "I hope you will understand. I have not been inside a church for many years."

Tom was dumbfounded …

The coach turned off the freeway and Miss Pyn marveled, remembering that then, and even now, she was puzzled that she should reveal to a stranger something as personal as her feeling about the church. All she knew about the man was that he sometimes worked in the church garden. Why was she drawn to reveal her spiritual state of mind to him?

The coach made stops at several terminals as the driver announced the airlines to be found at each one. Finally, Miss Pyn was the last passenger on the coach. "Our last stop will be the International Terminal," the driver reassured her. The coach stopped, and Miss Pyn took her first real step on her journey to England.

The International Terminal was comparatively small, with five or six ticket counters for various airlines offering travel service to several countries. Miss Pyn found the British Airways desk at one end of the building. There were two prospective passengers arranging their tickets ahead of her. Although she had traveled to many places by air over the years, this trip was the one she had anticipated for her whole adult life. "Now at last," she thought, "it really is about to begin. I must remember to appear quite casual."

"Good afternoon!" A young woman in a trim airline uniform graciously greeted Miss Pyn. The clerk appeared genuinely pleased to see her.

"Good afternoon! My name is Pyn. I believe that I have a reservation on your plane to London this afternoon."

"Oh yes, Miss Pyn. Would you mind waiting a few moments? Our supervisor asked to be informed upon your arrival."

"Not at all. I have waited many years for the moment of our departure. A bit longer will hardly matter at all."

Without a word of explanation, the apparently efficient attendant departed to an inner office while Miss Pyn nervously wondered if there was going to be a further impediment to her journey.

Presently another woman emerged from the inner office with a bright welcoming smile. Miss Pyn thought that this handsome young woman seemed vaguely familiar, but she was not certain where she might have met her. Her smile was most welcoming.

"Good afternoon, Miss Pyn. I'm so happy to see you, and so very pleased that you will be flying with us today. Perhaps you don't remember me?"

"Oh yes! Now that I hear your voice, I believe that I do. It has been a number of years, but I think you must be Jennifer -- Jennifer Grey."

"As always, you are precisely correct. I was in one of your earlier groups of student assistant librarians; although, in my time, we were not yet called 'librarians.' That came later. Miss Pyn, you're not due to board for some time yet, and I have some relief time. Why don't we sit and chat a bit in our waiting room for special passengers?"

"How very thoughtful! That will be very nice indeed."

Jennifer led the way to a comfortable lounge with a fully equipped bar.

"We can talk here. I don't expect many special passengers this afternoon. May I serve you a glass of sherry?"

"Thank you, but I think not. I wish to be very alert when this flight commences. I have waited some years for this day."

"Yes, I know. I remember your plan to visit England was well formed even before the time I studied with you. By the end of my second year in the library student assistant program, I knew that your English expectations were infectious! I developed similar plans."

Miss Pyn smiled with delight. "I remember your keen interest in English literature, but I did not suspect either your desire to travel to England or my influence in that direction."

"As it turned out, your influence was rather profound. When I went off to the university, there was no question of what my major would be. Only English Language and Literature would do."

"That is certainly reassuring," Miss Pyn replied with some hesitation.
"However, while such study can undoubtedly result in a true enlargement of the mind, an undergraduate English major is not very useful for career preparation."

"Oh, I had fully expected to continue my education at a graduate school. I thought I might follow your example and study Library Science. I did need some income before I could continue in grad school. British Air needed a summer replacement, and I was fortunate to qualify."

"That was good fortune indeed, and I see you are still with the airline."

"Yes. I'm very fond of my work, and they've sent me to England several times for training. As a member of the firm, I can take my vaca ... that is, my holiday in the UK."

Miss Pyn smiled at Jennifer's use of British English. "How very nice, Jennifer! So you have been to England before my first visit! But today I shall finally get there."

"I'm happy for you, Miss Pyn, but actually your arrival there will be tomorrow."

Miss Pyn shook her head. "While that is literally true, I shall not sleep on the plane; so I can think of it as the second part of today."

"If you say so, Miss Pyn." Jennifer smiled indulgently. "Would you like a cup of tea? I know we have English Breakfast and Earl Grey Tea."

"Thank you, yes. I should like a cup of Earl Grey as long as it is not decaffeinated. I feel that decaffeinated tea -- especially Earl Grey -- is at least a mistake, if not an abomination."

"The tea is Earl Grey," Jennifer assured her. "And it has not been tampered with."

"Good! That will be very nice."

"May I pour? Would you like it with milk? Or should I say, would you like it white?"

"On this side of the Atlantic, it is 'with milk.' When I arrive in the U.K., I must remember to say 'white.' Thank you! You pour the tea very well, Jennifer."

"Don't you remember, Miss Pyn? You taught us how to pour tea properly."

"Of course! How good of you to remember."

"But now," Jennifer announced, "I must return to the reservation desk so that I'll be able to escort you onto the aircraft when the time comes. But please stay. You'll not be disturbed here."

The quiet peacefulness of the lounge recalled to Miss Pyn those wonderful late summer afternoons when she could ride her bicycle in the countryside and find rest in the churchyard garden.

"Good afternoon. It is Miss Pyn, is it not?" Tom was once again working in the garden, pruning shears in hand and spent blossoms in a basket.

"Yes, you are quite correct. I believe I remember that your name is Thomas, and that it has been several weeks since we last spoke. I have enjoyed a number of afternoons resting in your garden since then."

"I'm pleased that you were able to be here. Technically, it's not my garden. It belongs to the church. I'm lucky enough to be able to putter around in it now and then. Lately other duties have kept me busy elsewhere. But today I'm doubly pleased. I thoroughly enjoy every opportunity I have to work here, and a chance to have a chat with you adds to my delight."

"I too am pleased to be here. It is an especially lovely afternoon."

As Miss Pyn sat on a garden bench, Tom apologized. "I hope you will excuse me if I finish the project I've begun. I need to cultivate several roses just over there."

"By all means. I shall enjoy observing your technique."

Tom knelt and began working the soil around the roses. After a few minutes, he exclaimed, "Oh! I've forgotten my special cultivating tool! Could I trouble you, Miss Pyn? These days, I find it rather difficult getting up and down in the garden."

"Not at all! Where might I find your tool? Do you need to describe it to me?"

"I don't think I need to. It's on a little table all by itself; just inside the church door."

Miss Pyn hesitated, dismayed.

"You apparently do not remember what I said when last we spoke here in the garden?"

"I certainly do remember that you prefer to remain in the garden and not go into the church. I didn't think that you would mind helping me by getting a small hand tool that is just inside the church door on a little table. You don't need to enter the church if you'd prefer not to; it's only in the vestibule."

Miss Pyn stood up slowly and walked across the road toward the front of the church. When she could no longer see him, Tom, pleased with himself, smiled. After some time, he began to wonder what was keeping Miss Pyn. Presently, she returned with the cultivating tool in her hand. She looked a trifle distraught.

"Is this the tool you require?"

"Thank you. It is. I wondered why it took you so long. Couldn't you find it?"

"It was exactly where you said it would be. So I did not have to break my resolve and enter the church. However, there was some singing and I paused to listen."

"Oh yes. Some members of the choir are practicing a new song for Sunday. It's new to them at any rate."

"I recognized the song," Miss Pyn confessed. "However, I have not heard the words for it for ... for some years. They were spoken to the congregation for my ... my father's funeral." She paused, and then hurriedly explained. "I believe that it is based on a passage in scripture, in the *Old Testament.*"

"That's right! It was suggested by, I believe, the ninety-first psalm; and its title is 'On Eagle's Wings.'"

"Yes, I remember. I had to ... to remain and listen. I hope I did not delay your project. If I did so, I am sorry; but I was unable to leave."

"Not at all! The roses will be here tomorrow, and even if I can't be here they will survive. What is important is that you heard some good music. That is, if the choir was any good. They sometimes are. The first time I came to this church, at the end of the service, the members of the choir were invited to remain for rehearsal. I remember thinking that it might have been better if they had had the rehearsal before the liturgy."

"I found that the choir was quite good," objected Miss Pyn. "Certainly with that song!"

"They truly are much better than when I first heard them," Tom replied. Then he gazed earnestly at Miss Pyn. "But I'm more interested in your resolve. Would you like to tell me about it?"

The notes of the sacred song echoed in Miss Pyn's thoughts -- interrupted by a voice over the public address system announcing the arrival of a flight. She started, and then realized that it was not yet time for her boarding. Besides, she thought, Jennifer would call for her. She thought again about that afternoon in the

187

church garden and remembered that she had begun to suspect that Tom was not exactly what he appeared to be. How would the church gardener know that the choir was rehearsing? And even if he were the sexton, would he know that the choir's new song was based on or suggested by psalm ninety-one?

"I wonder," she challenged him, "how is it that, as the caretaker of this lovely garden, you know so much about the activities inside the church?"

Tom laid down his precious tool. "It is true that I am the caretaker of this garden, but I am also the caretaker of a bit more. The fact is, I am the one who looks after the church and the congregation. They call me Father Tom. I suppose I should have introduced myself formally when we first met, but I saw no reason to do so; and after you left with your definitive pronouncement I knew I was right in not revealing my profession lest you'd be put off and might never again rest in this garden."

At first Miss Pyn stared in disbelief. "I suppose," she finally admitted, "that I can overlook your rather clever disguise, since it was not premeditated. However, I suspect that your conduct this afternoon was not entirely without forethought. I wonder, for example, why, when you came to work in the garden, did you not bring your cultivating tool with you?"

"I guess I have to confess that I've hoped you would come to the garden one day, and I might need an excuse to bring up the subject you left me with the other day."

"And what of the choir practice?" Miss Pyn demanded.

"That was purely coincidental, or should I say providential? Neither the practice nor your visit was -- or were -- scheduled for today."

"'Neither was' is precise. However, the issue here is not English usage, but it is your premeditated conduct."

Miss Pyn smiled to herself, remembering as she now sipped her tea, how uncomfortable Tom appeared to be once he'd been found out. She looked at her watch, wondering when the plane would be ready for boarding, and then relaxed, recalling that Jennifer had said she would call for her at boarding time.

She remembered that before Tom could utter another word she had mounted her bike and with a farewell wave headed for Seven Oaks, thinking she would let him wonder about this little episode for a while. Then perhaps, when she next saw him, he might be repentant.

The next time came rather soon. In fact, the next afternoon, Miss Pyn again visited the church garden. Tom was working among the roses.

"Good afternoon, sir."

"Why, Miss Pyn! Hello there! I didn't expect to see you quite so soon. I was scheduled to be away this afternoon, but my appointment was cancelled. So I'm pleased to be here and I'm pleased to see you."

"I, too, found some unexpected leisure. Since it turned out to be such a marvelous afternoon, I decided to ride out to your garden. I trust that I am not intruding?"

"Of course you're not intruding. I'm very glad to see you. Perhaps we can continue our conversation?" Tom rose, took off his muddy gloves, and pointed to a wooden bench surrounded by roses. "May we sit on this bench?

"Now then, I believe you were about to tell me why you've not been inside a church for so long."

"Most certainly I was not about to explain that to you or to anyone! In fact, I was about to ask you to explain your premeditated conduct of yesterday."

Tom looked a bit worried, until Miss Pyn smiled, and they both realized that sometimes after speaking our minds we tend to hear in reply only that which we expect to hear. Then, they both laughed.

"I confess that I had planned to greet you yesterday just the way I did," Tom admitted. "I hoped that my little charade would help us initiate a talk that I feel we should have. I had no other motive. If I offended you, I'm sorry -- truly."

"I did not find your little charade, as you call it, offensive," Miss Pyn reassured him. "I was only startled and puzzled by it. It certainly served its initial purpose. I did enter at least the vestibule of the church. I must admit that I did not find that repugnant."

"I'm pleased with at least that much. Now may I ask you to tell me the rest, or must I wait somewhat longer -- even though you were the first to mention the subject."

"True, it was I who ... who first spoke of it ... and I have not the slightest idea of what prompted me to say that to you! I suspect I shall have to tell you the rest sooner or later. Even though I have not confronted this for many years, I suppose this may be as good a time as any other."

Tom asked gently, "Would you like to stroll in the garden as we talk?"

"Thank you! That would be very nice indeed."

As they started out, Miss Pyn exclaimed, "Just look at that very red rose over there! The petals are almost like velvet. It calls to mind the red roses in my father's garden at our church. I remember that he said they were 'Crimson Glories.'"

"You're right! I found a metal tag on one that said it was 'Crimson Glory.'"

"I suppose," Miss Pyn insisted, "that I shall have to satisfy your curiosity about my remark the other day. There is not much to say. At the end of our second year at the university, my classmate Carole and I were planning to study in England during our third year. However, I received urgent word from home that my father, while helping our neighbor, had had a serious accident. On returning home, I learned that he had died on the way to the hospital. Two days later, during visiting hours at the funeral home, Michelle -- the twin sister of my friend, Michael Hughes -- introduced herself, explaining that she had read of my father's accident. While she was sad to learn of father's death and commiserated with me, I was very pleased to meet and visit with her. Afterward, I remember so well, we chatted at a special place along the river. It was there that she told me that Michael -- who I had expected would soon return home from Korea and would most likely become my fiancé -- had two weeks earlier saved a wounded pilot and two wounded soldiers by flying a medivac helicopter to the base hospital. In doing so, he had sacrificed his own life."

"Pyn ... may I call you Pyn? It's difficult to believe that you or anyone could endure two such losses in so short a time. I think I'm beginning to understand."

"That was not the entire matter!" Miss Pyn objected. "At least Michelle came to my father's funeral to offer support. The moment I could no longer endure the pain came during the reading of the psalm. Today, the choir singing the song, 'On Eagle's Wings,' recalled the psalm. It proclaims that the just will be protected by angels. The words I remember were: 'You need not fear the terror of the night, nor the arrow that flies by day; though thousands fall about you, near you it shall not come.' I could not accept that! I remember pleading with Michelle: Where was the angelic protection of our dear ones promised by the psalm?"

Tom looked dismayed at the anguish in Miss Pyn's face. "I wish I could say I understand. There are not many human beings who have endured such pain. I can only imagine how deeply you must have felt your loss. You must have felt utterly abandoned by God."

"No!" Miss Pyn shot back. "No! God did not abandon me. I abandoned God! I wanted nothing more to do with one who would not keep his word. Even now,

193

while the pain is rather remote, I am not able to accept the idea of a just and caring God. Except for the few moments today, I have not been inside a church since my father's funeral."

"Pyn, you baffle me! I feel I should attempt to explain the inexplicable. If I say that God has a plan for each of us that we can seldom see yet alone understand, you would not find that a satisfactory answer. I could say that your eagerness to abandon God, though understandable, is simply not possible."

"How can you say that? I have lived quite a few years now outside the church. And -- I might say -- quite successfully."

Tom smiled at such self-confidence. "Surely your work in the library and your work with the student program give ample testimony to the success and the worth of your life here. One could say that your contribution to the community has been most generous. In truth, you are probably quite a good Christian without realizing it."

"How can you say that I am a Christian -- unwitting or not -- when I say that I have abandoned God?"

Tom's reply was gentle but firm. "I can say so because I know that it is just not possible to abandon God -- because every breath we breathe depends on

God. I'd say that if you truly have abandoned God, you must no longer exist; or if you do exist, then you are dangerously close to Satan's own sin of pride."

"If I care not for God, I certainly do not care for Satan! I simply cannot understand the concept of a loving, just, and caring God in the light of my experience!"

After this outburst, Miss Pyn was quiet for some moments. The stillness in the garden underlined her thoughtful silence. Then she spoke: "Yet I am intrigued by your notion that we are wholly dependent on God. Even when we wrong others? How can that be?"

Tom thought for a few moments before going on. "A standard definition of sin is 'thought or action in pursuit of a mistaken good.' Sometimes the sinner has to be straightened out. Look what happened to Paul on the road to Damascus."

Miss Pyn looked skeptical. "He deserved to be struck down because he was harming human beings -- but one has to admire him for acting on his convictions."

"Both before and especially after Damascus. Would you agree?"

"I suspect I must agree, but I confess that I do not know much of Paul's later life."

Tom was secretly delighted by Miss Pyn's eager curiosity, and continued with enthusiasm. "That's not difficult to fix; his letters are especially enlightening and they may offer some help in understanding your dilemma. After Damascus, Paul brought Christianity to the Gentiles - - so much so, that he is known as the Apostle to the Gentiles. Yet he had to endure serious suffering."

"Why? Was not his experience on the road to Damascus enough to reconcile him to the Christian way?"

"Most probably, yes! However, he tells us, in effect, that he had to become part of the redemptive act. At first his response to suffering was impatient. He wrote in his second letter to the Corinthians: '... a thorn in the flesh was given to me, an angel of Satan, to beat me, to keep me from being too elated. Three times I begged the Lord about this, that it might leave me, but he said to me, 'My grace is sufficient for you, for power is made perfect in weakness. ... I am content with weakness, insults, hardships, persecutions, and constraints, for the sake of Christ; for when I am weak, then I am strong.'"

Miss Pyn, much to her own surprise, had been listening with rapt attention. She observed: "I gather that through his suffering Paul cultivated patience. How is that effort, as you have said, participation in the act of redemption?"

"The writings of Saint Benedict would answer your question better than I can. On the one hand, I suspect that, since you have spent most of your adult life outside the church, you're not conversant with the Benedictine rule. On the other hand, I know from what I have observed and what I have heard, you have had to be extraordinarily patient in the library -- especially with the student librarian program."

Miss Pyn felt somewhat uncomfortable with such praise. "Not really. The students, for the most part, were quite bright and studious. There were a few times when my patience was tried, but I realized that in those rare instances the problem resulted from youthful inexperience. I believe that, before we were distracted by your reference to my conduct in the library, you were about to advance our discussion with the ideas of Saint Benedict."

"Oh yes! I believe that Benedict's thought can cast light on both matters. In the rule of Saint Benedict we find the following: 'We shall through patience share in the suffering of Christ and so share in his kingdom.' So you see, despite your resolve to be otherwise, I believe you've been an unwitting Christian all along."

Miss Pyn reflected for a few moments before replying. "Your thoughts and those of Saint Benedict and Saint Paul are entirely too overwhelming to be fully comprehended in so short a time. I shall need time -- much time to consider it all. So for now, good day!"

Reluctantly, Tom returned to the roses. He knelt in the grass at the edge of the flowerbed. As he bent low over the roses, his figure cast a peculiar shadow over the plants as they moved and fluttered gently in the wispy breeze. What a strange shadow it was. Sometimes it appeared to be a perfect letter "S." At other times, as the breeze nudged the stems and flowers of the roses and quivered the rose leaves, it became an unmistakable letter "J." An "S" -- perhaps for solace, or satisfaction, or maybe for sorrow; and then magically a "J" appeared -- perhaps for joy.

The silent figure was immobile for many long minutes while the shadow moved and changed and then moved again. A casual observer, strolling along the road beyond the stone wall of the garden, would see only a gardener in his garden tending lovely roses. Had the stroller noticed the marks of moisture in the rich earth at the base of the brilliant Crimson Glory just in front of the motionless figure, he undoubtedly would have concluded that gardening was indeed very sweaty work. In truth, there were beads of perspiration covering Tom's brow. "The sweat of labor," the stroller might think, "brings its own rare satisfaction and its own rare reward."

This observer, unknowing and unfeeling, would have been mistaken. Those few who understand with the human heart would know. They certainly would know that the fatigue of toil sculptured here was not merely that of muscle and bone. This fatigue could come only from the toil of a steel-hardened will, an iron-forged mind, and a well-tempered heart irrevocably determined to conclude finally and at last a monumental and overwhelming task. Those able to see -- to see and understand as well -- would find here in this garden a figure bent in exhaustion, to be sure; but cast simultaneously in intense sorrow and in even more intense joy.

Up the roadway at the curve on the crest of the hill, Miss Pyn paused. She turned, looked back, and dismounted from her bicycle. She gazed at the sculptured figure of Tom in the churchyard garden below for many long moments. The sun behind the frozen figure created a magical, even mystical silhouette. Then, at last, Tom looked up. At that precise moment, Miss Pyn knew. Oh, how she knew; and she understood as only she could understand.

With her hair highlighted and glistening in the soft sunlight, she raised her arm high, high above her head, as high as she could reach and, still keeping a gentle loving curve to the sweep of her arm, she waved ...

gently, ever so gently. For five full minutes, she waved and waved until an approaching farm truck chugging along the road forced her to remount her bicycle.

In the evening sunlight Tom's face was radiant. His wonderfully infectious smile broke across his pensive face just as he looked up. High on the hill, at the curve in the road, Miss Pyn, looking wistfully sad and troubled, could not see the expression that would have gladdened her heart. Even the most insensitive observer of the human spirit, passing in the road close by Tom, could not help but know that here indeed was the face of a very happy man.

Miss Pyn thought, "Oh Thomas ...Thomas, I am such a fool, such a silly fool. I am so dreadfully sorry. Could you, would you, will you ever be able to bring yourself to forgive me? Will you ever again have a word, any word for me? Will I ever again be able to say anything at all that you will listen to, and understand?"

In the lowering light, Tom studied the disappearing figure of his beloved Pyn moving over the rise of the hill and down the curving road. And he gazed long ... after her. Only now, after using the phrase for many years, did he understand the true significance of the words, "Dearly beloved." She had been lost, and he had been able to help her rediscover her spiritual life.

Jennifer Grey returned to the lounge to announce, "It's nearing departure time. I suspect you would like to come to the plane with me."

"Of course! I am delighted that you will accompany me."

As they began their descent to boarding level of the terminal, Miss Pyn had a question. "I have often wondered, Miss Grey, if your family could claim relationship to Sir Charles Grey, who gave the world, with the help of Mister Twining, the classic Earl Grey Tea?"

Jennifer smiled. "It would be very nice to know that we might be descended from a British aristocratic family, and it would be even nicer to have our very own tea! But, I regret to say, there is no evidence, that we can find, of a connection between our generation of Greys and the famous Lord Grey."

Miss Pyn responded softly, "Perhaps one day you may discover a connection. Do you have other relatives still residing in England?"

"We do have some cousins living there. In fact, I called one of them just a few minutes ago after I learned about your travel today. Her name is Emily; she is a delightful young woman not quite my age."

"May I ask why you called her?"

"Oh yes, she is a librarian at Ealing Broadway. I thought you two would have something in common. I saw no reason that you should arrive in England with no one to meet you when I have a cousin who is also my good friend and lives not far from Heathrow."

"You are entirely too thoughtful! It is true that I have no one to meet me when I arrive in England. Despite a few misgivings, I thought I should have little or no difficulty traveling there because British and American English are almost the same. I am nearly overwhelmed. This is entirely too considerate of you, and perhaps too presumptuous of me to impose on the generosity of a person I have not yet met, even if she is your friend and cousin."

"Emily was delighted to learn of your travel to London. While you have not met her, you are no stranger to her. I first told her about you when she began her work as a librarian some time ago. She has been hoping to meet you ever since. So in a way, you are not really a stranger at all."

"You know I have long thought of my travel today as a dream journey, but your thoughtfulness and your cousin's generosity have raised it beyond any expectations. I shall not be able to thank you ever! I shall always be indebted to you."

"Believe me, Miss Pyn, there is no need to feel that way. I know there are many among your former student librarians who would want to do at least that and much more for you. Now come, I should like to have you meet your flight attendant, Beth."

They stepped off the jetway into the aircraft and were met with a welcoming greeting from a handsome and capable young woman: "Good afternoon! Welcome to British Air. Hello, Jennifer! This lady must be your special passenger?"

"Yes, she is very special. Miss Pyn, I should like you to know Elizabeth Farnsworth, and I'm pleased that she will be your attendant during your flight. Beth will take good care of you. I know you will enjoy this flight, and I'll look forward to greeting you when you return. Now I must return to the boarding desk. So goodbye!"

Miss Farnsworth escorted Miss Pyn to a roomy aisle seat. "I think you'll find this seat satisfactory, at least for now."

Miss Pyn smiled, "I am certain I shall. Thank you, Miss Farnsworth."

"You're welcome. If there is anything you need, please feel free to ask me. And may I ask you to call me 'Beth,' as everybody does."

"I thank you, Beth."

Miss Pyn settled in her seat and relaxed for only a few minutes. Most of the other passengers were still getting settled in their seats, when Beth reappeared. She said with a smile: "Captain McGuire asked me to invite you to move forward to first class where there are several empty places, so that we'll have better ballast in flight. That is, if you don't mind."

"Of course I will not mind, but why ask me?"

"Perhaps he overheard Jennifer say you are so special. So come with me, and I can help you bring your things."

They moved forward into first class, and Miss Pyn took several more steps on her wonderful journey of a lifetime even before the door on the great plane closed in preparation for departure.

The Captain's voice came over the intercom. He introduced himself, and promised good weather all the way to London. He predicted a smooth, fairly quick flight which would arrive at London's Heathrow Airport at about 9:30 a.m. Greenwich time. There would be a brief stop at Dulles International Airport and then non-stop up the east coast, across the Atlantic, over Ireland and on to London. He promised that he would point out the green fields of Ireland as they passed over them shortly after breakfast time. Then he invited all the passengers to listen and watch the attendants as they explained the safety features of the aircraft.

Following the explanation, the Captain's voice came on, indicating they were third in line for takeoff. After only a few minutes the plane was airborne. Miss Pyn, at last, was off to London!

The landing at Dulles was easy, and after a short time the plane was airborne and again off to London. When the seatbelt sign was turned off, Beth reappeared. "Would you like headphones, Miss Pyn? You could hear as well as watch the movies."

"I am not interested in either film, but I would enjoy some music. Might there be some classical music?"

"Oh yes! We offer a good selection of works by composers from Bach to Chopin and beyond -- including some contemporary works. I think there's enough variety to last the entire trip."

"Thank you! That is delightful. However, I hope the music is not too dreadfully contemporary."

"You needn't worry, Miss Pyn. The contemporary works will come at the end of the tape, and we will be at Heathrow, or nearly there by then. So you could just turn off the music."

Miss Pyn adjusted the headset, found the correct channel, and listened to almost all of Bach's *Jesu, Joy of Man's Desiring.* "How wonderfully appropriate," she thought, "that the beginning of my journey should be tempered by my favorite Bach melody!"

Presently Beth again appeared and offered the dinner menu. "Would you care for a cocktail or a glass of wine before dinner?"

"I should like a glass of sherry, providing it is not too sweet. For dinner, let me see … of course, since I am traveling to England, I must try the Dover Sole. Do you agree?"

"Yes. It is an excellent choice, Miss Pyn."

The dinner was as Beth had promised, and Miss Pyn savored it to the very end. When the dinner settings were cleared, Beth made another appearance. This time she offered a blanket and a pillow.

"I really do not expect to sleep tonight, but I had better accept them in case the air temperature might warrant the use of the blanket. And the pillow would be comfortable. Thank you!"

"You're very wise, Miss Pyn. We're about to leave the coast and head across the ocean. The temperature is likely to drop. If you need anything, just signal me."

Miss Pyn nestled under the warmth of the blanket as the plane continued across the sea. As she listened to a marvelous performance of Beethoven's *Ninth Symphony*, she thought about that symphony and that performance. To play and sing that masterpiece of music and poetry required both talent and skill. The members of the orchestra and choir could not be inexperienced, however talented they might be. Each participant had to devote years to study, practice, and performance to be able to play or sing that work.

"I think," she mused, "that on average, each performer must have invested at least ten years of preparation before undertaking that concert. It is almost beyond comprehension to realize that since there were one hundred musicians and another one hundred singers, they collectively devoted two thousand years of effort to produce that work -- the kind of artistry about which the English poet John Keats would have observed, 'A thing of beauty is a joy forever.' It is in truth the blending of two masterpieces: Beethoven's music and Schiller's 'Ode to Joy.'"

As the plane continued its flight, and a new symphony began with soft music, Miss Pyn again remembered her own time of joy.

It had been several weeks since her last encounter with Tom. She had biked up to the garden and found it deserted. Initially, she found the empty garden most pleasing; she could collect her thoughts undisturbed. She found a bench further into the garden.

The quiet of the afternoon inspired reflection. She looked forward to challenging Thomas' confident pronouncements made on the day they had last spoken in this garden.

She thought: "I might have difficulty disputing the saints, Paul and Benedict, but surely Thomas' notion of an unwitting Christian may be a fallacy. It may even contain an inherent contradiction. Even if I cannot dispute it, a lively discourse could follow. I shall be prepared for his arrival."

After some minutes, her reflection was interrupted by the song of a wren high in a tree at the edge of the garden. "That little bird must find this afternoon pleasant too," she thought. "Perhaps it is singing in praise of its surroundings -- an anthem of tranquility that reminds me how much I should enjoy the peace and beauty of this place."

She looked around and realized that she had not seen this part of the garden before. Among the red roses, she saw a perfectly beautiful white rose in full bloom. "What a stunning flower! It is absolutely breathtaking -- an aristocratic, even regal specimen surrounded by a coterie of crimson courtiers. My, how very lovely!"

She continued to enjoy the blossoms and the bird song for some time. Then, she wondered aloud: "With all this beauty in the world, why is there still sadness? I suspect that Thomas would remind me of Saint Paul. I wonder ... But why is Thomas not here? He usually is by this time. Oh God, I hope he is all right! Oh, what ... what have I said? I can't believe that ... that I really said what I have said."

She sat very still and pensive. After a long while, Tom appeared.

"Hello, Pyn! I saw your bike at the entrance to the garden. It's an unexpected pleasure to find you here. How are you?"

"Good afternoon Thomas! I ... I am not entirely certain how I am. Some time ago I looked forward to continuing my discourse with you. Now I ... I am not at all certain."

"I'm on my way to the church. I'm to lead the Benediction Service that ends our forty hours of adoration. Since I know how you feel about entering a church, I won't invite you to join us, but you are welcome."

"Thank you! Not today, Thomas, but someday -- perhaps quite soon."

"Did I hear you correctly? Did you say what I think you said? If so, it's an answer to my prayers for you."

"I should have suspected that it was your doing -- your fault, I should say!" The expression on Miss Pyn's face belied her attempt to sound angry, and prompted Tom's quick reply.

"I've hoped for this news for some weeks now! But it's surely not entirely my fault, as you put it. I'm certain that many folks have been praying for you for a long while -- your family, your friends including Michael, and surely some of your students in the library. My part was quite modest, but I am overjoyed for you!"

"It is all rather puzzling," Miss Pyn explained. "As I rode my bicycle here, there was no sign of what was about to happen. I saw no lightning. No one appeared to me when I entered the garden. No voice spoke to me from a bush as I sat thinking. I just quietly prepared my arguments to refute your notion of an unwitting Christian. Failing to see you, I inadvertently thought: 'Oh God! I hope he is all right!' It was then I realized I had uttered an unwitting prayer. I not only had destroyed the most convincing argument I had constructed to defeat you, I realized that all this time I have been mistaken. Everything just came together and fell into place. I prayed not only for you; I prayed for my family, my friends, my students, my benefactors who are numerous, and I prayed for Michael and I prayed for myself. I prayed simple prayers -- I asked the angels and saints and Our Blessed Mother to protect you, and help me to endure all that will happen to me. I asked that whatever anxiety, discomfort, and pain I might experience, however modest, could become part of the redemptive process."

Tom had listened to this startling account with surprise at first, and then with delight. "My dear Pyn, I'm most happy for you and for all your benefactors, as you call them. You sound as if you expected a great miracle to help you see the light. But you yourself said that Paul needed to be struck down only because he had hurt people. I don't think that you ever persecuted anyone.

"You and all of us need to be content with the unnoticed miracles that occur every day in our lives! But now I must leave to lead the Benediction Service. Bless you! I hope to see you soon."

"You will!"

Many minutes passed before Miss Pyn realized that Rachmaninoff's masterful *Rhapsody on a Theme of Paganini* was issuing forth from her headphones. That haunting Rhapsody filled her with a melodic joy that never ceased to move her spirit, no matter how often she heard its strains. It always reminded her what a great joy it was to hear, to feel, to see, to breathe, to be alive.

The plane continued its careful race toward the sunrise. With the swiftness of a jet, daylight filled the passenger compartment of the plane. As it did so, Miss Pyn remembered that during the weeks and months that followed her reconciliation she had seen Tom from time to time. Perhaps one day, she would be able to tell him exactly how she had felt that evening which now seemed so long ago.

One day after Mass, Tom had greeted her and asked, "Would you do something for me, Pyn? I've noticed that you sometimes have a tennis racket with you on your bike. My tennis game is quite poor. Would you consider giving me some pointers on the court?"

Miss Pyn happily agreed, and they met for several sessions of tennis. She suggested that, to execute the serve, he toss the ball high and almost scratch his back with the racket before reaching up to serve. Then, she added that he needed to pivot into position to return the ball as it crossed the net toward him. His game improved quickly -- so quickly during those sessions that just now she began to wonder if Tom had thought up another charade for her benefit. She wondered too if some additional practice in perfecting her own game might have been helpful before the day Thomas had won their subsequent match.

Miss Pyn remembered that day very well, and she smiled as she recalled thinking as she approached the tennis court: "How very nice this day is! Surely, were I to say that it is magnificent I should feel guilty of an understatement. Oh, I had better not say that to anyone, including Thomas. I wonder what prompts such whimsy in me. Perhaps it is Thomas. However, the day is lovely -- very."

In truth, it had been a rare bright July day. The gentle rain of the previous evening had freshened everything. The day's cobalt sky was punctuated by occasional white tufted clouds that accented the blue background and the green that dominated the landscape. The blues and greens were given new form by soft transparent breezes that quaked the leaves of hickory and oak, enlivened silvery aspen, and startled a slumbering crimson maple.

Soon Miss Pyn and Tom had finished their tennis match. Although she had lost, she felt exhilarated because she had nearly won the first game; did in fact win the second by overcoming a three-point deficit; and lost the third game only with a final tiebreaker. Tom not only felt triumphant, he was happy to have won the match even though his left eye had been troubling him ever since his ophthalmologist had recommended that he have a specialist examine his eye.

Exhausted, they relaxed at the umbrella table on Tom's patio. "Thomas, we could have some of the cheese I brought for our post-challenge celebration. There are English water biscuits -- sorry, I mean crackers -- that should go nicely with either the Stilton or the French Brie."

"That's wonderful! There I go sounding like you, Pyn. Only I guess I should have said, 'That is wonderful,' to really sound like you."

"Are you making fun of me, Thomas? That is not very nice. You should try to avoid splitting the infinitive 'to sound ' with the word 'really.' However, 'to sound really like you' would do very well, you know. You see, if you insist that I speak pedantically, I shall become the pedant -- so there!"

"I'm not making fun of you, even though I'm sometimes tempted to tease you. No, I do enjoy -- do love really -- your precise use of English. I should imitate your diction and syntax more often. However, I've a contribution to make to our celebration. I've found a very special bottle of Niersteiner."

"Thomas, you should not, you may not, you will not use special wine today! I know you feel particularly triumphant in victory because I came so close to upsetting you, but there will be other days. I shall have my revenge. Besides, how should I feel if we drink up all

214

the very good wine when you win the match, and there is none left when I should win? Have you such confidence in your skill? Are you so convinced that I shall not win again, ever? Remember, when we first played, I was the better player! Is there none of the Piesporter left? We could have it."

"Yes, there is Piesporter. It's almost as good as the Niersteiner, but in this part of the country Niersteiner is more difficult to get. So it's a rather rare vintage, and for this special occasion -- which has nothing whatever to do with my victory today -- we will have it! You are still the better player. You play with finesse. I'm more like a Neanderthal player with a strong club for a racket. So Niersteiner it will be -- even if you say I 'should not, may not, will not' or even if you hope I could not -- I insist, I shall uncork the treasure."

"Well, I shall say this -- you sometimes sound as if you have the will of a Neanderthal. I shall enjoy the Niersteiner, but may I know why this is such a special day? Tell me, *s'il vous plait.*"

"In good time, my friend, in good time. First I shall get the wine, the cheese, and the biscuits -- that is, the crackers." Tom smiled slyly. "I'm so sorry, dear friend, but I could not resist. I really couldn't."

Her look was devastating. Then came that delightful smile, and they both laughed.

When Tom returned with the Niersteiner, Miss Pyn persisted.

"Thomas, you still have not explained why this day is so special. May I know?"

"It's special, Pyn, because I have good news. I've learned that I'll be leaving my little country parish and going on to wider pastures. I'm supposed to be a shepherd, you know. Bishop Nichols wants me to go to Rome for further study and for as yet unspecified duties."

"Oh, Thomas! I think that is wonderful news -- though many of us will find it disconcertingly sad, really. We shall all, however, be very happy for you even if we would rather weep for ourselves. Those 'other duties' give me pause. You will not be away for very long, will you?"

"I really don't know. I guess that much will depend on how wide the other pastures turn out to be. Right now the Bishop says that he doesn't have an urgent need for me. So he wants me to continue, as he says, to enrich my vocation and my value to the Church."

"I do not wish to sound disrespectful. But really, Thomas, while the Bishop may not have an urgent need for you, there are many people right here who do have perhaps an even more urgent need for your prayers and your guidance."

"You are too kind, dear Pyn. Rest assured, dear friend, that you will all always have my prayers. Other priests will come. Be they younger or older, they will offer good guidance for all the parish."

"When will you leave us?"

"Not for some months."

"While I am very happy for you, dear Thomas, I do not like it one bit. Could we save the Niersteiner for a happier day when you return? I do not like your happy news."

"Dear Pyn, I've opened the bottle already. We must toast our good fortune now, for the wine will not keep."

"Your good fortune, you mean."

Just then flight attendant Beth interrupted Miss Pyn's concentration. "Good morning, Miss Pyn. Would you like a warm towel to freshen up with? We are just about to cross Ireland. I think we'll be hearing from our Irish captain. The flight won't take much longer. I'll come along with customs cards in a few minutes."

As Beth had expected, the captain called attention to the lovely green fields of his ancestral homeland. There was little doubt why the land below was called the "Emerald Isle."

217

Miss Pyn did not mind the interruption of her thought. The memory of that special day with the Niersteiner would return soon enough. While part of it was a joy to remember, the rest of it was very painful, even after all this time.

The great jet continued on its way. As she had promised, Beth again appeared with the card that could be filled out before landing in order to expedite customs clearance. Then suddenly, there it was, etched on the sea below. Miss Pyn exclaimed: "The 'sceptered isle ... set in the silver sea'!"[4] Although she had promised herself that she would be calm and casual, she couldn't hide a very satisfied smile.

As the plane circled for landing, Miss Pyn saw some London landmarks. Some of them she could identify; others were wholly new. But then she saw the unmistakable river. After only a few minutes, she felt touchdown. At last she could see her very first London sight from the ground. It proved to be rather disappointing. It was a milk delivery truck of the same model and even the same color as those she saw every day delivering milk in Seven Oaks. The truck even had the same company name on it. She thought: "Could it be that the jet has turned around in circling, and returned to The States?"

---

[4] William Shakespeare, *Richard the Second*

Then she noticed, as the plane taxied further, many other airplanes with markings indicating they had come from many parts of the world; and she knew she must be in London.

A short time later, Miss Pyn walked along the jetway into the terminal, where she collected her one piece of luggage and then entered the customs line. As she waited, and other travelers joined the line, she saw that she was fourth in the long line, and again thought of Joe's luggage advice for overseas travel and realized how good it had been.

Then she remembered the reaction of one of her student librarians who had studied in England during her junior year at university. Her very positive report had concluded with: "Those English people -- they are so polite even when they don't want to be polite!" Perhaps she would now be able to verify that observation.

A handsome uniformed young man greeted her at the customs desk. "Good morning, madam! May I please see your passport? May I ask what brings you to our country?"

"Primarily, I am on holi ... or should I say 'vacation,' so that you will know that I am authentically American?"

He replied with a broad grin, "Both terms are English. We do, however, tend to use 'holiday.' May I ask how long you expect to stay here?"

Miss Pyn thought of saying, "Not long enough," but she thought better of the idea and replied, "I expect to stay about a month, and because I am a librarian I hope to visit many of your best bookshops and publishers in the hope of finding some treasures for our library in Seven Oaks."

"I take it that your Seven Oaks is not in Kent?" He said that with a sly knowing look.

Miss Pyn readily admitted: "We do have many places with names similar to names in this part of the world. As you know, some are very familiar -- with 'new' added to the name: New York, New Jersey, New London and even New England come to mind. Unfortunately, Seven Oaks is not among the better-known places."

As he stamped her passport he graciously continued: "I do hope your stay with us will be successful and that you'll enjoy your holiday ... er... your vacation!"

Miss Pyn continued walking toward the reception area in the direction of the meeting point. There were several people awaiting arrivals, including some holding up signs for individuals or for taxies or limousines. From among them, she heard "Miss Pyn?" and was momentarily startled. She then said to the smiling young woman who had apparently spoken her name, "Yes. But how did you know?"

"Hello! I'm Emily, Jennifer's cousin! After Jennifer's description, I'd know you anywhere with your beautiful red hair -- except perhaps in Scotland. Jennifer has said that nearly all of your students were envious of your red hair. I'm so happy to meet you at last!"

"I, too, am very pleased to know you; and I think that you are entirely too generous in meeting my flight. But I confess I am relieved that I need not face this country and its Underground system unaided."

"I am pleased to provide that aid. May I take your bag? We've not far to walk to my car."

"Thank you, but I can manage nicely. Professor Epworth, who is retired and who prefers to be called 'Joe' while he volunteers at our library, offered me extensive instruction in luggage-handling during overseas travel. That is why I have only one case."

In a short time, they arrived at Emily's little Ford. Miss Pyn began to enter the passenger side as she would an American vehicle. Then she exclaimed, "I must remember that you do many things differently over here!"

"Oh yes. For a moment I thought you hoped to drive my car," Emily teased. "But you had better get accustomed to our traffic before you attempt that."

"Of course, I should not think I would ever operate any vehicle in this country. You are too kind even to suggest that I do so. I do, however, maintain a current operator's license and for some years I have planned to purchase a convertible red Alpha Romeo; but the convertible season where I live is rather short and the cost of the automobile is rather expensive. So I have not as yet realized my ambition."

"I'd suspect that any plan to purchase an Alpha is definitely ambitious, Miss Pyn."

After a few moments, they left the airport car park and were on the road toward London. Miss Pyn observed, "You certainly do things differently here. Many of my countrymen would think that all this traffic is going the wrong way. I do hope this journey is not too long and difficult for you."

Emily laughed. "I drive this way quite often -- collecting colleagues, friends, and sometimes family. It's a relatively short, convenient drive. First we'll take this carriageway for a short time. Then it merges with a motorway, which is our version of what I believe you call a 'freeway.' Then after that, a bit further on, just before Hammersmith, we'll travel north on another motorway, the London ring road toward Ealing. In a few minutes we'll be there."

"Is Ealing very far from the vicinity of The British Museum? I planned on looking for lodging in that area. I believe that Cartwright Gardens is not very far from the part of London I wish to explore."

Emily maneuvered the car onto the motorway, and then replied, "For many visitors, Cartwright is an excellent location. Along one side of the Gardens there are three large residence halls for university students. But along the crescent that borders the rest of the Gardens there are places that welcome lodgers -- several B & Bs and at least one small hotel. Oh, you do know what 'B & B' indicates?"

Miss Pyn laughed. "Perhaps when you come to visit us, you'll be delighted to discover that there are Bed & Breakfast establishments in my country as well. And from your description, I think I should be able to find something comfortable here in your country."

"You probably could find suitable lodging, but I'd like to propose something quite different. Ealing Abbey is also my parish church. There is a wonderful couple in our parish that occasionally welcomes lodgers into their home, and it's a short walk from the Abbey."

"Oh my goodness! The possibility of staying in a residential neighborhood near London is certainly most attractive! However, I do feel that I am imposing on the generosity of you and your countrymen much too much already."

"Not at all! The Stablers take in lodgers from time to time, and all the people I know at the Abbey will very much like to know you. The area around the British Museum is an easy short ride on the Underground from Ealing, and I'll admit that for me such a ride is often conducive to reflection. At Cartwright Gardens nearly all the people you'll be likely to meet will be students preparing for end-of-term examinations, or transient individuals pursuing other business. You'll not find them typical London residents."

"I must say that your arguments are most persuasive. I shall accept your thoughtful recommendation reluctantly, providing that your fellow parishioners find me acceptable. I feel that I shall never be able to thank you and others adequately."

"I'm certain we'll all be very pleased that you'll meet so many of us who come from an ordinary English neighborhood. We'll soon be there!"

The road in Ealing onto which Emily turned could probably not be accurately described as "ordinary." The roadway was wider than is usual in London, and the lots on which the houses stood were spacious, with both front and rear gardens. While there were a number of shade trees along the road, there was also sufficient sunlight to encourage many examples of the celebrated London gardens overflowing with roses. These flourished in front of sturdy multi-story homes of individual designs vaguely reminiscent of Edwardian architecture. Each front garden was defined by an individual wall and garden gate. Whether the walls were low or high, the roses were always visible and, as Miss Pyn observed, often stunning.

They stopped in front of the Stabler home. The stone wall was accented by an impressive Spanish arbor and gateway leading to the garden that must have been the envy of the entire neighborhood. There were roses of every color grouped together along a multi-colored flagstone walkway. Near the front entrance to the house, Miss Pyn noticed a patch of plants that were just emerging. She didn't recognize the plants, but she hoped they would flower during her time in London. So she made a mental note to ask her hostess about the plants.

Helen Stabler opened the door in response to the door chime. "Good morning, Emily! I suspect that this lady is the person you called about. I am most pleased that we are able to offer accommodations today."

Emily proudly presented her companion. "Yes, Helen. I'd like you to know my cousin's friend, Miss Pyn.

Like me, she is a librarian, but with considerably more experience and expertise than I. She plans on visiting here in the U.K. for about a month."

Miss Pyn grasped Helen's hand. "I am happy to be here, and delighted to be able to stay in a London neighborhood. That is, if I am not too much of an imposition."

"Not at all! We're very pleased to welcome Americans who are acquaintances or relatives of our neighbors. It affords us opportunity to learn about our friends across the sea."

"And I," Miss Pyn responded, "wish to learn about the countrymen and the environment of the authors of my favorite literature. I am afraid that I will not bring you much knowledge, for I am a rather ordinary American."

"But you are exactly the kind of American we would like to know better!"

"I am already beginning to suspect that you are thoughtful and too kind. Would you not agree, Emily?"

"Did I not tell you, Miss Pyn, that you would like Helen and she would like you? But now I should leave, because I'm due at the library soon. When you come to Ealing Broadway, Miss Pyn, you will be able to find me in the library just opposite the head of the stairway leading to the second level. I hope you'll come and visit. For now, goodbye!"

Mrs. Stabler turned eagerly to Miss Pyn. "Now that we've finished the introductions, I'd like to show you your room. It's our favorite room in the front of our home right on the first floor. Oh, I should remember to say to you 'our second floor.' Perhaps you already know that in England our first floor is one flight up the stairs from the ground level?"

"I do, of course -- from reading Conan Doyle and other authors; but it is nice to be reminded of that."

They climbed a stairway to the second level of the house, along a hallway into a brightly colored room with several windows looking out to the street below. It was what might be called a bed-sitting room -- with chairs, a writing table, a nightstand, and a comfortable bed. On a dresser against the wall was a vase of freshly picked roses from the front garden.

Miss Pyn exclaimed, "This room is a delight, and the roses are perfectly lovely. I thank you for both!"

"Your bath facilities are just there, and further along the hallway you'll find a kitchen that is quite well equipped for your use at any time. We've even recently added a refrigerator. They are becoming more common in this country, you know."

"I certainly did not expect to find such excellent lodging anywhere in London. I am very pleased and grateful."

"Thank you. I trust you'll be comfortable. If there is anything you find you need, just knock on the door of our living quarters."

"I believe I shall be fine. I come equipped with a guidebook and London maps, including a map of the Underground. I shall explore!"

Helen Stabler laughed delightedly at Miss Pyn's enthusiasm. "When would you like to begin your exploration?"

"I would like to begin immediately, but I think that to do so would be rather imprudent. I have had an arduous journey."

"Was your flight very difficult?"

"Not at all. The flight attendant said that the captain would like me to travel in the first-class section of the plane."

"That must have been quite pleasant!"

"It was very pleasant. The seating was comfortable, and the attendant most thoughtful. The music all night long was delightful. Of course, I could not sleep. And the night before, I had been so excited with anticipation that I was hardly able to sleep at all. So if I may, I would like to relax in your lovely garden for a while. Then I shall unpack and organize my things, and get my notebook in order for a record of my impressions."

"By all means," Helen replied. "You're most welcome to enjoy our garden."

"Thank you. Then I shall retire early so that I will be fit for tomorrow's grand entry into London."

Early the next morning, Mrs. Stabler was in her front garden. "Good morning, Miss Pyn! May I ask where you plan to begin your exploration?"

"Well, my earliest recollection of London dates from the time I saw a motion picture. It was a war film set in England. I think it was called *Waterloo Bridge*. I distinctly remember the bridge itself. I should like to begin there."

"Whether you choose to begin at the north end of the bridge or the south end, the Underground will take you to either."

"I should like to approach the bridge from Waterloo Station."

"My husband, Ted, would say that is an excellent choice. The bus at our corner will take you to Ealing Broadway, where you can take the Underground east to Tottenham Court Road, and then south to Waterloo Station. From the station just walk north. You'll pass The Royal National Theatre, which includes the Olivier Theatre, and then on to Waterloo Bridge."

Mrs. Stabler cautioned: "The bridge at Waterloo is not quite the bridge you may remember from the film.

Although it was proposed to open in 1815, at the time of Napoleon's Waterloo, it's a modern utilitarian bridge. It's not very romantic, but it is very useful. Hundreds of people cross it everyday. If you wish to see an old-fashioned ornate bridge, Westminster Bridge just upstream is quite lovely."

"I certainly shall see it -- if not today, then another day. Thank you very much for all your thoughtful directions. Before I leave, I should like to say that your garden is lovely indeed. I do not recognize the little plants that are just emerging near the door."

"They are rather unusual -- especially the striking purple color which this variety has. We call them 'Michaelmas Daisies.'"

"'Michaelmas Daisies'! What a quaint name!"

"They bloom near the end of September around the feast day of Saint Michael. Elsewhere they are sometimes called perennial asters, but I much prefer 'Michaelmas Daisies.'"

"I have a very special interest in the feast of St. Michael, especially now that I am able to understand implications of the life of the spirit. I have had a sense of the significance of Saint Michael's Day ever since I learned that my very good friend who died in Korea and his sister were born on the feast of Saint Michael. Now it means so much! I shall not be able to see the

Michaelmas Daisies in bloom during my visit here, but perhaps I shall be able to purchase some plants after I return home."

Mrs. Stabler protested: "But those would not be the same plants! You must have a souvenir of your visit with us. I know! Emily mentioned that she hopes to see you next year at the library meeting in America. I shall gather some seeds in the fall, and perhaps she'll be able to give them to you next year."

"That would be wonderful, and too generous!"

"I can't guarantee that they'll be exactly the very same color -- perennials are like that -- but if they grow, you will have a direct connection with us, and you're certainly most welcome to share our flowers."

"Thank you! Now I must begin my exploration."

"I'm sure you will enjoy it. Here is your key; you may come and go as you

please."

"Thank you so much! I do not expect to be very late. Goodbye."

Miss Pyn moved along the walkway toward the bus stop. "I must remember that in England the sidewalk is called 'the pavement,' and the street is called 'the road.'"

A few doors along the road an older gentleman tending his garden greeted her with a smile, "A good day 'tis for takin' a walk, m'am!" Miss Pyn smiled her agreement and then, remembering several people she had seen in wheelchairs in air terminals on both sides of the Atlantic, she thought, "Every day is a good day for walking for those who are able to walk."

The bus arrived at the corner just as Miss Pyn approached the bus stop. The ride to Ealing Broadway with its District Line terminal was quite short, and when the conductor announced her stop, she alighted and walked toward the Underground.

At the ticket window, Miss Pyn purchased an Underground pass for one week, as Helen Stabler had suggested. She boarded the train and found a comfortable seat -- one that would allow her to study the District Line chart above the windows on the opposite wall. She was confident she could follow the route of the train with little difficulty and she hoped that, since an unidentified voice had cautioned "Mind the gap" as she climbed into the train, the same voice would announce the location of each stop as the train approached it.

Just before the train began to move, a distinguished-looking gentleman, with a briefcase and walking stick, entered the car and took a seat near Miss Pyn. After a few moments, he addressed her: "Excuse me, madam. I believe that you are a visitor."

"Yes, I am. But how did you know?"

"Your North American accent confirms my suspicion. I decided that you must be a visitor when I noticed that you are carrying a guidebook and maps of London and the Underground. I believe that I should warn you that, while London is quite safe as large cities go, there are pickpockets around watching especially for visitors. You will probably notice in some Underground stations a warning that pickpockets are active in the area. I would advise you to keep the guidebook and maps out of plain sight and consult them only in a safe place."

"I appreciate your advice, and I thank you."

"You are most welcome. I believe that you are an American? Some years ago, I traveled to your country to the city of Chicago. There I was greeted by many strangers who evidently recognized my English attire. They offered me directions and advice. Whenever I see an American visitor I try to reciprocate their thoughtfulness. May I ask your destination, madam?"

"I am traveling to Waterloo Bridge, which I believe is an excellent introduction to London's city center."

"It is that! In just a few stops, you can change trains for the Circle Line. It is especially good for visitors, because it runs in a circle -- a rectangle really -- connecting most of the railway stations. Even if you were to take an Underground train in the wrong direction, you would eventually get to your destination. The north end of Waterloo Bridge is a short walk from either of two stops on the Circle Line."

Miss Pyn found this stranger's advice a bit confusing, and responded, "I had hoped to approach the bridge from Waterloo Station."

"In that case, the Circle Line will not serve. It connects the railway stations only north of the river. It does not cross the river and connect to Waterloo. You will have to remain on this line until you reach Tottenham Court Road. Then take the Northern Line southbound to Waterloo."

"Thank you," Miss Pyn said with relief. "I think that is what I had figured out I should do. It is reassuring to learn that you agree."

"You're most welcome. My name is Cedric Overbrooke. May I give you my card? You'll see that I am an investment banker. I suspect that you wouldn't be interested in investing in pound sterling."

"You are quite correct. I am Miss Pyn. I am a librarian, and the only investment I shall be able to make will be in a few books for our library in the United States."

"I offer you my card for another reason. All my colleagues in the office and also their secretaries know the city center very well. So if you have questions or need directions give us a ring, and someone will be able to help you."

"I thank you! That is most generous and reassuring."

"Not at all. I shall alert the office that you might call. We are approaching Tottenham Court Road. Remember to take the southbound train. Good day, and enjoy your stay in London, Miss Pyn."

Miss Pyn stepped off the train and headed for the Northern Line. A young woman walking beside her addressed her: "Excuse me, I noticed that you chatted with Lord Overbrooke. Have you known him very long?"

"Only for about twenty minutes. We met on the Underground at Ealing. He apparently recognized that I am a visitor and offered me valuable advice about travel in London."

"His thoughtfulness, especially toward visitors, is widely recognized. May I ask where you are going?"

"Of course! I am going to Waterloo Station. I wish to cross the bridge into the city center."

"That is a wonderful introduction to London. You will be able to see most things from the bridge. I'm headed to the station too. May I walk with you?"

"By all means. I wish to chat with as many London residents as I can during my short visit. I am puzzled about one thing. You Londoners have a reputation for reticence concerning strangers. Yet two of you chatted with me in the short time I have been here, even though you knew that I am a visitor."

"We certainly could not be reticent with our cousins from North America! Well, here we are; just as the southbound train approaches. Remember to mind the gap!" She gave this warning with a sly smile. "We'll be at Waterloo in just a few minutes."

As they sat down, Miss Pyn said, "I thank you for your assistance and your company. I do not even know your name. I am Miss Pyn. I am a librarian in the small town of Seven Oaks in the United States."

"It is a pleasure to know you. I'm Judy Browne, on my way to the law office where I work, just down from the station. Since we are nearing the station we'd best say goodbye now. If I ever get to your part of the world, I shall try to find you. Good luck! Have a safe journey, and enjoy London!"

With that, they stepped off the train and their ways parted. Miss Pyn thought, "What a wonderful young lady!"

Miss Pyn left the Underground Station and started in the direction of Waterloo Bridge. She passed the Olivier Theatre, making a mental note to be sure to check the performance schedule to see if the offerings during her stay in London might include a play that would be of interest to her.

Continuing along the way, she passed The Royal Orchestra Hall and, at last, walked onto Waterloo Bridge.

The sight was exactly as she had expected. Downstream from the Bridge, she could see Christopher Wren's magnificent dome of Saint Paul's Cathedral; upstream, Westminster and Big Ben were clearly visible. "Everyone," she thought, "who has long hoped to come to London and has seen over and over again pictures of these two London landmarks must have the same breathtaking feeling I now feel. What an absolute joy this sight inspires!"

As she walked along, she passed many busy Londoners on the way to who knows where, apparently completely oblivious of the freshness of the air, the grandeur of the river, and the glory of those architectural monuments. She felt that she was inclined to stop every one of the bridge walkers and ask if they were aware of what joyous feeling they could experience each time they stepped onto this wonderful bridge.

Instead, smiling to herself, she just continued on her way toward The Embankment and the steps down to it. At The Embankment, she chose to walk upstream in the direction of Westminster. Along the way she sighted an inviting bench, and she decided that here would be a good place to rest after a long walk.

She sat, and for some minutes she observed Londoners and visitors coming and going along The Embankment. Then she noticed, just across the walkway opposite her comfortable bench, a monument with the name "Cleopatra's Needle." At first, like many other visitors, she thought that here was yet another treasure that the British must have confiscated from Egypt. Later she would learn that Cleopatra's Needle was given to the British by a grateful Egyptian government in modern times, and the monument actually had nothing to do with Cleopatra.

She suddenly realized that it was nearing noon and that she was hungry. So she rose from the bench and walked on in her quest for lunch. Some distance upstream along The Embankment, she spied what appeared to be a floating restaurant and soon after that, a floating pub. Bright letters on the side of the boat spelled out the name of the pub: "The Tattershall Castle Paddlesteamer." Miss Pyn decided that this was indeed an appropriate site for her first lunch in London.

Mounting the gangplank, she noticed several bars at various levels on the vessel. She chose the one offering buffet lunches and a good view upstream of

Westminster. As soon as she entered the sunlit room, she was greeted by a young servingman.

"Good afternoon, madam. May I serve you a cocktail?"

"If you offer a sherry that is neither too sweet nor too dry, I should like that in a small glass."

"By all means, madam! We offer a fine sherry that is probably exactly the sherry you'd like."

"Thank you. I shall like that!"

"Is there anything else I could serve you, madam?"

"No, thank you. I shall order lunch at the buffet in a few minutes."

Miss Pyn took her sherry and found a table that afforded a full view of the river and Westminster. As she sipped her sherry, she found the gentle movement of the water and the soft breeze along the river very restful. "Some people are very fortunate," she thought. "They could come here every day for lunch in this marvelous setting."

Presently, she finished her sherry and went to the buffet, where she was greeted by a handsome servingman. "May I help you, madam?"

"Yes, I have read that in England I could find a jacket potato for lunch. I should like to try one."

"We have some just out of the oven. Here is a very nice one. Would you care for anything else?"

"Yes, please -- a small serving of your seafood salad."

"An excellent choice! May I suggest something to drink?"

"Just some ice water with lemon will do nicely, thank you!"

Miss Pyn returned to her table to enjoy her lunch, the view, and the restful river. Just as she was finishing her meal, she noticed a familiar figure enter the buffet bar and head straight for her table.

"Miss Browne, how nice to see you again so soon!"

"Hello, Miss Pyn. I'm so glad that I had an errand to run in this area this afternoon! So I stopped at The Tattershall on the chance I might find you here. I remember you said that, after crossing Waterloo Bridge, you'd come this way."

"This is a lovely surprise! Do sit down. May I get you something?"

"Thank you, no. I seldom take anything at lunchtime. However, I can visit with you for a few minutes before I must return to the office."

"It is so good to enjoy my first lunch in London on this vessel in the company of a London resident."

After Miss Pyn completed her lunch, she announced to Miss Browne, "Now I shall explore Trafalgar. Would you care to join me?"

"I would very much like to, but I must return to work. However, I can show you the way."

"Thank you so much! You certainly make a visitor feel most welcome."

After leaving the boat, they walked on for a while toward Trafalgar. Miss Browne suddenly stopped. "I must say goodbye here. This is where I turn toward the office. It has been a pleasure meeting you, Miss Pyn. I hope you will enjoy the rest of your visit to London."

Miss Pyn paused to watch her new friend leave, and thought again, "What a wonderful young lady!" She walked on, and there it was: Lord Nelson clearly in command of the great Square. Everything was exactly as she had pictured it: the tall monument, the lions, the fountains, the pigeons and the people feeding them -- all in front of the National Gallery; and over to one side of the Square, Saint Martin-in-the-Fields. She thought fleetingly of the many hours of wonderful music The Academy Orchestra of Saint Martin had brought to her for years. She thought it unlikely that she would be able to see and hear the Orchestra and its famous director during her stay in London, but perhaps she might get a glimpse of The Pearlies on the stage behind the church.

Miss Pyn knew that the Pearlies sometimes gave brief performances dressed in costumes resembling the attire of medieval fruit and vegetable sellers called "costermongers." Their costumes have hundreds and even thousands of white pearl buttons sewn on them – thus the name "Pearlies." Miss Pyn thought, "No wonder that they are very successful fund raisers for charities. Just the sight of their costumes is impressive!"

Miss Pyn decided to rest for a time on an inviting bench in the Square. She sat studying the formidable gathering of Londoners and pigeons. A few of the birds wandered over to see what this newcomer might offer -- one alighting on the bench right next to her. They all soon realized that this person had nothing to give them, so the birds quickly dispersed to see who else they might harass.

Miss Pyn turned her attention to the fountains, admiring the figures of the lions and thinking that those lovely fountains surely must keep Trafalgar cool even on the warmest London days.

As she thought about the Square, she remembered the words Joe the gardener had spoken to her before she left Seven Oaks: "You will discover that there is always much that is forever new ... but also that much in England is familiar, very familiar indeed." Joe was so perceptive.

Glancing once more at Saint Martin-in-the-Fields, Miss Pyn regretted that she must move on. Accordingly, she walked along Whitehall, passing Parliament and continuing on to Westminster Abbey.

She paused at the entrance to The Abbey, and thought of the more than a thousand years of history in this one place: "Surely I cannot appreciate all of this in just one afternoon. I shall limit my visit today to the Poets' Corner." Just inside the door, she saw a gentleman attired in a red and black robe, and asked if he were an usher.

The gentleman laughed and replied: "We certainly respect that title, but in England we are usually called 'vergers.' Our duties include those of an usher, yet we are expected to do more. May I assist you, madam?"

Miss Pyn was delighted to explain: "Yes, please! I am a librarian from America. I should like to begin my study of The Abbey at The Poets' Corner."

"Yes, of course! It's just there on the other side of the Abbey. At this time of day you may walk across the nave without disturbing anyone. You'll see the Tomb of Geoffrey Chaucer. The Poets' Corner begins there. Perhaps you know that Chaucer's Tomb is not where it is because he was our first great poet. Rather, it was placed there for other reasons: He lived nearby, and was a member of The Abbey Parish. As such, he was entitled to be interred in The Abbey. Moreover, he served a number of our monarchs in various capacities, including that of ambassador. Thus, his tomb is where it is. The recognition of his poetry came later, as did the designation of 'The Poets' Corner.'

"As you pass the main altar, notice the Coronation Chair just behind the altar. Did you know that the first coronation occurred on this site in 1066? The Chair, however, did not arrive until 1301. Since 1308, nearly every English monarch has accepted the scepter in that Chair."

"I did know about the Chair, but I was not aware of its long tradition. Thank you for increasing my knowledge."

After only a few moments and a few steps, there it was: The Tomb of Chaucer! It did now and for all time mark the beginning of The Poets' Corner. Nearby was The Shakespeare Memorial. Miss Pyn knew that Shakespeare's remains were in Stratford-Upon-Avon, but it was most appropriate that England's greatest poet-dramatist should be memorialized here.

Next she saw The Tomb of Charles Dickens. The verger had said that it was the most popular because his prose was widely read even today. It too belonged here not only because there are other prose writers represented, but also because there are passages in his work that have the ring of poetry.

Then she wondered if her favorite modern poet was represented here. She knew that the remains of Gerard Manley Hopkins were interred in the cemetery at a suburb of Dublin in Ireland, and she hoped that one day she would visit there. Then she found it! The Hopkins Memorial! She was overjoyed, and instantly many lines rushed through her mind. Which of the many lines would be most appropriate? Perhaps a line from the poem "Pied Beauty" -- "He fathers-forth whose beauty is past change: Praise him."

She marveled that this very Roman Catholic poet -- a convert from Anglicanism who was influenced by another convert, John Henry Newman -- should be memorialized in this Abbey. True, the Abbey was originally Benedictine, but was now very Anglican. "Perhaps one day," she mused, "but not likely in my lifetime, the principal English prelate will be The Cardinal Archbishop of Canterbury and the churches will be reconciled. The introduction of the vernacular into the Roman liturgy -- English for English-speaking countries -- was probably a good step forward."

Miss Pyn interrupted her reflection with the thought that it must be getting on toward teatime and she had better be on her way. After deciding to revisit

245

The Poets' Corner another day, she left the Abbey and walked to the Westminster Tube Station. She boarded a southbound train, changing at the District Line to Ealing Broadway and after a short bus ride from Ealing Broadway, she was near West Ealing Abbey in less than an hour. Although she had hoped to visit the Chapel there, she thought that she had better go directly to the Stabler home.

Helen Stabler greeted her as she entered. "Good afternoon, Miss Pyn! I do hope your visit to the center of London was most enjoyable."

Miss Pyn was eager to share her delight: "It certainly was all and more than I could expect in one day. I started at Waterloo Bridge, as I said I would. Crossing over, I saw wonderful sights both up and down the river. I then headed for Trafalgar Square. On the way, I lunched at The Tattershal Castle Pub. On the Tube, I met two friendly and generous Londoners who offered me directions and encouragement.

"After lunch, I went to Trafalgar Square -- which I found overwhelming, yet exactly as I expected it to be. I would have been happy to spend the rest of the afternoon there, but I was eager to visit Westminster Abbey. So I went there. As I entered the Abbey, I asked the verger for The Poets' Corner."

"Of course! I should have known! Did you visit the historic chapels?"

"I shall be sure to visit them the next time I go to the Abbey. Then I expect to study all the treasures and continue my visit to The Poets' Corner. However, one morning I shall leave quite early, because I hope to find a very special place along The Strand."

Mrs. Stabler was delighted with Miss Pyn's report. "It seems you've had a wonderful day! Now, have a restful evening."

During the night, a soft rain sharpened the colors of the houses and left a silvery patina on trees, gardens, roadways, and walkways. The early morning sunlight transformed it all into a mass of sparkling jewels. "Indeed," Miss Pyn thought as she stepped with crisp cadence along the pavement in the deserted streets, "Sunday morning fresh with the ablution of a midnight rain is truly a rare treasure. What a delight this is! I should like to absorb it all, every bit of it -- the houses, the doors, the stained glass, the gardens, even the gentle breeze, the silence, and the graceful curving roadway. All of it could become part of me and I of it. However, I must hurry along or I shall be late."

She crossed over the road, turned at the corner and walked along the side of Ealing Abbey, an inviting

Benedictine church. Miss Pyn climbed the stone steps of the church expecting to greet Father Jack.

The previous Sunday Miss Pyn had attended an early service. The elderly priest had said Mass in a way that reminded her of an old-fashioned Latin Low Mass. It was not really so conservative, for it was in English; but there was little participation by the congregation.

She had admitted her disappointment to her hosts, the Stablers: "I found it strange that there could be a liturgy celebrated in a Benedictine Abbey with almost no singing."

Helen Stabler had smiled. "No doubt you had Father Will. He is very old, a gruff saint to be sure, but our faith tells us that all the important bits are there and the miracle is just the same. We thought you wanted only an early Mass. Had we known you would appreciate something contemporary we would have recommended Father Fisher at the nine o'clock liturgy. Would you not agree, Ted?"

"Oh yes, of course. Quite."

"Father Jack, as the young people like to call him," Helen had continued, "is a cheerful, quietly saintly man with no pretense whatever. He was eighteen years in India working among mostly poor Catholics in the south and west where there are parishes said to have been established by Thomas the Apostle. He is, of course, older than the young people he has attracted to regular Sunday service. He organizes outings and occasional good works projects. His rapport with the young and theirs with him is puzzling. He is a very simple man and there is about him an aura of the mystical that resonates with the contemporary spirit of India."

"It's more than an aura, my dear," Ted Stabler had snorted. "The man is a menace. He seems to be able to know exactly what I'm thinking every time I meet him."

"Now Theodore, you ..."

"I know exactly what you are going to say -- I must not disparage a man of the cloth. Am I right? Well, I don't wish to disparage anybody. It's just that the man is a menace. Whenever he greets me, he seems to know all that I'm thinking. If that were not enough, sometimes he seems to know what I will be thinking in a minute or two. It's chilling, Miss Pyn, very chilling -- almost Gothic."

Miss Pyn was not at all certain whether Ted's analysis was Gothic or accurate or fanciful. She did reflect that some people are extraordinarily perceptive, while others have limited depth of thought. Perhaps Ted's anxiety might be understood in this way. His literal-mindedness accounted for much, very much.

Ted had persisted, "I'm not at all comfortable addressing a priest of the church as 'Jack.' It is not at all respectful."

"Yes," Helen had explained, "Father 'Jack' is a bit too contemporary for Ted. Father Jack's full name is 'John Fisher.' He prefers to be called 'Jack' by everyone. He says he is not like either of his namesakes. He does not aspire to be the Archbishop of Canterbury -- even if he were of the Anglican Communion, which he deeply respects. Certainly, he says, he does not believe he is called to the holy martyrdom suffered by his other namesake under Henry the Eighth. Some of his brothers in the Abbey believe that he might have achieved a contemporary martyrdom among the very poor of India had he been permitted to remain there. Instead, the Abbot -- with extraordinary insight, a modern psychologist would say; or with divine inspiration, a traditional theologian would say -- called him home because, as the Abbot said, "Our house needs the freshness of the philosophy John must surely have acquired these many years. Has it really been eighteen years?"

"I'll say this much for him," Ted could not restrain himself. "He certainly has drawn young people into very active membership at the Abbey. But he still gives me the shivers. Whenever he speaks to me, I feel he knows too much."

"Ted, you know very well that you've not given Father Jack any time at all. When you really know him, you'll find him a kind, simple, cheerful, happy man whose holiness does not show in the least. It's just there; and after a while, those who have dealings with him just come to know it's there.

"Miss Pyn, you will find that Father Jack is a very interesting person. I hope you meet him while you are here. If not at the Abbey, perhaps I could persuade him to come to lunch or tea."

At this, Ted had snorted and grumbled, mumbling something about going to the British Museum on that day. Helen continued, "I know you'll find his liturgy much to your liking and not at all radical, despite what Ted says. That is, of course, if you're at all conversant with contemporary Catholicism."

Miss Pyn recalled her own experience: "I find the new church most satisfactory. Many years ago, I left a very old church with priests who prayed mostly with their backs to the congregation in a language that, ironically, most of the participants did not understand -- an old church with rules, regulations, and canons that were inflexible, often requiring a tribunal to adjust. Then not long ago, I discovered a new church overflowing with vigor, light, and fresh love that I am slowly becoming accustomed to and learning to treasure.

"I suppose," she admitted, "those of you who remained with the church during the years of renewal perhaps did not notice the change because it came about gradually. My renewal was of a different sort -- private, personal, and sometimes bitter. When I did discover that the church was indeed shockingly new, I came to it with a fresh insight that I once thought was not possible. I suspect that Father Jack's liturgy will be exactly what I would hope to experience with a man whose personality and character have the depth and richness you describe. I suspect I shall not be disappointed."

Now as she approached the door of the Abbey, she wondered, "Could my response to Helen's description of Father Jack have pleased either Helen or Ted? Well, I will soon know." She stepped out of the sunlight into the deep shadows of the vestibule.

At the door of the church, there stood a vestment-clad priest greeting worshippers as they entered. Miss Pyn greeted him enthusiastically, "Good morning, Father! Surely, this is the day the Lord has made -- it is such a beautiful morning!" But then she thought of what Ted had said about this friendly priest, especially when with a warm smile he replied: "Good morning! You must be a visitor. You are most welcome."

Thinking that Ted might indeed be correct about this priest's powers of observation, Miss Pyn replied, "Yes, I am from America. But how did you know?"

"There's no mystery about it," he smiled. "I've not seen you before at this Mass, and your outgoing greeting reminded me of North Americans I've known in Canada, in the U.S. and in Rome -- and of course, your pronunciation. After Mass, if you can remain here for a few minutes, there are a few people I'd like you to meet."

"I should like that, very much. I have come to England to learn all that I can."

Miss Pyn found a pew halfway up the aisle -- close enough to the altar to see and hear the celebrant, and far enough away from the choir loft so as not to be overwhelmed by the organ. After a while, the entrance procession moved up the aisle. Father Jack addressed the congregation: "Before we begin, I should like you to know that this morning we have two important visitors. The first is Father Melrose. He is a young Anglican priest who is with us studying to become one of us by joining our Benedictine community. I have invited him to preach today's homily. The other visitor comes to us from America. You will know who she is the moment she opens her mouth. Please make her and Father Melrose feel welcome." With that, he led a brief applause.

Miss Pyn was self-conscious when she responded to the prayers of the liturgy, but she felt most welcome. Young Father Melrose's sermon about reconciliation was most reminiscent of Tom's admonition, "Pyn, you must learn to forgive yourself!" -- uttered long ago.

After the final blessing, Miss Pyn sat in meditative silence for some minutes while Father Jack put vestments and chalice away in the sacristy. Presently, he walked down a side aisle, pausing briefly at a group of young people who were obviously waiting to meet him. He then stopped at Miss Pyn's pew. "I'm sorry. I don't believe I heard your name; but if I have, I'm afraid I've forgotten it."

Miss Pyn was happy to respond, "My name is Miss Pyn. I am a librarian from the United States. My home is located in the town of Seven Oaks, which is in the midwestern part of the country. All my adult life I have planned on visiting here, and at last I have arrived."

Father Jack seemed genuinely delighted. "I'm very pleased that you are here! There are some young people I'd like you to meet and who, I'm certain, would be pleased to know you too. If you would care to follow me."

Father Jack led the way and Miss Pyn followed him out a side door into a covered walkway that marked the edge of the Abbey garden. There, a group of young people waited. "Here are some of our young friends of the Abbey. I'd like you all to know each other. I'm delighted to have you meet Miss Pyn from the States. I suspect that, as a librarian, she has been a friend of our country and our literature for some time. I'm sure you will enjoy knowing each other. Miss Pyn, I'm pleased to present: Josh, Roland, Jennifer, Fred, Sally, Penny, Jane, Emily, and Tony. They're among our most active young friends, and they are here this morning to plan next month's activity, which will be an outing and picnic to the Cotswold village of Burford. We'd be very pleased if you would join us."

The new friends all enthusiastically agreed, which made Miss Pyn once again feel most welcome. Then she recognized a young woman in the group.

"Hello, Emily! I am very pleased to see you again! Father Jack, I have already had the pleasure of meeting Emily. Her cousin Jennifer, a former student in our library program in America, arranged to have her meet my flight at Heathrow. Since then, we also encountered one another at the library at Ealing Broadway. As librarians, we have found that we enjoy many of the same authors. She has graciously offered to drive me to Victoria Station when I begin my trip -- or should I say pilgrimage -- to Worthing next week in search of any atmosphere there to enlighten me regarding Oscar Wilde's play, *The Importance of Being Earnest.*"

Miss Pyn then responded to Father Jack's invitation: "I would be most pleased and delighted to accompany you to the Cotswolds -- for several reasons. I have been a student of England and English Literature for many years since my college days. I had planned to study here during my junior year of study. I was not able to do so, and ever since, I knew I would come some day. Since I am here, I should like to know as many of your countrymen as possible. Then too, our library in Seven Oaks is a fine house on a hill, built by a man who, as an English lad, worked as a farm laborer in The Cotswolds. When he became prosperous in our country and wanted to build his house on the hill, he imported stone, and even stonemasons from The Cotswolds to build his house on land that he called 'Whitewood Wold.' So you see why I am so eager to visit The Cotswolds. I should be very pleased to accompany you, but unfortunately, about the time you will be having your picnic I shall be boarding the plane to go home to

America. I thank you very much. I know that somehow I shall get there during my remaining time here."

Father Jack replied, "Speaking for all of us, I'm sorry you will not be with us at Burford where there are used bookstores that would interest you, I'm sure. But there is someone else I would like you to meet, Miss Pyn."

He turned to the young people: "Would you all excuse us? I'll return in a few minutes. I'd like to introduce Miss Pyn to Father Rick."

They walked out into the semi-cloistered garden that was wonderfully peaceful and quiet this Sunday morning. Seated in a wheelchair beneath a flowering tree near a small pond, an elderly monk was reading his breviary. Father Jack spoke softly, "Father, I would like you to meet a countrywoman of yours who is visiting. Then, if you will excuse me, I should return to the youth group meeting. Father, I know you will be pleased to meet Miss Pyn."

Father Rick looked up. "I'm happy to know you. I trust you will forgive an old man who is unable to rise to the occasion. Please sit a moment so we can have a chat. It's not often I can learn of things about our country these days."

"I am delighted to meet you too, Father. I certainly did not expect to meet an American in an English abbey."

Father Rick laughed. "Presently, I will tell you how that came about. But first I should warn you about that bird nervously fidgeting over there in that tree. You needn't be alarmed! The bird is a kind of watchman. If I were to collapse, I think he would alert my brothers. A romantic might call him my guardian angel, but I think that would be a bit much. His story might interest you.

"Two years ago a young monk found that bird when it fell out of the nest and was abandoned. Young Albert cared for the bird; he found a box to put it in, washed some worms to feed it, and gave it liquids with an eyedropper. The bird survived and became attached to Albert, who had some difficulty convincing the bird -- whom he called Peeper -- that it was a wild thing. He finally did convince it, but the next year Peeper returned.

"During that year, Albert completed his undergraduate study and I got to know Peeper. When Albert left for graduate study, he placed Peeper in my care. Though he often looked for Albert, Peeper seemed to accept our new arrangement. Only I suspect that he thinks that he's the one who looks after me instead of the other way around. He'll keep a wary eye on you until he is convinced that you are all right. I'll calm him down a bit with an explanation, but he'll remain there ever watchful."

With that, Father Rick turned toward the tree and raised his hand. "Peeper, this lady is a new friend from across the sea who has come to visit. There is no need to be alarmed."

Miss Pyn was amazed; the bird became visibly less agitated.

"Well then," Father Rick continued, "You would like to know how I became an English Benedictine monk. Actually, I'm not an English Benedictine; I am an American Benedictine living in an English Abbey. I joined the Benedictine community when I was quite young. After I took my solemn vows, I thought I could serve members of my generation in the military. Perhaps I wanted to see more of the world. So I asked permission to volunteer for one military tour of duty. This was granted, and thus I was able to satisfy my patriotic sense as well. I did see some action, and some things that no one should see. I did get to Asia and I was able to end my tour of duty, taking a discharge there. It was then that I met Father John Fisher in India. After that, I happily returned to my Midwestern American Abbey.

"My life and work at the Abbey was very fulfilling for a number of years. I had served my country, and continued in a life of service and prayer. When the Viet Nam era enveloped our country, I was unable to accept the 'patriotic' arguments in favor of sending American military personnel into that country. Other than my conscience, I had no reason to worry. I had already served and, as a monk, I was not obliged to serve any more. Yet, I had enormous reservations.

"Some young men protested; others left for Canada. I felt that, as a monk, I could not protest. Nor could I leave the Abbey. I prayed over my dilemma for some days, and then I remembered my friend from India who had by then returned to England. I sought and received permission from both abbots to come to Ealing, and work and pray here with my brother monks at least for the duration of the war. By the time the war ended, I was so much a part of this community that all my superiors agreed that I could remain here."

Miss Pyn responded with her own story. "Yours is a most remarkable story, Father. During much of that time, I was simply tending the library in our town of Seven Oaks -- all the while hoping and planning to come here. I had planned on spending my junior undergraduate year studying English literature in England with my college roommate, but that was not to be. I am here now at last, and I hope to learn all that I can during this short holiday."

"You've come to the right place," Father Rick assured her. "London offers just about all one could hope for. Ealing is a quiet place for reflection; it's away from all the richness and turmoil of London, and it offers relatively easy access to the heart of things in town in one direction and to many other places in other directions."

Miss Pyn was grateful for this encouragement, and explained: "I am here in Ealing through the good graces of an acquaintance who found lodging for me with the Stablers. They are most gracious hosts."

"Oh yes! I know Helen and I've met Ted. He has decided opinions, as I recall."

"You are quite correct about Ted; but they are both very generous people." Miss Pyn observed the beauty of the garden around them. "This garden is not only peaceful, it is very well planned. Each plant is vigorous and clearly shows that it belongs here. I know the English climate is particularly suited for horticulture, especially flowering shrubs and roses; but this garden is simply wonderful."

"On behalf of my brothers, I thank you! However, the Benedictines have been cultivating the soil on this island quite regularly for well over a thousand years -- ever since they arrived in 597 with Saint Augustine, bringing Christianity to England. We certainly should have learned how to garden by this time! This part of the garden isn't cloistered, as you might have gathered. I'm here most pleasant days; and you're most welcome to stop by and chat, or just rest. I'll even tempt you to come again: Growing in the flowerbed on the other side of the path are some special plants. While they are relatively common in this country, they have a special association for me. When you return, I'll be pleased to explain. I've certainly enjoyed our little talk."

"As have I!"

"As I've already said, you're most welcome. Listen! Did you hear Peeper chirp? He's repeating my invitation to please come again. That bird now knows that you're a friend."

"I shall certainly call again." Smiling, Miss Pyn walked out of the garden in the direction of the Stabler home.

Early the next morning, Miss Pyn was again on her way to Westminster Abbey. The day was perfect for exploring, and Miss Pyn enjoyed her ride to town center. Although she had planned on going to the Abbey, she knew that she simply had to take advantage of the unusually bright warm sunny London morning. And so she walked along, stopping briefly at Trafalgar Square.

This morning, the atmosphere of the Square was quite different; nearly everyone seemed to be hurrying somewhere. She stood once again admiring the fountains and the lions.

A voice nearby said, "Good morning! You must be a visitor too."

Miss Pyn turned, and saw a woman of perhaps her own age quite primly dressed. "Yes, but how did you know?"

"Your American accent confirms my conjecture. My surmise, however, was predicated on my observation that we two seem to be the only people in the Square who have the leisure to stop and admire the qualities of Trafalgar this morning."

"That is an excellent observation, and your accent suggests New England to me."

"You are quite correct! I'm a visiting scholar on sabbatical leave from my college in the greater Boston area where I lecture on Middle English Literature. I'm here to research a medieval treatise devoted to arboreal agriculture for a modern publication of a collection of Medieval English manuscripts. The treatise was originally copied at Westminster Abbey, and there are copies quite nearby -- in London at The British Museum, in Oxford at The Bodleian, and in Cambridge at Corpus Christi College."

"How very interesting! I am simply on holiday from our library in Seven Oaks in the United States where I am the librarian. I am pleased to say that we have a set of *The Middle English Dictionary.* A friend of the library was a friend of one of the editors of the dictionary. When our friend's friend retired, he gave our friend his personal copy of the dictionary. When our friend retired, he thought the dictionary would be of more use in our library than on his shelf. He was correct. The dictionary is used quite often. If you are ever in our part of the world, you would be most welcome to use our dictionary."

"I thank you! In Boston, I do have a set, but it is good to know where another is available. By the way, my name is Keefe, Kathryn Keefe. I'm usually addressed as Professor Keefe, but my best students call me Dr. K."

"Our library patrons always call me Miss Pyn. Even my best students in the library student program invariably address me as Miss Pyn."

"Well, how do you do, Miss Pyn. I should be pleased if you will call me K. or Dr. K, as you wish. Have you a particular destination in mind this morning?"

"Yes. This morning, I plan to make my second visit to The Poets' Corner in Westminster Abbey. But since the Abbey will not be open to visitors for some time, I thought I should look for a place along The Strand."

"I suspect I know what it is you expect to find along The Strand. So may I join you in your quest?"

"I shall be pleased with your company! But may I know your suspicion, or your conjecture?"

"Oh no! Not just yet. I shall tell you if my thought is correct in due time. For now, I shall honor an academic practice that is seldom followed by many of my colleagues. That is, not to reveal one's thought until one can be certain that the thought is correct or well-founded. So for now, let's just walk along."

They walked on in the direction of The Strand. As they walked, Dr. K. said, "That church must be Saint Martin-in-the-Fields."

"It is. Do you know why it is called 'in-the-Fields'? I suspect that, when the first church was built, this area was an undeveloped field between the towns of London and Westminster. While the church building has been replaced, the name of the parish remains the same. If you are here one afternoon, you might see and hear The Pearlies give a performance as part of their efforts to raise money for charity."

"Are those the folks with the white buttons sewn all over their costumes? I've heard of them."

"They are, and their performances are delightful and very successful."

They continued on toward The Strand. Presently, Dr. K. inquired, "Are you a student of modern British history? My knowledge of British history covers medieval times up to the Renaissance."

"I am not a student of British history," Miss Pyn admitted. "I do read English literature, and I also read about English literature. Thereby I acquire some knowledge of places in England. For example, this Square is Trafalgar Square. Lord Nelson lost his life as his men defeated the French at the Battle of Trafalgar, and he is immortalized in the statue atop the tower in the center of the Square. The battle occurred about ten years before Waterloo. I suspect that most people know that Napoleon lost the battle at Waterloo."

"Oh, I believe so!"

"Yes, and Waterloo Bridge, which is quite near here, was at least planned, if not begun about that time."

They continued on toward The Strand. As they approached it, Dr. K. pointed out the Adelphi Theater along one side of The Strand. "That theater is rather well known for musical productions."

"You are quite right," agreed Miss Pyn. "Andrew Lloyd Webber is very popular with Americans. Oh! Look across the road and up a bit. See! There is Simpsons In

The Strand. I have been told it is an excellent place for a meal."

"I think I should like to have tea there one day. I wish you could join me!"

Miss Pyn responded with regret. "I realize our busy schedules probably would not permit that, as lovely as it would be. I read that Thursday is the most popular day because the shops are open late on Thursday, and that attracts fashionable visitors from the suburbs. Look! Over there is the Savoy Hotel, and next to it is Lancaster Place! The roadway next to it runs down to Waterloo Bridge."

"Ah! Now I can share some of my knowledge of the Middle Ages with you! Lancaster Place and the Savoy Hotel are very important historically. The son of King Henry III -- John of Gaunt, Duke of Lancaster -- lived in The Palace of Savoy during the fourteenth century. The palace was destroyed by peasants in revolt."

"Thank you! That is very informative. My knowledge of English history is derived from literature, and begins with the Renaissance and Shakespeare. However, I have read *The Canterbury Tales*, which I enjoyed immensely."

Thus encouraged, Dr. K. continued, "Chaucer's pilgrims were on the way to visit the shrine of the martyr, Thomas Becket, at Canterbury. Even though Chaucer know John of Gaunt well, he did not write of the events around The Savoy."

"The Savoy Hotel is very impressive!" Miss Pyn was now eager to display some of her knowledge of The English Renaissance. "Just across Lancaster Place is Somerset House. The Duke of Somerset lived in this place, perhaps in Shakespeare's time. If you have not seen the modern structure from the riverside -- as I did when I walked across Waterloo Bridge earlier today -- I suggest that you walk onto the Bridge and look up and downstream to see some of London's famous landmarks, and then look back at the imposing facade of Somerset House. It is a very fine structure. The building also houses The Courtauld Gallery of quite modern fine art."

The ladies continued their stroll along The Strand. Across the road from Somerset House they saw the west end of the Aldwych Arch, or Crescent, containing theaters and government houses of countries like India and Australia. They noticed a median in the roadway on which they saw the church of St. Clement Danes, with a statue of its famous parishioner, Samuel Johnson, who had lived not far from the church.

Dr. K. observed, "The name of that church suggests that there must have been a settlement of

Danes near here. I suppose that just as 'in-the-Fields' continued to be part of the name of St. Martin-In-the-Fields, so too 'Danes' continued long after the Danes departed. But why do you suppose Samuel Johnson is remembered here?"

Miss Pyn was delighted to explain: "Johnson is not only memorialized here, he is also buried in Westminster Abbey in The Poets' Corner. He was the poet who wrote *The Vanity of Human Wishes*. He was also the critic who wrote *The Lives of the Poets*. Perhaps above all he was the lexicographer who compiled a modern dictionary of English long before Webster did so for American English."

"My word! What an accomplished man! I must read more about him!"

Continuing their stroll, they saw on the left The Royal Courts of Justice. Miss Pyn observed, "That is a most impressive structure. Judging from the many windows and turrets in that large multi-story building, there must be close to one thousand rooms there."

Opposite the Courts they came near the home of the legal profession, The Temple -- quite near the end of the Strand. Gazing just beyond The Temple, Miss Pyn exclaimed, "There it is! My destination at last -- Twinings Tea Shop at number 226 The Strand!"

Dr. K. stopped abruptly. "So! My initial supposition predicated on my first impression appears to have been well-founded. I suspected, from the moment I first saw you, that you were more than likely heading in the direction of Twinings Shop."

"How could you suspect that?"

"That is no mystery," was her smug reply. "I just knew that, like me, you appeared to be a connoisseur of fine tea, and so your destination had to be Twinings."

"And so I am, and so it is."

"Furthermore," teased Dr. K., "could there be any other really important place along The Strand?"

"You are quite correct," replied Miss Pyn with a smile. "Just look at that shop with a lion over the door! It has been in this very place for almost three hundred years. Although much around it may have changed, the shop has remained -- a testament to durability and stability."

"Well said. You are beginning to sound like an historian."

"Not really! I suppose," continued Miss Pyn mischievously, "if I had said that it was 'testament to steadfast stability' you would probably accuse me of attempting to sound like an English poet from The Middle Ages trying to construct a line of alliterative verse."

270

"Not unless you were to say, 'It was a striking statement of steadfast stability.' In which case," Dr. K. teased, "I think even you would agree that perhaps you were trying a bit too hard."

"Well, however it may be said," insisted Miss Pyn, "the presence of that shop in this place is most impressive. It has been right here since before our country was founded."

"Yes, and it even predates our celebrated Boston Tea Party, which began it all. I should not think that Twinings had any involvement in that party."

"You are right!" agreed Miss Pyn. "In fact, I have read that The East India Tea Company's tea was thrown into the sea that day. But perhaps we should have come here a little later this morning. The shop will not be opened for some time."

"That's just as well, for I must get to my research. The British Museum Library should be open by the time I get there. Then later, you remember, I shall travel to Oxford and Cambridge."

"I do remember your plan, and it reminded me of my plan made many years ago. I had planned to visit Oxford and Cambridge too. However, my time here in England is so short that I have to postpone those visits, and hope for another time here in the future."

"I do hope you'll be able to do so, and I hope we shall meet again. For now, I guess we must say goodbye."

"I thank you for making my stroll along The Strand so very interesting. I should continue my exploration of Westminster Abbey. Goodbye, and remember that if you ever come to Seven Oaks you will be most welcome; and you can consult our *Middle English Dictionary*."

The two friends parted. Dr. K. continued north toward the British Museum Library, and Miss Pyn west toward Trafalgar. The scene at Trafalgar was quite different when she reached there. The people were no longer in the great hurry of early morning. Some could even relax; and instead of viewing them with a bit of envy, Miss Pyn decided to join them. Later, after a relatively short time she was once again at the entrance to Westminster Abbey.

The verger said a cheerful, "Good morning! It's so nice to see you again so soon. Have you come to visit The Poets' Corner again today?"

"Yes, but I promised my London friends I would visit at least some of the chapels."

"Very good! You may begin just to your left at either the chapel of Saint Andrew or the one of Saint Michael. Then if you walk along the back behind the main altar, you will encounter a number of royal tombs and chapels before you arrive at The Poets' Corner. Enjoy your visit."

"Thank you. I know I shall. "

With no hesitation she walked directly into the chapel of Saint Michael. Miss Pyn suspected that there must be several Saints Michael, as there are several Saints Andrew. As she entered the chapel, she realized that this chapel must be dedicated to Saint Michael the Archangel, but she thought about other saints named Michael -- including the one she had known personally. She clearly remembered that Father Hart had written that his associate and her friend must have given his life much like the martyrdom of a saint. She prayed for Michael and for her many other benefactors, and meditated peacefully for some minutes.

Then she thought that it must be time to see other parts of The Abbey. Next she came upon the tomb of Queen Elizabeth the First. The tomb was an impressive monument commemorating the monarch who gave her name to an important period of English literature and history, The Elizabethan Period. That was the time, Miss Pyn remembered, of The Spanish Armada and the glorious age of English drama -- the plays of Marlowe and Shakespeare. She remembered, too, that Shakespeare wrote a play about the victory of the first

Tudor King over King Richard the Third at the Battle of Bosworth. Perhaps, she thought, the character of King Richard was portrayed in the play rather more villainous than that of the actual king. After all, the play was presented during the rein of Elizabeth, whose grandfather was the one who had defeated King Richard.

The tomb and chapel of Elizabeth's grandfather, Henry the Seventh, was nearby in the center of that part of the Abbey. On the other side of the Henry chapel she saw the tomb of Mary Queen of Scots. Miss Pyn was well aware of the historical irony of the proximity of the tombs of the two queens. Elizabeth had managed to do away with Mary, who was executed and buried in The Tower of London.

Miss Pyn recalled that Elizabeth's successor was Mary's son, James the Sixth of Scotland, who became James the First of England upon Elizabeth's death. It was James who had his mother's tomb placed in Westminster Abbey. James also decreed that his mother's favorite chapel in Falkland Palace should remain as it was in her time. Miss Pyn remembered that it was during the reign of James that Shakespeare retired from the theater; and then, thirteen years later, still during the reign of King James, Shakespeare's collected works were printed in *The First Folio*.

Then she thought she had engaged in enough historical reflection, and it was certainly time to seek out The Poets' Corner. Accordingly, she passed the tombs of Edward the Third and Richard the Second, and was once again at the tomb of Chaucer at The Poets' Corner of the Abbey.

As she had suspected, John Milton was memorialized here. She remembered the moving conviction in the poem, "On His Blindness": "They also serve who only stand and wait." She quietly hoped that, during the years of her own spiritual blindness, Milton's observation could apply to her.

Then she saw the William Wordsworth memorial, and she remembered her favorite lines: "'Tis a beauteous evening calm and free/ The holy time is quiet as a Nun/ Breathless with adoration." Surely, she thought, those lines provide a perfect setting for quiet meditation.

Miss Pyn was not surprised to find the Jane Austen memorial here among the great poets, musicians, and other artists. She not only frequently read Austen's novels, they were among the books most often requested by the patrons of the Seven Oaks Library.

Even though she had discovered the Hopkins memorial during her first visit to The Poets' Corner, she wondered if other more contemporary poets were honored here. She was pleased to come upon the T. S. Eliot memorial. While she was not entirely comfortable with Eliot's conviction that the world would end "not with a bang but a whimper," she was impressed with the striking imagery found in lines such as "Let us go then, you and I / When the evening is spread out against the sky / Like a patient etherized upon a table."

Miss Pyn was very pleased to find that so many of her favorite authors were represented here. She thought she would look for her favorite Romantic English poet. Although she knew that John Keats was buried in Italy, she thought he should be memorialized here; and she was delighted to come upon the Keats memorial. Many memorable Keats lines raced through her mind, but only one would be perfect for this time in this place: "A thing of beauty is a joy forever." Surely, she thought, very many artists here and elsewhere have filled the world with things of beauty that have brought everlasting joy.

Once again, Miss Pyn did not want to leave The Abbey and The Poets' Corner, but she knew she must do so -- especially since she wished also to visit the chapel at Ealing Abbey. The familiar ride on the Underground and on the bus took the usual short time, and she soon climbed the steps of the Abbey at Ealing.

She looked forward to a quiet meditative rest in the lowering evening light of the Abbey chapel. On entering the chapel, she noticed on her right an unusual depiction of The Blessed Mother. Mary was seated next to a table. Gathered beside her were several young children. Each child had an obvious injury. The Holy Mother was clearly caring for and consoling each of them. Miss Pyn was deeply moved by this striking icon in alabaster. She reviewed the titles she remembered for Mary -- The Immaculate Conception, The Mother of God, The Blessed Virgin Mary, The Mother of Perpetual Help, and even *The Stabat Mater.* All these titles seemed to set Mary above the rest of humanity, and rightly so. But here in this chapel was a study depicting a perfectly human mother caring for children.

Miss Pyn thought about this iconic presentation for some minutes. She wondered if her own reconciliation would have happened sooner if she had only come to have known this nature of The Holy Mother earlier. Never mind, she was now reconciled; and she was most grateful to have had this experience.

As she meditated, her eyes grew more accustomed to the soft light of the chapel; and she was astounded to recognize a familiar figure seated in the first pew near the altar. Quietly, she walked up the aisle and whispered, "Thomas."

Tom, who had just closed the book he had been reading, looked up in astonishment. "Pyn! I see you've made it to England! Why didn't you write?"

"It did not seem appropriate because I was not able to travel to Rome to visit you, and I did not think that you might be able to visit me here because of your work in The Vatican."

"Actually, I'm on my way to Vienna on a mission for The Vatican. I'll leave from Gatwick the day after tomorrow. I stopped here to visit some friends at the Abbey. They will let me borrow a car tomorrow so I can visit the Cotswolds. Would you like to come with me?"

"I should like that very much! The young people in the parish here have invited me to join them on an outing they are planning to the Cotswold town of Burford next month. Unfortunately, I must return to Seven Oaks by that time. So I had to refuse their kind invitation."

Tom was delighted. "We could leave after Mass tomorrow. Shall we meet here then? It is so good to see you here, Pyn! For now, I have to join my friends in the Abbey dining room. See you tomorrow!"

"I shall be here."

After gazing once more at the image of The Blessed Mother caring for the children, Miss Pyn took her leave and walked in the direction of the Stabler home.

The next morning, she once again met Tom and they were off to The Cotswolds. Although the drive took some time, to Miss Pyn it seemed like quite a short ride, and soon she and Tom strolled along the Burford Village high street. They noticed, down a side lane, a pub called The Stone Carver, with doors wide open beckoning patrons, and a chalkboard proclaiming the bill of fare that featured "A Ploughperson's Lunch."

"Are you hungry, Pyn? That place looks much too interesting to pass up. We could at least have a drink if the food doesn't appeal."

"It is rather early for either; but I agree, Thomas, it would be very good to look in -- especially before many patrons appear."

The building was very old, with a low door, a stone floor and dark hand-hewn oak beams. Ancient diamond-shaped leaded-glass casement windows had unusually deep polished oak sills displaying many intricately carved stoneworks so beautifully detailed that surely they qualified as works of art. A plate-rail near the ceiling beams displayed more pieces of masterful stonework. Two securely locked glass cases contained more pieces that were clearly of even greater value.

"What things of beauty are here displayed," mused Miss Pyn. "With such exacting craftsmanship, they bring joy to this world! I wonder who made them and why they are here -- here in this pub. They make it a kind of art museum. I suspect there is a story here."

They moved to the bar. It too was a masterful work -- the front carved red oak, the top crosscut oak, both with a deep patina of age and generations of hand-rubbing. The barmaid was pretty -- perhaps twenty-four, with black, black hair, pure white complexion, and a voice that carried the melodies of Wales.

"Good mornin'! May I serve you and the lady, sir? Perhaps a shandy or a sherry? We have some excellent ales too." She broke into a magnificent smile that added new warmth to the soft golden glow that filtered through the leaded glass windows.

"The missus, that's my old auntie, who runs the business here, says that when patrons of quality come in I should address them proper-like. Was that all right?"

Miss Pyn only smiled her unmistakable acquiescence.

"I calls her 'the missus' so that the regulars always know that she's the boss and that I'm not here just because I'm her relative, even though I think they all know it and yet they are always well mannered despite their knowin'. What can I get ... er ... what may I serve you?"

"A glass of sherry would be just lovely, as long as it is not too sweet or too dry for this hour of the morning."

"I've got just what ... that is, I have an excellent medium sherry, madam, that I believe should be to your likin'. Some of my locals drink it in the mornin'. Others drink it all day and even all evenin' long. It's very popular hereabouts. And sir, what can I ... ah, what may I serve you? We have lagers and ales -- some all the way from London."

"I have no desire for a London brew. I always try the local product. Have you a local bitter that your regulars like?"

"There is 'Fields,' as we calls it. It has a bit of authority, so I don't usually offer it to visitors, especially to gentlemen. Wouldja like a taste?"

Before Tom could reply she drew a small amount into a half-pint glass, saying, "Now try this while I pour the lady's sherry."

When she brought the sherry, she asked Tom, "Well, whatja think of it?"

"I've not yet tried it."

"Why? Does it look too strong?"

"No. I await the toast. What is your name? Will you join us?"

"My name is Lynn, sir, with two 'n's.'"

"That is a very pretty name for a pretty young woman," Miss Pyn said.

"Thank you, ma'am, but the missus thinks it's too common for our proper establishment. If you're still here when she comes down with the lunchtime food, you'll probably hear her call to me from the stair as 'Linda.' Then when she sees you, she will call me 'Melinda' cuz she says it's a more refined name and better for patrons of quality to hear."

She smiled apologetically to Tom, "No, I thank you, sir, but I'm not allowed to indulge while I'm on duty, and it really is quite early too. So thank you so very much, but no."

Tom raised his glass and proclaimed, "Cheers."

Miss Pyn responded with *"L'chaim."*

"Yes, to life."

"Skol."

"Nazdrowie."

"Salute."

"Prost."

"To us!"

With glasses raised, Miss Pyn and Tom looked at each other in frozen silence for what seemed to Lynn a long time. So she added, *"Slainte,* as me old dad used to say." And she raised her imaginary glass to join the toast: "All the best to the two of you together."

Tom, who had begun to raise his glass at Lynn's Irish toast, looked at Miss Pyn with a hint of sadness in his face while she gazed at the glass of sherry on the bar before her for some moments. Lynn began to fear that she had said something wrong, and blushed a little. Tom, perhaps sensing her embarrassment, quickly drank his taste of bitter. And the moment passed.

"Ah, that bitter has a bit of authority in it all right, but it's mellow and creamy. A man could very soon get used to drinking that. I'll have a pint of it if I may."

"Of course, and as the missus would say, 'Tis my pleasure, Sir.'" With a delighted smile, she drew the amber liquid until the creamy head was overflowing, trimmed the pint and handed it to Tom with a sprightly "Cheers!"

Miss Pyn looked again and again at the stonework. "Lynn, why is this pub called 'The Stone Carver'? Perhaps because of all of the beautiful carvings that are all around us?"

"I know only a little," replied Lynn with a conspiratorial glance, "but they say it's named for the person who made them in his shop that was once in this very building. There are those who say that, on certain days when the sun begins to set and casts an eerie light through the leaded glass on that little table in the corner near the fireplace, the carver can be seen sitting at that table."

She continued almost in a whisper, "I have not seen him cuz I dare not look over there. I asked my dear auntie to be excused from workin' alone here at that time of day. She agrees, but probably because the place begins to fill up about then. I know the regulars don't ever sit at that table, even when we're crowded. Some say, too, that on special days they see not only the carver, but his beautiful lady sitting with him. So you see why I don't wish to look that way at sundown. Even at other times, it gives me a chill to look over there.

"Even when forward young fellows say -- probably to vex me," she confided, "that the lady resembles me, I refuse to look. I really don't know, but old William, who usually comes in about now, knows the story, and loves to tell it."

"What is William's full name?" asked Tom with growing interest.

"I don't believe I know that. He never uses it, even though he talks like a real gentleman. Oh yes, I heard him called 'Harding' once. That must be it, 'William Harding.' He should be here soon."

Miss Pyn continued to study the stone carvings. "Thomas, they are beautiful. It is difficult to believe that such gentle soft lines could be wrought in stone." She moved to the window, examining the work more closely.

Tom continued to study his pint o' bitter. "This fine bitter is called 'Fields' you say. Is that the name of the brewer?"

"No," laughed Lynn. "I was told his name was Hickson. Mr. Hickson thought nobody would drink 'Hickson's Bitter,' so he named his brew, 'The Flavors of the Fruits of the Fields.' Nobody would drink that either, 'til his brother joined the brewery and cut the name to 'Fields.' Now it's very popular."

All this time, no one else had entered the pub. Tom was beginning to wonder with whom this very popular bitter was popular, when a man, in an obvious hurry, entered and called out "Mornin' Lynn, a half bitter please."

"Fields?"

"You bet! On a day like this, only the best will get the thin blood movin' right. Cheers, one and all!" He paid, and after some deep gulps, he and the bitter were both gone. Tom was convinced.

Miss Pyn returned to the bar. "We noticed that you will be serving a 'Ploughperson's lunch.' Is that something special? I have not seen that offered before."

"No, not really. It's just a regular Ploughman's with a 'Politically Correct' name. I learned about 'P.C.'

from my cousin who lives in Chicago in America. I thought it might attract attention. I guess it did."

"What else will you serve?"

"Well, our pub fare is like other pub fare, only ..." Lynn raised her chin proudly, "we think it's much better. The Missus no longer makes the steak and kidney pie or the pork pie. The firm that makes them now does very well, but they're not quite as good as those me auntie used to make. She still makes the shepherd's pie and the chicken casserole, so those are always very good, and she supervises all the rest.

"You'll find her sausage rolls are the finest anywhere. Oh yes, on some days we offer smoked trout -- it's very good. If it's on today, I'd recommend it heartily. Do try it. It's the best in the Cotswolds."

Lynn glanced at the door. "Here comes Mister Harding -- Ol' Will."

The man entering the pub appeared to be an impressive gentleman, but of limited means. He stood comfortably straight and carried a finely carved walking stick with a silver top. He paused while his eyes adjusted to the changed light.

Tom spoke. "Mr. Harding, I believe."

The old gentleman looked puzzled and a bit reluctant to speak. Finally he replied, "I am sorry, sir, but you have the better of me. I do not believe that I have had the pleasure of your acquaintance. Is there something I might do for you?"

"My friend and I would like to have a chat with you. No doubt you can tell we are Americans. We're interested in the history of this pub. We've been told that you know most things about the village. May we stand you to a pint of 'Fields'? I find it an excellent brew. May we sit over by the window?"

An eager smile warmed the old man's face. "Call me Will, as everyone here does. I am very pleased to learn you are Americans. I shall tell you why in a few moments. That table over there will be just fine. When the lunchtime rush begins it will be the quietest place, and if that proves unsatisfactory we can always move to the back garden. It will be getting comfortably warm as noon approaches. Your offer of a pint is most gracious, sir, but would you make it a half please? At my age, my days are measured in pints. It seems that half pints not only delay the inevitable, but stretch out each day as well."

Tom asked Miss Pyn if she would like another glass of sherry. She pointed to her half-filled glass, "This will do nicely just now, thank you, Thomas."

When Tom returned with the drinks, he said, "I'm sorry, sir -- Will -- that I failed to introduce us. May I present my friend, Miss Pyn, and I am Tom Zimmerman. We're here, as you say, 'on holiday.'"

The old gentleman took Miss Pyn's hand in his; and with a smile in his sharp blue eyes, he said, "I am very pleased to know you." Looking at Tom and still holding Miss Pyn's hand, he added, "You know, when I awakened this morning I knew that something perfectly wonderful would happen to me today. So it has! Now I must tell why I'm so glad you are Americans.

"These days everybody calls me Ol' Will. Nobody uses my full name. I'm addressed as 'Harding' only for official matters like taxes. When you called my name, I thought that you might be from Inland Revenue come to ask some embarrassing questions.

"So, Tom, your name is Zimmerman. Do you know that in German the 'Zimmerman' is the 'room man' -- the expert finish carpenter who completes the job as it should be done. You don't happen to be a carpenter, are you?"

"Unfortunately, I'm not; but the person I most admire, or I might say even revere, was a carpenter for much of his life."

"I am so relieved that you are visitors -- generous visitors at that, that I should like to propose a toast. To your health, good sir, and to that of your beautiful lady! All the very best, cheers!"

Again Tom paused, his glass in mid-air for just a fleeting moment. He and Miss Pyn both looked uncertain, but they quickly drank the toast while the old gentleman drank deeply, if only a small amount of his half.

"Now then, what may I tell you?"

Miss Pyn put down her sherry glass and began: "I am a librarian in a small town in the Midwestern part of the United States. I have been intensely interested in your country, its history and lore for all of my adult life; and Thomas is interested as well. We have found the Cotswolds Villages especially fascinating."

Ol' Will nodded his approval.

"The library that I direct is constructed of Cotswolds stone. It is a beautiful old mansion that stands on a hill, commanding a view of the entire town. The grandfather of the family who gave the people of Seven Oaks our library lived in this Cotswolds district as a lad, and left here a young man after working several years as a laborer. In later life he became wealthy, and imported Cotswolds stone and two Cotswolds stonemasons to build his house on a hill. Today it is our town's treasure."

"So we were attracted here," Tom continued. "And when we saw this pub we could not pass it up.

We'd like to know as much of its history as we can. How did the pub get its name?"

Delighted by their interest, Ol' Will took a deep breath and began, "Well, I'll tell you, its name and its history are much the same story. It is at once a simple and strange story -- so strange that if it had not happened, few people would believe that it ever could have happened.

"I think I remember that the great Polish author, Joseph Conrad, wrote that 'the human heart is vast enough to contain the whole world; it is valiant enough to bear the burden.' Perhaps the simple story I tell of the stone carver touches on only the tiniest part Conrad's grand observation, but in my mind it adds another dimension to it -- rather like a freshly revealed facet on a fine gemstone."

As if to forestall any doubt in his hearers, Ol' Will leaned closer to them and said, "I witnessed the last part of the story because I became a very close friend of Christopher, one of the principal participants in the story. Much of what I did not observe, I learned from my friend. Other details I heard about from very old-timers who knew the beginning. The rest I was able to ferret out from documents and old news accounts."

Satisfied with this preamble, he settled back in his chair, took a sip of his bitter and continued. "The story began during the latter part of the nineteenth century, when a man of some means came to the Cotswolds in search of a new life. He came from Ireland and, while he had prospered there, his wife of not yet fifteen years had died there. He wished to be away from his memories of Ireland. He was not originally Irish. Some say he started in France; others say he was from Spain, like the early Celts. He was, everyone agreed, from the continent. Speculation about his French or Spanish origins was probably based only on the name of the man's beautiful daughter and nothing more.

"Father and daughter took up residence on a fine farm he had purchased over in the direction of Stow-on-the-Wold. He would not be only a gentleman farmer; he had some knowledge of farming and he could learn more. So he would be his own manager. He did learn, and for over five years he managed very well. He was accepted by the farming community and was thought to be a worthy asset to the district.

"His daughter Belinda, who was just thirteen years old when she and her father came to the farm, grew in wisdom and beauty during those marvelous years. She became the favorite of everyone at school. She was talented as well as beautiful, accomplished in music -- voice as well as piano, and she was fluent in French and Spanish as well as English. With so very much natural endowment and cultivation, one would expect that she would be envied by many jealous rivals. Instead, her gentleness, her engaging smile, and her eagerness to help her schoolmates prompted a respect and even affection in all whose lives she touched."

Ol' Will paused, picked up his glass, looked very pleased and began to sample the bitter again, slowly, like an expert taster. Tom looked puzzled. "I don't understand why her name suggested their country of origin."

"If you will reflect for just a moment, Thomas," Miss Pyn interjected, "surely you will remember that the first part of Belinda's name is from the French and the second part is Spanish, both meaning beautiful."

Tom smiled his thanks. "Your story of this twice beautiful lady promises to be very interesting. Will you continue it, sir?"

"It's my pleasure. Among her admirers at school was Christopher, the son of the family that lived and worked here on this property for generations. The Stancrafts were stonecarvers for longer than anyone could remember. Well known, their work was in demand throughout all the Cotswolds."

Ol' Will paused for a sip from his glass. Tom followed his example, while Miss Pyn looked thoughtful. "That family may have been crafters in stone for more years than one would imagine, even before Norman Times. The Old English or Anglo Saxon word for 'stone' was 'stan.' Could it be that the family name derived from the family occupation?"

"Well, sir," said Ol' Will raising his glass, "You are not only a gentleman; your lady is a scholar."

"Not really," protested Miss Pyn. "I am only a student of things English, especially of our language. I cannot be at all certain of how old the full name 'Stancraft' could be without further research, and perhaps not even then. My surmise is born only of informal speculation."

Tom differed. "The lady is indeed a scholar. I am ceaselessly amazed by what she has learned in her library."

As the men praised her, Miss Pyn blushed a little. "You both are entirely too extravagant. May we hear the rest of the story? Belinda interests me."

"Of course. Where was I? Young Christopher was a handsome lad who served his apprenticeship in his father's shop even as he went to school. It certainly seemed he would finish his apprenticeship by the time he would be twenty.

"Belinda was by this time a grown woman -- a year younger than Christopher. Her beauty even then was a legend. Her coloring was rather like that of our pretty Lynn here. Belinda was a natural beauty whose image was not only striking, it lingered in the memory of all who beheld her. Her eyes, her lips, her nose, her chin were well nigh perfect and perfectly proportioned; and she was wonderfully cultivated too, even then.

"The two young people became very close friends and in time, as those things happen, they thought they should like to live their lives together." Ol Will's listeners nodded, and for a moment focused their attention on their glasses.

Ol' Will waved absentmindedly to two young workers who greeted him as they entered the pub, and returned eagerly to his story. "So they proposed marriage to their parents. Christopher's father and mother objected. Under no circumstance should he even consider the thought until after he served his apprenticeship and was established in the business. They agreed he was a good son – dependable, a good worker, and generally sensible. They loved Belinda, as did everyone. They had great praise for her beauty; but no, any such plan would have to wait. Only Christopher's mother had a troubling thought she shared with no one, 'Could Belinda's beauty be too great?'

"Belinda's father was adamant. The boy was nice enough and handsome too, but even when he finished his indenture he'd be only a stone carver. While she -- not only the daughter of a prosperous landowner, but also a young woman of rare beauty, talent, and cultivation -- could expect to marry much higher, someone of greater means and expectation. Besides, Christopher with all his industriousness would never be able to support her in the degree and manner to which she was accustomed, and which she deserved. No, this could not be.

"Her father proposed instead that she continue her education on the continent. Belinda was dismayed, but she reluctantly agreed to spend one year in a French convent school for women of 'good' families. After that, she would study music in Spain for another year, providing she could come home on holiday each Christmas. Father and daughter were each convinced that the other would have a change of heart in two years.

"Ah, me!" sighed the storyteller. "Such hopes each had! Well, as you can imagine, the parting was difficult; but the young people were consoled with the thought that Christmas was not too many months away. The second parting, after that first Christmas, was even more difficult -- they knew their next meeting would be a whole year away. Belinda's father still maintained his strong feeling against his daughter's love for

Christopher, but he agreed to have the young man and his parents see Belinda off to her school. So with great sadness they parted. Christopher's mother hugged and kissed the young woman she still hoped would become, in time, her daughter-in-law. Then she turned away quickly so that no one would see the grave frown on her face and the tear that ran down her cheek." Ol' Will's sudden frown seemed to echo the mother's feelings, and instilled in his listeners a foreboding that made them urge him to continue.

"Well, my friends, perhaps because many letters traveled across the Channel in both directions, the year passed quickly. It was again December; Christopher was nearing the end of his apprenticeship, and Belinda could soon be expected home -- this time from Spain. There was such joy in the village! Belinda could stay only a few weeks and, yes, Christopher was not yet established; but it would not be long before the two years would pass. There was great anticipation and great expectation in those two young hearts! Everyone knew Belinda's father loved his daughter very much. Surely he could be persuaded. Surely he must be persuaded."

Despite their feelings of apprehension just seconds before, Tom and Miss Pyn couldn't help feeling a surge of hope and optimism at these words. Her eyes alight, Miss Pyn urged, "What happened?"

"Well, my dear lady, the ship left the port of Cadiz on the high early-morning tide of December twelfth bound for Bristol. Belinda and ninety-six fellow passengers expected an easy passage home to England.

"Just out of the Bay of Biscay, high winds came up -- winds that grew into a fierce winter gale. The ship traveled no further. All were lost."

"Oh!" cried Miss Pyn, and now it was she who frowned, and perhaps it was a tear that she surreptitiously brushed away. Tom said quietly, "Go on with your story."

"The entire village was very sad that Christmas," continued Ol' Will, shaking his head. "Christopher and his parents were devastated. Christopher's mother wept silently, praying for her son and for Belinda. Christopher's father said little, but each day he gave his son more and more work. The young man would survive ... in time.

"Belinda's father could not or would not be consoled. He was convinced that if he not been so adamant, had he not insisted on his daughter's two years of virtual exile, she would not have been lost at sea. He brooded and he drank a little too, often neglecting his farm.

"During the dark winter evenings that followed, Christopher found solace in continuing his work on a carving, a very special carving that he had thought of designing for the beautiful lady he had hoped to marry. Now there would never be that special occasion to mark with this gift of his art. Nor would there be a beloved one to treasure and find joy in his gift, and delight in his artistry.

"Nonetheless, he decided, he could finish the work by April, in time to mark her birthday. Despite his grief, he worked and worked, and indeed he did produce a carving worthy of his lost love."

"What a sad and beautiful story," whispered Miss Pyn.

"Ah, yes," replied Ol' Will. "But you must hear the rest of it." And when Tom suggested that another half pint would ease the telling, "Don't mind if I do!"

He sipped some of the coppery foam and continued, "Well, the years passed; and Christopher's father, exhausted by a lifetime of hard work and suffering the pains of continual exertion, was forced to give up his work. Christopher's mother had always hoped to see her son one day find happiness, but the following winter she fell ill and died suddenly of acute bronchitis. Through it all, Christopher worked as hard as ever anyone could. And each winter he designed and carved another gift to be ready in the spring for the birthday of his would-be bride.

"I met Christopher the year his father died. I was a young man; and I was very interested in his exacting beautiful craftsmanship -- by that time it was celebrated throughout the Cotswolds and was very much in demand. I thought, it turned out presumptuously, that I might imitate if not equal his artistry. I soon learned that I lacked the gift. I had not the talent. So I went off to learn how to fight a war."

Ol' Will went on with a wry smile, "Fortunately, the war ended before I became a fully qualified officer. However, before I left for training, I had learned about Belinda's father. His prosperous farm was then fully mortgaged, and he was alone and unable to work; he was nearly destitute.

"I did not return for two whole years. By that time Christopher had carved two more treasures for Belinda's birthday. On my return, I learned that the entire village knew about Christopher's birthday gifts for Belinda; each April everyone looked forward to that year's creation."

Ol' Will's smile became very gentle. "While I was away, Christopher had taken in his destitute might-have-been father-in-law, because, as Christopher said, 'he had no one, and no place to go.' Well, Belinda's father was wholly dependent on Christopher for nearly ten years.

"During those years, I saw Christopher often. Each year, I admired his artistry more and more, and we became close friends. In fact, to my surprise, he asked me to serve as executor of his estate since he had no close relatives. He said that while he expected to live a good long time yet, the failing health of Belinda's father reminded him that he needed to plan ahead.

"I often stopped by the shop after the workday for a chat with my friend. We both smoked tobacco in those days and we'd sit of an evening, meerschaums in hand, addressing life's problems and speculating about the meaning of existence." Ol' Will's gaze shifted for a moment to a far-off place. Then he leaned back and continued to reminisce.

"One evening -- I remember it so well -- I asked about his long devotion to Belinda. He said his faith supported it, and his certain conviction that he would meet her one day in heaven and she would be even more beautiful."

It was some moments before Ol' Will's gaze returned to his listeners. He looked away again for a while, and he said rather brusquely, "Well, you'll be wanting to hear the end of the story. When Belinda's father finally died, a deep irony of life was revealed to me! That's when the old-timers told me, because I was Christopher's friend, that Belinda's father forbade the marriage of the young people because he believed that Christopher could never support his daughter! Ah, but the deeper irony became apparent years later.

"Life continued, and Christopher continued to produce his annual treasure. Then, one night, Christopher died peacefully. It fell to me to settle his affairs. What I discovered was truly amazing.

"Years earlier, when Christopher took in Belinda's father, he discovered that he had many outstanding debts. Christopher, the 'young man of questionable reliability,' mortgaged this very property that had been in his family for generations in order to pay those debts that Belinda's father had incurred!

"After Christopher died, there was a small amount yet outstanding. Rather than risk losing this property, I decided to sell the carvings. But I was perplexed. Should I sell them to a dealer, who would most likely, over time, sell them to many buyers and so scatter the collection, thus diminishing its aesthetic impact? Or could I somehow preserve the collection?"

Lynn, busy now with noonday customers, glanced occasionally at the three figures so engrossed that they seemed far away from the bustle of the pub. "Ah," she thought, "Ol' Will has them under his spell." And indeed, Tom and Miss Pyn waited eagerly for him to continue.

"After a while, I realized that the debt could be met by selling only a few pieces. I did this. I myself bought two, which I keep at home; but they are already willed back to the collection. Even after the sale there are still over sixty uniquely beautiful statements of devotion carved in stone."

He looked around with affection at the carvings that surrounded them. "So ... when Lynn's aunt and uncle offered to lease the property and promised to develop a respectable public house that could support the collection in a manner worthy of its artistry, I thought that would be a fitting end to this story -- to keep the works in the place where they were created.

"Now you see, the story of this pub is a simple, powerful love story."

With a steady hand in a graceful movement Ol' Will raised his glass, looked first to Miss Pyn and then to Tom, and took a long drink ever so slowly. He set down the nearly empty tankard and continued.

"Are the ghosts real? I leave that to others to decide. I have not seen them. Of course, I am not ever here at sundown; nor shall I ever be. I need nothing more than the aura emitted by these wonderful studies in stone to verify the tale of Christopher and Belinda."

"What a grand story," whispered Miss Pyn with a voice that was nearly tearful, although she would never admit it. "What will happen to this wonderful memorial?"

"There is a Trust. This building and the collection are its principal assets. With revenues from the lease so far, the Trust has purchased the building next to this. It too is leased. After the revenues accumulate we will remodel that property into a suitable place for the collection. The pieces you see here are only a small portion of the entire collection. Remember, there are well over sixty carvings."

The old man slowly rose. "Ah, the long sitting makes the bones stiff. I must leave now, or my granddaughter will be most upset with my tardy return. I hope you enjoyed the story of these beautiful carvings. I bid you both good day and God speed. If you come again next year, God willing I shall be here."

With that, the old gentleman was gone. Miss Pyn and Tom sat in silence for many minutes, sometimes looking at each other with puzzled thought-filled eyes, sometimes looking out of the window or at the stone work -- all the while utterly oblivious of the rising chatter of the lunchtime patrons that swirled around them.

Presently, Tom spoke: "I don't believe it. I don't believe it, I say."

"Thomas, you must," Miss Pyn said earnestly. "How could you not believe that beautiful story? Why, Mr. Harding knew Christopher and, in the end, handled his affairs."

"I believe the old gentleman's story, every word of it. What I can't believe is that we are here in this place, at this time, and that he was just here and told us that incredible story. Why? Perhaps we'll never know."

"Perhaps we shall ... in time. On the other hand, it is such a wonderful story, do we really need to know with our heads, or can we just 'know it' with the understanding of the heart?"

Raucous laughter at a nearby table roused them. "You know, Thomas, when Mister Harding left, I thought I could not even move for a long while -- yet alone eat -- but I find now that I am quite hungry, and I think that I see the smoked trout Lynn urged you to try, just there at the serving counter. Shall we?"

"Yes! *Manjiare*! Oh, I mean, let's eat! Evidently I've been in Italy too long. Let's take our lunch into the garden away from all this talk and smoke. That trout looks very good. I will have it and a jacket potato. You see, I can speak the language here sometimes too."

"And I shall have chicken with salad and a jacket potato; I am hungry. But Thomas, are you not forgetting something?"

"I don't think so. Oh, all right. I'll have some of that cold mixed vegetable salad with it. Honestly, Pyn, sometimes you sound like my mother."

Miss Pyn simply smiled as Tom paid for their lunch.

In the garden, Tom offered to get their drinks. "Would you like another sherry?"

"No, thank you. One glass of sherry so early in the day is quite enough. I think I should like some white wine -- a Piesporter, or ... remember your bottle of Niersteiner! On second thought, Niersteiner should await another day, a very special day. Oh, I know! I shall have a glass of sweet Italian white vermouth and lemonade. I have wanted to try that combination ever since I heard a smart young lady order it in London. I suspect that it should be an excellent accompaniment for my meal."

Tom returned to the bar, leaving Miss Pyn all alone in the garden. Ol' Will had been right; the sun had warmed the air nicely, and the garden was very quiet in sharp contrast to the chatter inside the pub. The seasonal planting was underway but not yet finished. Miss Pyn suspected that Lynn did much of the planting during her free time. She noticed flats of geraniums, impatiens, and marigolds near the potting shed at the back of the garden.

Primroses of all sorts of boisterous colors were already in bloom as though waiting eagerly to enter into a vigorous sporting competition along the borders of the garden. The tea roses showed so much promise, with enormous buds ready to spring forth, that Miss Pyn regretted wistfully that she could not be here in this garden in a day or two to witness the grand inauguration of the season of roses.

She frowned as she remembered once again how joy seemed, forever and always, tempered by the bittersweet; for when the roses bloomed, Spring -- the season of nature's new life -- must be gone for yet another whole year.

The garden was a special place, she decided, as special as the pub. It was terraced, and at every level there were little gardens, sometimes tiny gardens, that were perfect beds for all kinds of lovely flowers that accented the terraces and defined spaces ornamented by individually carved stone tables with comfortable modern chairs. Carved benches punctuated the various levels of the terrace, and the legacy of Christopher's artistry became beautifully apparent again.

At the back of the garden, covering the southwest corner, were tall lilacs of many shades in full bloom. Every now and then a southerly breeze whisked up a soft scent of lilac that graced the entire garden.

Miss Pyn thought, "This place is too beautiful for a pub garden."

Tom returned with their drinks. Miss Pyn thanked him, adding, "This place is enchanting, Thomas, is it not?"

"An enchanted garden! I've always thought an enchanted garden had to be a private place, a secret place, not the back garden of a public house."

"Oh, but we are all alone here just now. It is very private for the moment. If we wish, it can be our secret place. What is more, we can store impressions and images of this special place in our memories -- so that tomorrow and next month and even next year, when we wish and remember, recalling the scent of lilac, it will be our private place -- our very own, very special secret place, ever so enchanting ... forever."

Tom thought, "What a rare being this woman is!" He smiled. "To be sure, friend Pyn, to be sure." As he picked up his cutlery, a delicate wispy breeze gently nudged the scent of lilac and the distant sound of music into the garden. Time surely had not stood still, but it certainly had not moved very quickly either.

"Pyn, that was the best trout I've ever tasted. It was marvelous."

Miss Pyn had to agree. "This luncheon was undoubtedly of the first order. I thank you very much, Thomas."

"Would you care for a 'sweet' is it, for dessert?"

"Yes, 'sweet' it is and no, I could not possibly manage the least bit more."

"Nor could I, though the desserts are very tempting. Pyn, I have a proposal to make. Are you willing?"

She smiled. "I suspect I had better hear what it is before I respond."

Tom began enthusiastically. "I know how very fond you are of what I call 'real music.' Ever since I came to Europe I've had a secret plan -- a hope, really. It's my fondest wish that one day you shall accompany me on a musical holiday. There are many great orchestras in Europe. My plan is to persuade you to come to Europe at Christmas. Then you and I could go to hear the very best. I have a friend in Vienna who can get tickets to the special year-end concerts at the relatively short notice of a year or so."

Miss Pyn had listened with misgiving. "Thomas, you are surely correct about my love of music, and your plan is certainly intriguing. However, it is not probable and certainly not practical."

"Not even if I tell you what I had in mind? We could go to Vienna after Christmas. Then on New Year's Eve we could go to see the operetta, *Die Fledermaus*. At the end of the second act, we could join the other members of the audience and drink a toast to the new year and to each other. Then on New Year's Day, we could attend the New Year Liturgy at Saint Stephen's Cathedral and worship with The Vienna Boys Choir. I've read that Haydn himself studied at The Vienna Choir School."

"Oh, Thomas," Miss Pyn responded in dismay, "that plan is wonderful -- even marvelous, but extravagant and wholly not possible."

"Wait! I'm not finished. After church we could go around the square a short distance behind the cathedral to the best coffee shop perhaps in all Vienna, and have a perfectly wonderful meal that you won't be able to forget. They have a magnificent buffet. We'd walk along the buffet accompanied by a serving person who'd take notes as we choose from among irresistible selections. Then we'd find a table, and in a few minutes our order would be handsomely presented.

"After all that, my friend says we could go to The *Schönbrun* Palace and hear hours and hours of Strauss music played and danced by the best Strauss dancers and musicians in the world.[5] You do like Strauss, don't you?"

"Of course, I like Strauss very much!" Miss Pyn seemed obviously impressed, but suddenly distracted. "However, that is not Strauss drifting our way from the other side of the garden. It is beautiful music, is it not? It is either a recording, or the playing of a very competent musician."

"Yes, I think it's, as you might say, 'just delightful.' I know that it isn't Strauss, but the melody is familiar. Do you know who the composer might be?"

"Oh yes, Thomas! Not many artists have been able to write such delightful melodies for a single instrument! When we hear such marvelous piano music, there are a select few composers who come to mind."

Miss Pyn continued earnestly, "The music we have been hearing is the work of the one artist who is, in truth, the poet of the piano. I believe the piece is Fredrick Chopin's *Etude in C Sharp Minor.* The form of his etudes is as challenging in music as is the form of the sonnet in poetry. Let us listen for a moment or two."

Tom was quite willing to gaze at the rapt expression on his companion's face as they listened.

---

[5] Tom is mistaken. Although the dancers from the opera ballet usually perform at *Schönbrun*, the New Year's concert is held in the Golden Hall of the *Musikverein,* the home of the Philharmonic.

"Oh!" Miss Pyn exclaimed. "On second thought, it is not the wonderful etude. I do believe it is the *Fantasy Impromptu Number Four*. You find it familiar because this work inspired a modern lyricist to write..."

"I think I know," Tom interrupted. "Something about rainbows?"

"Yes, it is the popular song, 'I'm Always Chasing Rainbows'."

Except for the music that was softly played and the scented breeze that moved gently through the garden, the afternoon was held in perfect stillness as though all the world was deep in thought. Not a bird chirped, not a squirrel scampered. Presently, Tom spoke. "I think you're hoping that Chopin and poetry would distract us from Strauss and Vienna."

"Oh, Thomas! There is not the least possibility that you and I could travel to Vienna next December. There is not enough time to arrange for tickets this year, and next year is much too distant."

"You're probably right again," said Tom with a sigh. "Come to think of it, I'll probably be able to leave Rome before then. My work should be finished, and I look forward to returning home. But we could always come back! We could fly into Da Vinci Airport. I'd show you around the Holy City and the ancient city of Rome, and we'd be sure to toss coins in the fountain to ensure your return. Then off to Vienna we'd go. Ok?"

Miss Pyn responded with an indulgent smile. "Thomas, you are absolutely amazing! A moment ago you wanted us to travel to Vienna. When I said that was not possible, you added Rome. I should think that we could not travel to either place this year or next. Certainly, we would do well not to count on it."

For some moments Tom's disappointment was painfully apparent in his silence. Frowning, he said, "Can't we hope?"

"Hope is one thing; presumption is quite another."

"Oh."

"I know, Thomas, that you are disappointed. Please do not be. Think of the joys and wonders of the moment, the delight in this very garden."

"I know, Pyn. I know. But I had other expectations. I have some others even for this afternoon." Tom gathered their belongings and paid the bill. "There are two more villages I'd like to show you. We'd best be off. It's nearly afternoon closing time anyway. First we'll drive to Bourton-on-the-Water. After that, we'll see."

The drive to Bourton-on-the-Water took little time along a country road. As they alighted from the car, Miss Pyn looked around eagerly. "My word, Thomas, this is surely a charming place! It is a lovely little village! Look at the stream running right through the center of the main square. No wonder it is named 'on-the-water.' Those little bridges are picturesque."

Tom was pleased. "I thought you'd like this place. See that building on the other side of the stream? Does it look at all familiar?"

"Gracious, with the addition of a verandah and a few French windows opening onto it, that could be the Seven Oaks Library!"

"I thought so too. I was quite surprised to see it, the first time I visited here. Of course, it would need several acres of garden around it."

Miss Pyn agreed. "It is startling, I grant you." She stared thoughtfully at the building. "Old Ben Thrust grew up in this part of England, and when he built his home in America he wanted to imitate the places he knew as a young man. He even imported stonemasons from here along with the honey-hued stone to construct the building that became the library."

"I have to admit, Pyn, there is no other place back home quite like your library. Now let's have a look at these quaint shops to see what treasures we can discover. After a while, we could find a tea shop -- or is it 'tea room'? I'll be ready for some tea before long."

"Thomas, you are incorrigible! We have hardly finished a perfectly wonderful luncheon, and you are already planning the next meal."

They strolled along the walkway -- two apparently unhurried and carefree tourists seeking solace amid new adventure in otherwise mundane lives. The shops offered treasures for all who sought unique and exciting but costly goods.

They crossed a footbridge over the stream that etched its path through the center of the square. On the other side, Tom noticed a costumed group of men.

"Look, Pyn, across the stream there are people with sticks or batons assembled for some purpose. Have you any idea what they might be up to?"

"I suspect, Thomas, they are Morris dancers lining up to begin a dance."

Tom hurried Miss Pyn over another little bridge to become part of an eager audience. The dancers moved symmetrically in well-rehearsed patterns that were likely part of a very old folk tradition.

"Pyn, I've never seen such dancing! It's not exactly the most vigorous, but it's carefully disciplined. It's neither classical nor modern ballet. Yet it reminds me of both."

"Yes, it is reminiscent of both traditions -- I suspect precisely because it is a folk dance with the same basic human movements. Is it not marvelous? The dancers are delightful!"

"They certainly are, but they'd better be very precise in their movements with those batons flying around! Somebody could get hurt!"

They watched for some minutes as the costumed figures performed several dances that were separated by brief moments of spirited applause from the appreciative tourist audience. The show was all the more delightful because it had been wholly unexpected, and gratuitous to boot. The impromptu audience dispersed, and Tom and Miss Pyn continued to stroll along the stream-severed center of the village.

"You know, Pyn, all that vigorous dancing does wonders for the appetite. Do you think we could begin to look for some refreshment? I think I see a tea place on the other side of the water. If we're lucky, it may have a back yard where we could sit. Oops, I should say 'back garden.' Anyway, we could go there and take our tea in the garden. It's a bit cool, but the sunshine is warm."

At first Miss Pyn hesitated. "It is rather early for tea, even for visiting tourists. We would most likely be alone. However, we can see if there is a garden. It would be rather pleasant in the sunlight."

The tea room was open for patrons, and it was most charming, with white lace and linen, silver and crystal amid much periwinkle blue all wrapped in curtain-softened yet brilliant sunlight. There was a garden too -- a spring-fresh dream crowded with lilac and early-blooming clematis and roses everywhere. It was warm in the sunlight, and as Miss Pyn had predicted, they were quite alone.

"Pyn, what is 'high tea'? Do you recommend it? What about 'cream tea'? That sounds intriguing."

"Oh, 'high tea' can be a formidable meal," cautioned Miss Pyn. "It is sometimes served in place of supper later in the day. Surely we do not need that! And 'cream tea' is not for the diet-conscious. As the name implies, cream tea confections are tempting and delicious, calorie-laden jam-coated scones covered with high-piled rich cream -- so rich that the best cream comes only from Devonshire. I should be content with tiny cucumber sandwiches, or if you must have a sweet, a 'Bath Bun' or a 'Sally Lunn' would do nicely."

Tom looked puzzled. "And what, dear friend, or who is 'Sally Lunn'?"

"The tradition is that Sally Lunn was a baker in Bath at the beginning of the eighteenth century who introduced her own version of the Bath Bun. Neither is very healthful; the Sally Lunn is less sweet because it contains none of the candied fruit usually found in the Bath Bun. This shop might not serve either."

"Would you care to take tea this afternoon?" So said the pert little waitress, quite obviously a country girl from the neighborhood. "We offer several kinds of afternoon teas. Our cream tea is very special."

"I suspect that it is very good," agreed Miss Pyn. "The surroundings, both here in the garden and inside, suggest that your teas could be nothing less than superb. Unfortunately, my friend and I need to be mindful of our diets. Might you have Darjeeling tea and a Bath Bun as well as a Sally Lunn?"

"Ordinarily we do offer both, madam, but unfortunately the Sally Lunns will not be ready for about forty-five minutes."

"We shall be pleased with the Bath Bun."

"May I suggest a bit of our special brandy-flavored marmalade and our country-whipped butter as accompaniment?"

To Tom's surprise, Miss Pyn acquiesced. "That will do very nicely."

"And just how diet-conscious is country-whipped butter?" he teased.

"Given the alternatives," insisted Miss Pyn, "butter is almost abstemious."

The serving girl soon returned to the garden with a light step, bringing a glistening tea tray crowded with tea service. Amid the delicate cups and saucers, two

317

magnificent Bath Buns and pots of brandied marmalade and country butter stood ready to be enjoyed.

"Is this tea Twinings, my dear?" inquired Miss Pyn.

"Oh yes, madam. We serve only the very best tea here because our guests are so discerning. I trust you and your gentleman will find it delightful. Here is a little bell. If you desire anything more, I shall be pleased to assist you." She left the garden with another equally light step.

Miss Pyn looked pleased and satisfied as she observed: "What a wonderful server and service!"

"And she is very pretty as well, I agree! That brandy-laced marmalade is interesting too."

They both enjoyed the tea, just as the serving girl had hoped. Miss Pyn found the Bath Bun with butter most delightful, while Tom thought the addition of marmalade a distinct improvement.

Tom attempted his invitation once more: "Pyn, would you reconsider our plan to visit Vienna next year? I'd be very happy if you would. We could start arranging things, and my friend could get the tickets."

"Thomas, you amaze me! When did your idea to visit Vienna or Rome become 'our plan'? Please believe me, I cannot make any such commitment at this time."

"Then I cannot hope. It's hopeless!"

"Oh, Thomas! Always remember what Hemingway's priest said, 'Sometimes I cannot hope, but it is never hopeless!' "[6]

"I'll try. I'll really try! But Pyn, there is one more place I had really hoped to show you. But I must return the car to the Abbey and join my friends at my last dinner before I leave tomorrow."

"Of course you must dine with them. I shall be able to see you off and say goodbye tomorrow."

Tom was pleased. "Would you come with me to Gatwick?"

"Yes. I believe I could do so, but only to Gatwick."

"Although I might still hope you would come along to Vienna, I promise it will be only to Gatwick tomorrow. But I've not told you where else I wanted to take you on this trip. Just now I have to turn the car toward Ealing and not toward Stow."

"Toward Stow?"

"Yes, toward Stow On The Wold. Do you remember -- Mister Harding mentioned it in his story about the stone carver. It's a very old village with an interesting history."

"Yes, I remember. The name means 'an elevated place.'"

---

[6] Ernest Hemingway, *A Farewell to Arms.*

"It is indeed elevated, and it has an interesting square with a pub or tavern with some history, and some lovely shops as well."

"An historical tavern?"

"Well, yes. The barman told me that King Charles actually fought on the stairway next to the bar, and was apprehended nearby. I didn't want to show you the historical tavern, however interesting it might be. I wanted to show you a lovely shop just off the square."

"A shop?"

"Yes. Since you won't come with me to Vienna, I thought we might find a keepsake there. Perhaps I could purchase a trinket or a broach or maybe a friendship ring that would remind you of me."

"Oh, Thomas! That is so thoughtful! Please do not take offense -- I must refuse your kind offer. Perhaps you have noticed that I wear no jewelry. Besides, I need nothing to remind me of my indebtedness to you. Have you forgotten that you helped me regain my spiritual life? I shall be eternally grateful to you."

"Well, I had hoped!"

As the beautiful afternoon began to wane, they drove on toward Ealing, listening to classical music on the car radio. The music filled the automobile and drifted out into the countryside, rich and vibrant. As the car sped along, Tom observed, "My word, Pyn, that music is certainly something special. Do you recognize it?"

"I do, and you must remember it too. It is Mendelssohn's *E-minor Violin Concerto* -- a singular work requiring expert performance."

"I think I shall not forget either the music or this afternoon. I do wish, though, that with your love and knowledge of classical music you'd reconsider my proposal to have you visit Vienna."

"I must not. I am unable to go anywhere on the Continent today or any day in the foreseeable future. I shall be happy to accompany you to the Gatwick Airport tomorrow, if you promise not to repeat your invitation to me to travel with you."

"Since I treasure your company, I promise I shall unwillingly behave. Here we are already at the Stabler home. Until tomorrow then, I wish you good evening!"

The next morning Tom was outside the Stabler home in a cab. "Hello, Pyn, and good morning!"

"Good morning, Thomas! My, you are punctual and in a cab as well! Are we to travel in style on your last day in London?"

"We will be riding in this cab only as far as Ealing Broadway for two reasons. One, my friends at the Abbey said one of their brothers would drive us to Victoria or maybe even to Gatwick. To tactfully refuse their generous offer, I said I had made other arrangements to get there. Hence this cab. Two, we have a plane to catch. Oh! I should have said, 'I have a plane to catch.' The Under-ground and the express train from Victoria should get us to Gatwick in plenty of time. I hope that you still are willing to accompany me to Gatwick?"

"Yes, since you corrected your statement of just who is catching a plane," Miss Pyn teased.

"Well, thank Goodness for that! We'll be at Ealing Broadway in only a few minutes! On second thought, we had best go directly to Victoria. Driver, would you mind taking us to Victoria Station?"

"I'll be most pleased to do that, sir. This morning things are quite slow. I'll be happy if I can find another fare there."

"Very well, take us there please."

"But Thomas, are you sure that the journey to Victoria will not be too costly?"

"I think not. Remember, we'll save the Tube fare; we'll take a train, and I have a plane to catch."

They rode on in silence through roads unfamiliar to them, arriving at Victoria in good time. Tom paid the cabman with a generous gratuity, and they entered the station.

"I shall purchase our tickets, Pyn -- a one-way for me and a round-trip for you. I must remember to ask for a return for you."

In no time at all and in what seemed to Miss Pyn a whirlwind, they were settled in the express train to Gatwick. As the train sped along, Tom asked, "How are you enjoying your visit to England, Pyn?"

"I find the people I have met here uncommonly friendly, and the places I have been able to visit very interesting. I am so very pleased that we were able to visit the Cotswolds yesterday; and there are other places I should very much like to visit as well. Glastonbury -- and of course Stratford and probably Bath -- would be on my list. My time here is so fleeting that I am already afraid that those visits will have to await another trip to England. Today I am even thinking that my visit to Worthing may have to be postponed."

"That's too bad, but you may be back another year. I think I know why you want to visit Stratford and Bath and possibly Somerset, but why Worthing? It's not a very well-known place. On the Channel, is it?"

"It is, though Brighton and Hastings are better known. However, you do remember that the main character in Oscar Wilde's play was found in the luggage room in Victoria with a ticket to Worthing in his hand. So Worthing is intriguing. As for Somerset,

Stonehenge is very near there, and Glastonbury is a bit further west."

"Oh yes, the ruins of Glastonbury Abbey. Do the Abbey ruins have anything to do with the King Arthur story?"

"Many people believe that the graves of King Arthur and his queen are located there. However, I have a question for you, Thomas. I have been to Westminster Abbey, and I found it to be an extraordinarily beautiful religious institution. Ealing Abbey is also a fine religious institution. Then there other abbeys in ruins, and other places -- country homes perhaps -- that are also called abbeys. Do you know how these places developed?"

"I certainly don't know all the particulars, but I have some knowledge of ecclesiastical history. Ealing is the easiest to explain. It's a modern abbey built during the last century. It did suffer some war damage during World War II, but it was not ruined. On the other hand, the ruin of some medieval abbeys came about after The Reformation, when King Henry VIII decreed that English abbeys would be abolished. Westminster was probably saved because it was already a parish church."

"Yes, and when I visited there, I noticed some royal tombs."

"Those are perhaps even more important to Westminster's survival," Tom observed. "The abbey contained the tombs of earlier monarchs such as Edward I, Henry III, and Henry VII -- and the Coronation Chair where English monarchs receive the crown. You already know, Pyn, that Glastonbury is a ruin. There are other ruins as well. For example, only the bell tower remains of an abbey at Evesham, not far from where we were yesterday. I don't really know about the country homes, but I suspect that such places were built on the grounds or the ruins of an abbey, and the name continued."

"That is a plausible explanation. But look, Thomas! We seem to be approaching Gatwick airport."

In only a few minutes they joined other passengers scurrying through the airport, and Tom declared, "We'll secure my boarding pass and then verify the location of the departure gate for Vienna."

They were soon settled at the correct gate and there were some minutes before Tom's departure.

"Well, Pyn, it won't be long now and I shall be off to work again; and you will be able to continue your holiday in London. You will continue your pilgrimage in this part of the world, won't you?"

"If you mean my sojourn here, I know I shall. If you mean my pilgrimage in this world, I have a few concerns. There is one thought in particular that gives me pause."

"What might that be?"

"Quite simply, it has to do with blessings. I have had many. Some are less obvious. They may be likened to the graces that Sir Alec Guinness labeled 'in disguise.'[7] However, I often wonder if my response to more obvious blessings is adequate. Is my gratitude sufficient?"

"Your very question suggests to me that you're indeed responding most adequately to the graces you have enjoyed. I'd advise you to avoid becoming overly scrupulous. Just embrace each opportunity, as it is presented, thankfully and joyfully; and act as you have been acting since your personal reconciliation."

"Thomas, I thank you again for your reassurance! I shall continue to pray for all my benefactors -- of which there are many; some not even known to me. Most of all, I shall pray for all of those who pray for me. Now, I believe that it is time for you to board the aircraft. So farewell, dear friend, and God speed!"

"Yes, Pyn, this is goodbye. One day I'll see you in Seven Oaks."

Tom walked to the jetway. At the entrance, he paused and turned -- hand above his head, he waved and stepped out of view.

---

[7] Sir Alec Guinness' Autobiography is entitled *Blessings In Disguise*.

At that moment, the words of another Thomas came into Miss Pyn's mind. They were words Saint Thomas More wrote in a letter to his daughter Margaret toward the end of his life: "Pray for me as I will pray for thee that we may merrily meet in heaven."

Without further thought, Miss Pyn hurried to catch the express train back to London. On the way, she thought her time in London had been so fleeting that she probably would have to plan a visit to Worthing some other time. At Ealing, she stopped only briefly at the Abbey to express her gratitude for a wonderful day, and a hope that Thomas' journey would be safe and successful.

At the Stabler home, Helen greeted Miss Pyn at the door, inquiring how her day and her visit had been. She assured Helen that all was going very well. Her outing to the Cotswolds was excellent, and her trip today to Gatwick was most enjoyable -- even though she had to say farewell to her friend, Father Thomas, who was off to Vienna. On her way back to London, she had decided that perhaps she had better trim her expectations and put off going to Worthing until some other time.

When Helen heard this, she was a bit disconcerted. "But just today Emily has so graciously called and said she had some free time before her holiday, which is due to begin the day after tomorrow. She would be very pleased to drive you to Victoria Station on the morrow so you can take the train to Worthing."

Miss Pyn was delighted. "I had better make the journey to Worthing, since Emily so graciously offered to help me get as far as Victoria. Worthing should be interesting."

"Emily said she'd be here at eight tomorrow. So have a pleasant evening."

"Here in your lovely premises, and with my exciting expectation for tomorrow, I certainly shall enjoy this evening. Thank you again for having me here."

Eight the next morning couldn't come soon enough.

Ever since she had been introduced to Jack Worthing, who had his name from a town called Worthing somewhere in England, Miss Pyn was convinced she must visit Worthing one day. She was not only interested in England, she was intrigued by the ancient practice of including the name of a town or district in the name of a person. When she discovered that Worthing was a town on the English Channel, she had resolved that one day she would visit there.

By the time she arrived in England, she had learned about other places along the Channel. She knew that Hastings, the town near the site of the famous battle at the time of The Norman Conquest, was far more important historically than was Worthing. She also learned that Brighton, with the famous pier and palace, was much more popular with tourists. Tourists both domestic and foreign flocked to its beaches in bathing costumes that were brief, exceedingly brief, or non-existent ... whether appropriate or not.

When she realized that her time in the U.K. was beginning to near its end, she had announced to her friend Emily that she would like to travel to Worthing. Emily had replied that though she would be going on a visit to Scotland, she thought Miss Pyn's plan was brilliant, and had insisted that she would drive Miss Pyn to Victoria Station.

The next morning, Emily drove her through the crush of early morning rush-hour traffic all the way to the front entrance of Victoria Station. "In this madness, I can't get any closer to the platform you will need. Remember, you must find either platform seventeen or eighteen. The Worthing train will leave from one or the other. Just go along to the back of the Station. There you will see the Gatwick Express at platforms fourteen or fifteen or so. Just beyond, you will find the train to Worthing. Goodbye! Take care; *Auf Wiedersehen*."

"Until we meet again," responded Miss Pyn. "And meet we shall, though it may be rather a very long time from now. Thank you, Emily, thank you very much for making these last days of my visit a time I shall not forget, soon or ever. I am sorry I shall miss you when you return to London. Do enjoy your holiday on Skye. I should very much like to travel there one day. Perhaps one day ... And Emily, thank you for making today's journey to Victoria so pleasant. I fear you will be late getting to the library."

"Please don't worry. I like driving, and besides, I have sufficient time. Furthermore, today is a short day at the library, so I can begin my holiday a day early and leave for Scotland this afternoon. I know I shall enjoy Skye, but I shall miss you when I return. For now, goodbye."

"Farewell, Em ... I may call you 'Em,' may I not?"

"Yes, you may, providing I am afforded the privilege of a familiar name for you as well. Let me see. How about 'P'? That's better. Yes, may I call you 'P'?"

Miss Pyn, remembering her friend Carol, thought for a long moment, fighting back a tear that Emily did not notice. "Yes," she nearly whispered, and then looked up with a grateful smile. "Thank you above all for your gracious invitation to return to London one day.

You must, of course, visit me in Seven Oaks so that we can plan my return together. Farewell!"

Miss Pyn waited as her new friend's smart blue car fought off busses and coaches and ever-lurking giant black cabs; it zipped around the corner and was gone. She thought she glimpsed Emily's wave, but feared that her own wave had been too late.

Then, a latter-day colonial undaunted and unafraid, she marched into Victoria. She had yet to encounter the nine-o-five London commuter, a species or perhaps even a genus all its own.

Victoria was surprisingly uncrowded, almost quiet. Miss Pyn missed several waves of the initial assault force that had descended into the maw of the Underground just before she entered beneath the grand vault of the station. The great clock announced 8:57. The enormous schedule board -- ever changing, and stuffed with places and times, and times and places -- offered nothing of Worthing anywhere, not even at platform seventeen or eighteen; or was it sixteen or seventeen, or eighteen or nineteen? To the untrained eye, the board was a hopeless maze, a befuddling warren of strange inviting but as yet inaccessible rail stops with quaint or startling place-names.

A search of the big board proved utterly futile. Better, Miss Pyn thought, to find the proper platform.

What did Em say? "The Worthing trains always leave from those platforms at the back of the station." During the short time she had known Emily, Miss Pyn learned that Emily was always right, always. Never mind that Em was the principal authority -- in fact, the only source for that conclusion, she liked her very much and strongly suspected that her friend was probably correct in her wonderful self-conviction as well.

She trudged on toward the rear of the station. Much of the terminal seemed to be quite new -- too new, in fact, for the grand old station Miss Pyn had expected to find. The romance she had learned to expect from her beloved books was all gone. She had not expected gaslights, and hansom cabs driving elegant and rich first-class passengers up to the elegant and richly appointed first-class rail carriages attached to formidable shiny-black steam engines earnestly puffing at the ready. Nor did she expect to find troops of men marching in formation along platforms -- soldiers or sailors most certainly, embarking on a celebrated expedition to somewhere, bringing civilization and British Common Law to a turbulent outpost at the edge of the world; or perhaps even putting an end to both Common Law and civilization for themselves and others in a very great or even a very little war – which, although always proclaimed "just" was never truly justified or justifiable. No, these were not her expectations.

But to find television monitors and stainless steel and chromium fittings in Victoria! -- chromium and steel highlighting contemporary tiles that could have been fashioned ... anywhere … anywhere at all. Oh well, she reflected, one could say all this modernization of Victoria was impressive ... quite, but not very.

The monitor could be useful, however. Perhaps it will indicate the platform for Worthing. The lettering looks rather large. At least that is something -- just one step closer and I shall be able to read it. Now then, it says, "Welcome to Victoria!" I would feel infinitely more welcome in Victoria if it would only tell where that _ _ _ _ _ _ illusive train to Worthing could be found.

Undaunted, Miss Pyn carried on, determination growing with each step. She could see platforms 15, 16, 17, 18, and 19 beyond the booths wherein ticket collectors awaited the eager commuters. She would ask one of the train people in one of the booths.

As she approached a booth she realized that she was too late. The 9:03 from Brighton had just zoomed in on platform 17. Before the train stopped, the advance guard had leapt off, hitting the platform on the run, hurrying toward the very ticket collector Miss Pyn was about to question. In moments, the entire troop of commuters swirled around everywhere, waving their marching orders in the faces of the ticket collectors or stuffing their passes into the limp hands of the bored ticket takers.

Miss Pyn hid behind a booth, peeking out around the corner awaiting her turn to pounce on the person in the booth. The fresh troops all charged on toward the entrance of the Underground; not one noticed her lurking there; not one thought her presence extraordinary.

At last, an opportunity! "Could you tell me where I might find the train to Worthing? It is neither on the notice board nor on the monitor. What I mean is that the platform designation for the train to Worthing is not to be found on either of those places. Could you help me?"

The large West-Indian woman in the booth looked very puzzled. She nearly said, "Tickets, please." That was surely what she always said at that hour of the morning -- little else. That was probably nearly all she had to say and all she wanted to say. But she checked herself, managed a half smile and asked, "To where?"

"Sorry, the noise is loud."

"Where do you wish to go?"

"To Worthing ... Worthing, that is."

Reaching for a battered, dog-eared book, the woman grunted, "One moment. Let's see: W-O-R-T-H-I-N-G -- is that it?"

"Yes! that is it. Just as in Oscar Wilde's play. You remember Ernest Worthing? He was found right here in the lost luggage room in Victoria Station. With a ticket to Worthing clutched in his little hand." More puzzlement. Miss Pyn's explanation fell on unresponsive ears. "That is it, however."

"That train doesn't leave until 9:21."

"I know."

"It will be on platform 18."

"Thank you very much." Miss Pyn turned toward platform 18, and the ticket-taker just shook her head muttering, "Tickets, please."

Miss Pyn pushed on toward the platform; the train on 17 was readied for later departure. Nothing was on 18. She thought she'd look at the empty platform anyway. She peered down the track. A train zipped along in the distance, rapidly approaching. She did not know that this train was the 9:05 -- forty-five seconds late. Doors began to open even before the long train reached the far end of the platform. The train was jammed -- several hundred, surely. The army of commuters poised in readiness -- every muscle, every nerve taut awaiting the signal to advance. The charge would be sounded momentarily -- the muted screech of the braking train. Even before the signal, point men and women armed with brollies and attaché cases -- some with lunch kits, some brandishing copies of *The Telegraph* or *The Times* -- leapt to the platform, eager to begin the day's contest.

Miss Pyn managed to scurry behind a pillar just in time to avoid the onslaught of the first wave of regulars who came on the heels of the first party. In no time at all, the entire platform was a sea of dedicated mercenaries, the would-be heroes and heroines of Threadneedle Street moving with swirls and eddies as a single body with singular intent toward the ticket takers and the passage to the Underground beyond.

They swished by her without pause toward the arteries of commerce, these corpuscles of the corporate world bringing energy and vitality to the business of the day. They were remarkably alike -- individual cells, to be sure, but together uniting into a swift stream providing sustenance to the financial life of the great city. Miss Pyn imagined how often the might of the 9:05 was repeated at Liverpool Street, Kings Cross, Waterloo, Euston, St. Pancras, and Paddington -- a grand stream inundating the city.

And she saw ever so clearly how remarkably alike they all were except for an occasional muted alien antibody -- an academic perhaps, swept along, but in another world, frantically searching for his ticket so that he might discover where he was going and maybe why he was going there; or a graphic artist, with portfolio, rushing off to catch finally and at last the most perfect light to paint still another time the perfect reflection of The Tower of London in The Thames at low tide; or a young actor heading for his job as haberdasher or bank clerk so that he could earn, one day, the right to delight the rest of humanity night after night by becoming somebody else in the self-contained real and fleeting world contrived and created on a very little stage in the West End; or a musician, instrument in hand, weary from last night's concert, pushing along -- who knows where -- perhaps to a school, a very proper city center school, to offer "musical instruction" to reluctant resisting first-formers so that he would be able to redeem his concert costume from the clothes-cleaning service for this night's concert.

They all rush on -- especially those who are most like one another. But why? Why do they rush on? Is it because they hope to get a better seat on the evening train?

The platform was now empty except for a few train people. Miss Pyn noticed a young man in a fluorescent orange vest. I wonder if that vest should be

337

called a 'waistcoat,' since a vest here is an undershirt. I suppose I had best not ask. However, she did say, "Young man, can you tell me where I should be able to find the train to Worthing?"

"No, luv," he said in a lyrical voice far too mellow and engaging for his years. "Sorry I am indeed, mum, but you see, now, I'm not one of the train folks. You'll be needin' a lad or lass in a blue uniform -- kind of official-like, you know. With some stripes, mum, if he or she has the benefit of experience and is likely to be knowin' anythin' atall. Just go along there lookin' for a guard."

Miss Pyn frowned. The young man broke into a smile as bright as the russet gold on the top of his head and the sparkle in his eye. "Of course, luv, surely I shouldn't be so daft. You are an American, now ain't you? You'll be recognizin' that the trainman you need to find is what you call a conductor and over here on this side we call a guard. I never could see, to tell what I believe is the unadorned truth, so help me, that those folks ever did anythin' that could rightly be called conducting or guarding anythin' -- anythin' atall, don't you see. But that's the way of it. Just look for the blue uniform. Good luck 'n God bless, mum."

"Thank you, young man. Thank you very much! And God speed." She was not entirely sure that was the appropriate response.

Miss Pyn looked in the direction of the Gatwick Express. No one could miss those bright sleek trains, the colors exuding the quintessence of swiftness and speed. There she saw a young man in blue -- no stripes, but he was young after all. His uniform was perhaps a trifle bright, but he was young and it was blue.

Miss Pyn clutched her things and began to pursue the young man. She did not want to appear too earnest in her pursuit. After she took only a few hurried steps, the young man opened the door of the American Airlines office near the end of the Gatwick platform. Oh my, she thought, that surely cannot be the correct uniform. I shall look for a different shade of blue.

Once again she gazed along the deserted platform. A little man walked along the platform slamming shut the doors on the now deserted 9:05. As he slammed doors closer and closer to where she now waited, Miss Pyn realized that he not only wore blue, the blue was highlighted by a gold stripe -- well, perhaps a yellow stripe. On second thought, the stripe could be silver. The closer the man came, the more the stripe appeared to be gray. Perhaps he would know where to find the train to Worthing?

"I say, sir" -- Maybe 'sir' is not the proper form of address for even a senior trainman, but the yellow-gold or silver-gray trim practically commanded it -- "could you tell me where I might find the train to Worthing?"

"But of course, madam." His accent was decidedly Italian, his manner that of a proper gentleman of the old school, of the prewar school. "You will find, madam, that the train to Worthing will depart punctually from platform 12 at the front of the station. Never fear, madam, you have plenty of time. You can easily make it there with much time to spare. Goodbye, and safe journey! Or as my countrymen say, *Arrivederci, signorina!*"

"*Grazie,*" sputtered Miss Pyn as she thought, what a perfect gentleman!

The gentleman was very pleased and replied, *"Prego."*

Miss Pyn was also very pleased -- very pleased especially since she had to rush off to platform 12, and would not need to continue a conversation in a language that had already exhausted her entire working vocabulary.

She moved in the direction of the front of the station as the gentleman trainman continued to slam doors. She approached the ticket-takers booths, once again passing under a clock that indicated that the time was 9:14. If the train to Worthing was due to leave at 9:21, she wondered, why do I have "plenty of time" to

340

get to platform 12 all the way in the front part of the station? She looked around for the gentleman slammer; he was nowhere to be seen. "I had better make another enquiry," she said aloud and then looked all about her once again to see if anyone heard her, especially the "Italian gentleman."

She found a booth. This time the booth was occupied by a young West-Indian woman. "Can you -- that is, would you be so kind as to tell me where I might find the train to Worthing which is due to depart shortly? I really should not miss it. Although I do not expect to be met in Worthing, the 9:21 is the only one I will be able to take today."

The young woman broke into a bright ingratiating smile as she pointed to -- of all things -- the Airlines office. How can this be? thought Miss Pyn. Surely the airlines cannot be expected to know the British Rail schedule. Oh my, she reflected, it must be my accent. She repeated her question once again, this time very slowly and very precisely.

Again the wonderful smile and the reach for the inevitable dog-eared book of schedules. "Would this be the place you are desirous of finding? Here, look in this book. Is that it?"

"Yes, that is the place! Where can I find the train that will take me there? I was told to look for platform 12."

"No, no -- perhaps you were misunderstood. There is no Worthing train from platform 12. Certainly not during the next hour or longer. The train will leave from platform 18, just there, in a very few minutes."

"Thank you very much!"

"You are most welcome."

Miss Pyn again hurried to platform 18, thinking this surely must be the correct platform despite the gracious assistance of the gentleman train guard. After all, both women had consulted the printed schedules and found the same information.

The train was undergoing preparation for departure. Near the end of the train, a trainman was on the tracks inspecting the couplings.

"Is this the train to Worthing?"

"That it is, mum. Any one of the last four cars will get you to Worthing, and it will leave before you can recite *Dick Worthington's Cat*." And he patted the first of the last four cars. "Take a tip from an old fellow. This car," he continued patting, "is a first-class car. At the other end, just before the loo, there is a compartment nearly as good as first-class, only it isn't. Most passengers don't know about that. You can ride there in comfort very likely undisturbed -- with fresh air to boot. Cheers, luv!"

"Thank you very much. May I enter the train?"

"You may indeed, mum."

Miss Pyn climbed aboard the train and settled in the compartment recommended by the "old fellow." My, this is comfortable and in plenty of time too -- four whole minutes before departure. There is enough room for my things on the seat. If others come, there is room overhead. She relaxed, took out her journal and began reflecting on the events of the morning.

After a few moments, she paused. I wonder why there are so few commuters here this morning. Perhaps Worthing is not a very popular destination. But this train stops elsewhere. Only four cars are going to Worthing. There are only two minutes before the train is due to leave, and no one seems to be boarding. Even though the rush hour has passed, surely there must be someone in the whole city of London who wishes to travel south toward Worthing.

She looked out the window toward platform 17. There she saw a guard with a whistle in his hand closing doors of the train on 17. He had stripes on his uniform -- many stripes. Miss Pyn gathered her things quickly, stepped out of the train and crossed the platform as fast as she could.

Just then, the guard's strident whistle re-echoed over the length and breadth of the platform as the train began to move.

"Is that the train to Worthing?"

"That it is, mum. There will be another train later on today. You may check the schedule at a ticket booth."

"Oh well, I shall try going to Worthing another time." As she walked toward the train that would take her back to London, she thought that at least Emily had been right as usual. She did say platform 17 or 18.

On the train to London, she wondered if there was any place she might visit before returning to Ealing. Then she remembered that Westminster Cathedral was not far from Victoria Station: That is a church I surely ought to visit. Soon the train arrived at Victoria and Miss Pyn hurried from the station. In a short time, she found Victoria Street and the entrance to the Cathedral.

Just inside the door, she saw a woman about to leave. She greeted her: "Good afternoon! I am a visitor from America. Are you a member of the parish here?"

The woman welcomed Miss Pyn with a warm smile. "I'm not a member, but I visit the Cathedral often, whenever I have free time at the office. Is there some way I can help you?"

344

"That is very kind. Since I know so little, there is not much I can ask. The Cathedral is quite large and beautiful, but the natural light seems quite dim."

"That's quite true, probably because much of the beautiful marble, which was imported from several places, is dark. On foggy days, which tend to be rare these days, the dark marble and the meager outside light make the interior rather dark. But today you should be able to see a great deal."

"I look forward to that. I have been to Westminster Abbey twice, and I have found it very enlightening, especially historically. Since I am a librarian, I found The Poets' Corner particularly intriguing. I suspect that the Abbey attracts more tourists and only some pilgrims; while the Cathedral attracts pilgrims, and only some casual tourists."

The woman agreed with a sigh: "Yes, most tourists don't realize what is to be found here. The Abbey is very old, while the Cathedral is a modern church. Yet there are some very old relics here. Your mention of pilgrims reminds me of the pilgrims who were on their way to Canterbury to visit the shrine of St. Thomas Becket. Even though Westminster Cathedral is not yet one hundred years old, it houses a bishop's miter that was worn by St. Thomas."

"I happen to know an American priest who has friends at Ealing Abbey, which is quite close to where I am staying in London. He says that his friends informed him that when the Abbey at Ealing was being established -- about the same time as this Cathedral was under construction -- there were those who thought monks from the Abbey could take the Tube to London on Sunday and sing in the Cathedral. Do you know if that developed?"

"I don't think so -- mostly because there is a renowned Cathedral choir that sings in the space behind the main altar, and I don't believe there are monks in the choir."

"Oh, well," Miss Pyn suggested, "perhaps somebody in Ealing may know more about that. Are there other things about the Cathedral that you think I might like to know?"

"You may find some of the chapels interesting. There is one dedicated to St. Andrew honoring Scotland, and one honoring St. Patrick and the Irish saints."

"That is interesting! I wonder why Ireland has a place next to Scotland as if it were part of the United Kingdom."

"There is apparently no objection to that," the woman assured her. "Just remember that the Cathedral was built before The Irish Free State separated from the rest of the Kingdom."

Suddenly, with a look of dismay, she announced, "I'm so sorry, I must leave now! I need to get back to the office. Do enjoy your stay in London and your visit in this church. Farewell!"

"Farewell, and thank you!" Then Miss Pyn thought what a gracious lady she had met: And I did not learn her name nor did I give her mine. Well, now I must see The Stations of The Cross.

Miss Pyn knew about the Stations from material she had read in the Seven Oaks library. She had learned that they were the work of the sculptor, Eric Gill, who began the project shortly after his conversion to Catholicism. The work took five years to complete and was greeted, as innovative works of art often are, with mixed reviews. Before long, the Stations became quite well-known and admired.

Miss Pyn was quite surprised. She found the Stations larger than she had expected: The sculptured figures are incredibly real, and the emotions they convey are deeply moving -- especially station number four that depicts the time when Jesus meets his Mother. They certainly are, as Gill had hoped, conducive to prayer.

She felt a certain kinship with the creator of these stations; for while her personal reconciliation was not exactly a conversion, it was rather like one. So she prayed for the artist and for Thomas' mission in Vienna. As always, she prayed for all her benefactors, especially those who pray for her. She might have enjoyed reflecting and meditating in that beautiful church for a long time, but she realized that the afternoon was fast approaching its end. It was time to return to West Ealing. She then remembered she could ride the District line all the way to Ealing Broadway.

Helen Stabler again met Miss Pyn at the door, and asked how she had enjoyed her visit to Worthing. Miss Pyn replied that she was sorry that she had not paid more careful attention to Victoria Station when she was there with Thomas just the day before. She confessed that she arrived at the platform for the Worthing train just as it was pulling out, and since the next Worthing train was not scheduled to leave for some time, she thought she had better devote the rest of her day in town to a visit elsewhere.

"Oh, that was too bad!" Helen lamented. Then she added, "If Emily happens to ask me about your Worthing trip, I'll just say you had an unexpected change of plans. But did you enjoy the rest of your day?"

"Oh yes, very much. I realized that when I arrived back at Victoria Station, I was quite close to Westminster Cathedral. So I went there and met a woman who explained many things I did not know. After she left, I studied the Stations of the Cross by Eric Gill, which I had read about at home. Those Stations are not only beautifully sculptured, they are deeply moving."

"I've often had a similar reaction to them. I'm pleased that your day went well. Have you any other plans for your remaining time with us?"

"I realize I shall not be able to visit Oxford and Cambridge as I had hoped, but I must visit the British Museum Library before I leave London. I shall try to do so tomorrow."

"There are several Tube stations in the vicinity of the Library, but none are very close by. That may be at least one reason that there is talk of moving the Library to a place next to St. Pancras Station in a year or so. The Tottenham Court Road stop is on the Central Line. Remember, you can board that line at Ealing Broadway. That is the most direct route. You'd exit into Oxford Street, which is quite busy. You'd cross Oxford and head up a bit to Great Russell Street, and the Library is a short distance to the east, and on the north side of the road.

Miss Pyn was a bit overwhelmed by all of these directions. After she'd taken out a notebook and pen, Helen was happy not only to repeat the directions, but added more: "For your return, I'd suggest that when you walk out of the Library you turn left and continue to the end of the building. Then go left again up the street alongside the Library to Russell Square -- which is not only quite lovely, it is part of Bloomsbury. I suspect that you know about the Bloomsbury Writers."

"I do know about some of their work. Our library contains two works by Virginia Woolf: *Mrs. Dalloway* and *To the Lighthouse*. We also have two works by E.M. Forster: *Howards End* and *A Room with a View.*"

"Those are among my favorites! Have you any Bloomsbury poetry in your library?"

"Oh yes! How could I forget Rupert Brooke's work, *1914 and Other Poems* -- especially since I saw his memorial just this week in Westminster Abbey."

Mrs. Stabler was delighted: "The work of The Bloomsbury group seems well represented in the Seven Oaks Library. You must certainly enjoy your work there! But you'll need more directions when you leave the British Library. You will walk diagonally across Russell Square, which will bring you to the Russell Square Underground Station. Take the Tube south one stop, and get on the Central Line to get back to Ealing

Broadway." Miss Pyn gratefully jotted down these latest directions, and bid Helen goodnight.

The next morning when Miss Pyn arrived at Ealing Broadway she decided that, since Emily was away on holiday, there was no reason to visit the Ealing Library. Instead, she went directly to the station and boarded the train. She found a comfortable seat and checked the map of Tube stops posted above the windows to see when she should expect to arrive at Tottenham Court Road.

Just as the train was about to move, a gentleman entered. Miss Pyn remembered that she had seen him on this train before. He greeted her: "Good morning! May I sit in this seat next to you? I trust that you are enjoying your visit here in London."

Miss Pyn gestured her welcome, and was delighted to have the opportunity to recount her impressions of London. "Oh hello! I am indeed enjoying London, but I also find it a challenge."

"Where have you been, and why do you find London a challenge?"

"I have been to Westminster Abbey twice, and along the Strand, and to Westminster Cathedral just yesterday. Each day has been interesting, and often inspired wonder. While I have visited several large cities in my country, I have not found any of them nearly so complicated and interesting as London."

'Yes, London is very large and many-faceted, with a long and interesting history. I take it you've not been to The Tower, which dates from 1066; and even before that time there was much history made in London."

"The Tower is one of several places I had hoped to visit. However, I shall have to plan on visiting them another time if and when I am able to return to England."

"I should think you'll be able to return some day, and I wish you well. What other plans have you had to put off?"

"Well ... I had hoped to see the Changing of the Guard at Buckingham Palace; although I might still get there. I had hoped to travel to Oxford and Cambridge and Stratford, and just yesterday I missed going to Worthing."

Her companion looked puzzled. "I can understand your first three choices, but why Worthing?"

"Do you know Mr. Wilde's play, *The Importance of Being Earnest*?

"Yes I do, and I think that now I understand your disappointment."

"I thought that a visit to Worthing would add to my understanding of the play."

"Precisely. But where are you off to today?"

"You may remember that I am a librarian. So some of my remaining time must be devoted to The British Museum Library."

"Of course. You may remember my name is Overbrooke. If you need any assistance during your visit to London, members of my staff will be pleased to help you."

"Again, I thank you."

"Not at all. We are approaching your stop at Tottenham Court Road. So farewell, and do enjoy your stay!"

"I shall!" Miss Pyn left the Underground and came up to the busy intersection where Tottenham Court Road meets Oxford Street and New Oxford Street. After a few attempts she was able to cross over to Tottenham Court Road, and proceeded north. A short way up, she found Great Russell Street and started in the direction of The British Museum. Then she saw it -- Bloomsbury Street; and she knew she must be heading in the right direction.

Then, there it was! The grand entrance to the Museum and Library with a great portico that could have accommodated the entire Seven Oaks Library and its entire grounds, including the lake. After some time, she found her destination, the famous Great Reading Room.

The room was larger than she had imagined. Books and bookcases were carefully arranged in an enormous circle.

A member of the library staff noticed her looking about. He approached her: "May I assist you, madam?"

Miss Pyn was delighted to reveal the motive for her visit: "I am a librarian visiting from America, and I am here primarily to observe this grand library."

"You are most welcome. We are always happy to welcome other members of our profession. Have you any first impressions -- favorable, I hope."

"All of my impressions are favorable, including the enormous size of your holdings. Nearly all of our collection at Seven Oaks could fit in one, or certainly no more than two of your cases in this room."

The librarian replied proudly: "The collection in this library is over two hundred years old, and we are constantly enlarging it."

"The Seven Oaks library is only a few years old, but we continue to add to it. In a good year we may add fifty to seventy-five books to the collection. During one or two years we even added over one hundred books, but we found that rather taxing."

"Your staff found it difficult?"

"I am the staff. Just this year, before I left for England, I acquired my first assistant."

"I see. For a while at least, you'd better not aspire to be like us. We accession sixty thousand books each year. We receive all books published in England, and others from elsewhere."

"That is an incredible number! I suspect that my newfound friend from Boston, Dr. Keefe, will have her scholarly work in your collection one day."

"The work will be here in our collection soon after it is in print. Do you know the subject of the publication?"

"Dr. Keefe is preparing a modern edition of a medieval manuscript devoted to arboreal culture. One copy of that manuscript is located in this library. If I remember correctly, another copy is at Oxford and a third is in Cambridge. Her work will be part of a collection of medieval manuscripts."

"Her name will certainly be in our catalogue if she is the general editor of the collection. Even if she is not the general editor, a work such as you describe will frequently have a catalogue entry that includes all the manuscripts in the work and the editor of each."

"I am happy to hear it. Then I shall actually know somebody listed in The British Museum Library Catalogue."

"I wish your friend success. Is there some other way I may assist you?"

"Thank you very much! You have been most gracious. I shall just look around this room for a few minutes."

"It's been a pleasure. Enjoy your time here, and the rest of your time in London."

Miss Pyn looked about the Reading Room for some time, and continued to be impressed. For a moment she thought she might also enjoy visiting the Manuscript Reading Room, but she remembered that admission there required a special pass which she did not possess. Then she decided that, if it was not too early, she might find lunch in the pub opposite the Museum entrance.

The Museum Tavern was just across Great Russell Street. It was already open for lunch and quite busy. As Miss Pyn entered, she noticed that the bill of fare included a ploughman's lunch. She remembered that she and Thomas had seen the listing of "ploughperson's lunch" at the pub in Burford, and had been amused to discover that such politically acceptable terminology was used even in the Cotswolds. Since this establishment is close to the Museum, she thought, perhaps they prefer the older terminology. At any rate, I should not indulge in such generous fare.

"What may I serve you, madam?" asked the young man at the counter.

"Your steak and kidney pie and the shepherd's pie are both very appealing, but I had better choose something lighter. I should like a small serving of that good-looking salad. It is chicken, is it not?"

"Yes, it is. May I serve you something to drink with the salad?"

"Might I have a small glass of Piesporter?"

"An excellent choice, madam!"

Miss Pyn carried her lunch toward some tables near the windows at the back of the tavern, and noticed a familiar figure alone at a table. She approached with a delighted smile: "Dr. K., I presume."

Dr. Keefe looked up and exclaimed, "What a happy coincidence! I didn't expect to see you for some time, and then only if we happened to meet somewhere on the other side of the Atlantic!"

"Yes, this is certainly a great pleasure! I thought by this time you would be away from London a day or even two. May I join you?"

"Please do. My work with the medieval manuscript here in the Museum has taken longer than I anticipated. I finally finished it this morning. The work with the texts at Oxford and Cambridge should be much easier now that I not only know the text of the treatise, I'm getting accustomed to the scribe's handwriting."

"You must be very pleased indeed," Miss Pyn responded as she placed her luncheon on the table. "I just completed my visit to the British Museum Library, and I found that it is enormous! A member of the library staff told me that for many years sixty thousand books have been added to the collection, and are still added each year."

"Well, that may be the reason why there are plans to move the Library to a new building next to St. Pancras Station -- at least that's what a librarian in the manuscript collection told me."

"I am so glad that I was able to visit the original location."

"Perhaps we'd do well to attend to our luncheons," teased Dr. Keefe. "This is an excellent Shepherd's Pie, and your salad looks very good as well."

The ladies ate their lunch in appreciative silence, oblivious of the many other lunch seekers around them. Dr. Keefe was the first to finish, and she assured Miss Pyn there was no need to hurry -- even though she had finished her own meal, she still had a refreshing drink she would sip. So they continued to enjoy their impromptu meeting without speaking, each reflecting on her London experience.

Eventually Dr. Keefe said with some hesitancy, "This time I think it is certainly goodbye. Tomorrow I'm off to Oxford. Unless you are planning a trip there, we'll not meet."

"I do regret that," Miss Pyn responded. "I too had planned to visit Oxford, and Cambridge as well; but I have had to alter my plan. I have found London both a challenge and a great delight. The places to visit in this great city are innumerable. I shall not be able to see The Tower and The Crown Jewels -- nor Parliament, Piccadilly, Baker Street, or Madame Tussaud's. My time here is just evaporating, or so it seems. I could name many more places I have read about and would like to visit, but I suspect that you know about most of those places and perhaps many more."

Dr. Keefe was flattered. She admitted that she knew interesting details about the places Miss Pyn had mentioned, but not many more. She said somewhat reluctantly, "This time it must really be farewell. Do take care, and enjoy what is left of your stay here and your life over there as well. May we meet again!"

Miss Pyn clasped her hand. "*Auf Wiedersehen*, and God speed thee on your way!"

After they parted, each went in her own direction. Miss Pyn followed Helen Stabler's plan, walking along the front of The Museum Library to Montague Street and up toward Russell Square. She hesitated before continuing on toward the Tube station. Instead, she thought, she should explore more of Bloomsbury. Eventually she crossed Russell Square to Woburn Place, which she remembered led to an important other Square -- Tavistock Square. She'd read that Tavistock was an important center in early Bloomsbury printing. The Hogarth Press was located somewhere around the area. She remembered that the Hogarth Press was established in the early twentieth century by Leonard and Virginia Woolf. She also recalled that the Press was first to publish the work of T.S. Eliot and that of Katherine Mansfield, as well as other famous authors. She did not expect to find any evidence of early printing at the Square, since all that had happened many years before. Yet, she thought, it would be rewarding just to see the area. In a way, it would be like visiting something historically sacred.

She walked along Woburn to Tavistock Square. As she walked, she thought about Eliot's poetry, and a little later she recalled Mansfield's story, *The Garden Party*. She wondered: If those two writers were unknown today, would any current publisher recognize the value of their work?

Some time later, she realized that the afternoon, like several other afternoons lately, was moving on -- and so she must move on as well. She walked back to the Russell Square Tube Station. She found the right train, and began her return journey to West Ealing.

At Ealing she was once again welcomed by Helen Stabler, who asked about her visit to the British Library. Miss Pyn confessed that she had found the Library and the collection of books nearly overwhelming. She had also learned that the Library would soon be moved into a new building.

"Oh yes!" Helen was apologetic: "I should have mentioned that early on. I believe its new location will be up toward St. Pancras Station."

"So I have learned. Even though I did not go along to St. Pancras, I did see a bit more of Bloomsbury. I went up to Tavistock Square."

"Then you were near the University and Cartwright Gardens."

"I did not go on quite that far. However, now that you mention Cartwright, it is almost ironic. Before Emily met me at Heathrow on my arrival in England, I had intended to stay at Cartwright Gardens. I am so pleased that Emily brought me here instead, and introduced me to you. I am grateful to you and John for your generous hospitality."

"You needn't feel indebted. We're pleased to have been able to do it."

"But I am very grateful, and I hope to convince you to visit my part of the world so that I could reciprocate your kindness."

"That is very generous of you. We have visited Nova Scotia. It is beautiful, and we know that the rest of North America, including your country, must be enormous. At our time of life, we're not likely to travel that far again. But Emily said she hopes to see you next year, so she can be our emissary. Don't forget -- I shall gather some seeds from our Michaelmas daisies for your garden."

Though Miss Pyn felt somewhat disappointed with Helen's response to her invitation, the promise of seeds delighted her. "That will be wonderful! We will maintain a connection that way. I shall not say goodbye as yet, since I do have a little time left to enjoy here. However, I shall bid you good evening."

In the morning, Miss Pyn walked out into the front garden and was greeted by Helen tending her flowers: "Another day in London, I suspect?"

"Yes. My time here grows short, so I thought I should once more visit The Poets' Corner and The

Tattershall Castle. It appears to be an excellent day for that. Then too, I think that I should try to see Father Rick before I leave London."

"By all means, do enjoy your full day. I shall enjoy my day here in the garden."

Miss Pyn boarded the train at Ealing Broadway, and even though there was no sign of Lord Overbrooke, she well knew the way to Westminster Abbey.

At The Abbey there was no sign of the verger either, but she knew exactly where she wanted to go. She crossed in front of The High Altar and paused before the Chaucer Tomb at The Poets' Corner. As she passed The Shakespeare Memorial she remembered that, in addition to Chaucer, Dr. Samuel Johnson and Charles Dickens were buried in The Abbey. For some time she recalled the poetry of Wordsworth, Keats, Hopkins, and Eliot. She thought again of her favorite novelist, Jane Austen; and wondered as well if the Bronte Sisters were memorialized in The Poets' Corner. She was delighted to discover that they were indeed.

Reluctantly, she left The Poets' Corner and The Abbey, wondering if she would ever be able to visit the place again. She walked to the Tattershall Castle, even though it was quite a long walk along the Victoria Embankment. Lunch was ready on board, and she was ready for lunch.

When the polite young man on the deck asked how he might assist her, she replied, "I should like a glass of Piesporter with a small serving of that delicious salad."

"An excellent choice! Where might I serve it?"

"Over there please, where I shall be able to look at the river upstream."

Miss Pyn enjoyed her lunch and the Piesporter. She studied the Parliament Building and Big Ben, and thought that this might be the last time she would see those grand symbols of England from her favorite boat on the river.

Perhaps I should have visited the Parliament, she thought. On the other hand, debates in either chamber over the finer points of British Law would not be of significant interest to me. There are many other places in London I should certainly visit rather than Parliament.

She reviewed her adventures in London, and remembered the many interesting people she had shared precious time with -- Emily at Heathrow, the Stablers, Father Jack and the people at Ealing Abbey, Thomas, Dr. Keefe, and of course Father Rick. She suddenly remembered that she should try to see Father Rick before leaving England.

So she gathered her things, gazed once more at the great river and Big Ben, and then walked to the Embankment Tube Station.

At Ealing she visited the Abbey chapel. She was pleased to reflect once again at the side chapel where the Holy Mother was depicted caring for and consoling injured and handicapped children. How fortunate she felt to have again that inspiring experience!

She then walked out to the garden to see if Father Rick was meditating there. She found him, and Peeper too, just as she had last seen them.

"Good afternoon, Father! How are you today?"

"Hello! I'm just fine, and so is Peeper! He's greeting you calmly because he recognizes a friend. We're both very pleased to see you."

"I am pleased to find you here before I have to leave England, which will be quite soon. My visit has been much too short. However, I did meet some wonderful people I shall never forget."

"Ah, yes. While there are fine people in many places, I've found that people here are most gracious. I believe you met an American here as well."

"Actually, there were two Americans -- Dr. Keefe from Boston, who lectures on Medieval English Literature; and Father Thomas Zimmerman, who is in Vienna today on a mission for the Vatican."

365

"Those certainly seem to be outstanding people. I am especially interested in Thomas. How did you meet?"

"I have known Thomas for some time. We met again in the Abbey quite by chance. He had no idea that I was here in England. He stopped here briefly to visit friends he had known in Rome. Now that I think about it, my first meeting with Thomas at his parish near our town of Seven Oaks was also quite by chance."

"I'm not sure that many of our meetings are entirely by chance. I'd like to know more."

Miss Pyn was happy to share her memories. "One day, a long time ago, I stopped to rest in a garden near a country parish church not far from town. There, I saw a gardener tending the plants. Some years before that meeting, I had learned on the very day of my father's funeral that my good friend had been killed in the war. I was bitter and indignant; in my sorrow I declared that I would abandon God, and I left the church forever -- or so I thought."

Miss Pyn paused for some minutes. Father Rick gently asked, "Do you wish to go on?"

"Yes!" she replied resolutely. "As I recall, that day in the garden there was a threat of rain. The gardener suggested that we should find shelter in the church. I told him that I would never enter a church, and I rode away on my bicycle. Some days later, I again stopped in the garden, and met the gardener tending flowers. He asked if I would help him by getting a tool he had forgotten to bring. It was in the church vestibule. Even though I did not want to enter any church, I did go. As I picked up the tool, I heard the choir rehearsing. They were singing the song I had heard at my father's funeral, and I stopped to listen.

"When I explained my delay to the gardener, he said that the choir was rehearsing a song that was new to them. Later, I wondered why a gardener would know such details about the choir practicing a new song.

"The next time I saw the gardener, I confronted him with my question. He admitted that he was the pastor of the parish, and worked in the garden for relaxation. After that, even though I had misgivings, I told him my story. He pointed out that it was not possible for me or anyone else to abandon God. After more intense discussion -- both philosophical and theological -- I agreed to enter the church and experience reconciliation."

Father Rick thought for some minutes. He then said, "Your account is amazing and edifying. I'm pleased to have heard it."

His reply encouraged Miss Pyn to continue: "So you see that I am deeply indebted to Thomas. He was instrumental in my regaining my spiritual life. He insisted that his help in my reconciliation was minimal; that surely the prayers of others -- of those I had served in the library and elsewhere, and most likely those of my father and my deceased friend -- had much more to do with it than anything he had done. Even so, I was very pleased to meet him here in the chapel."

"And did that meeting here go well?"

"Oh yes! Not only did we have a good chat, he invited me to accompany him on a visit to the Cotswolds the next day. I was particularly pleased, since just last week I had to decline an invitation to go there with the young people from the Abbey parish."

"That certainly was an unexpected opportunity."

"It certainly was, and we had a delightful time. He even wanted me to accompany him to Vienna."

Father Rick looked pensive. "Wouldn't you have enjoyed that too?"

"I'm sure I would have enjoyed it immensely, especially since I have never been to Vienna. However, I told him that I had to return to Seven Oaks and the library. I confess that my real reason for refusing his invitation was that I felt I could in no way ever intrude on Thomas' vocation. After all, there are very likely other souls that would benefit, as I have, from his spiritual assistance."

"Your determination surely took real courage and fortitude."

"Thank you, Father! Until just now, I was not certain that I had made the right decision. Thank you very much for your support."

"You're most welcome! The last time you visited here I promised that I would show you some very special plants we have in this garden. They're just over there across that pathway."

"I not only see them, I recognize them! In fact, Helen Stabler has some just like them growing in her garden. They are called perennial asters."

"Ah yes! When we put in that bed we had some extra plants, so I shared some with the Stablers."

"When I told Helen I would purchase some plants like hers for my garden, she said she would send some seed from her plants to me so that we would have a special connection."

"Then you would have a special connection with this garden as well. I don't believe I told you why those plants have a very special significance for me. In this country the plants bloom at the end of September, and so they're called Michaelmas daisies."

Miss Pyn suddenly gasped for air; it was some time before she could fully breathe. When she could speak, she said, "Father Rick, may I know your full name?"

"Of course! It's Frederick Hart -- but I'm happy with Rick."

Several minutes passed before Miss Pyn was able to reply. "Many years ago, Father, you sent me a note. However, the only name you had for me then was 'Needles.'"

"Glory be! I never thought I would see this day! I've prayed for you every day since I wrote that note. Do you remember it?"

"I do. The original is at home. I made a copy that I have in my luggage, but I always carry it with me in my heart. You began your note, 'Even though we have not met and the only name I have for you is Needles, we have a very special relationship -- we both have known and loved a saint in heaven -- the same saint.'"

"Yes, that's it exactly! That saint -- our mutual friend -- was Michael, who was martyred in Korea so long ago. Now that I've lived this day, I believe my life is complete, and I shall be happy to have it come to its end. I bless you, dear heart, and I'm grateful beyond belief for this visit. Go home to our country with my blessings. I shall be with you in spirit."

Miss Pyn left with a farewell gesture, but without another word; for she was unable to say anything ... anything at all.

During the morning of her last full day in London, Miss Pyn gathered her things and packed all that she did not expect to need that day and the next in the case she had brought to England. In the folding case Joe had recommended, she packed the few treasures she had found in London.

Later in the day, Helen Stabler announced, "A letter from Scotland came in the morning post for you, Miss Pyn."

"Thank you, but I do not believe that I know anyone in Scotland. Oh, it must be from Emily. She has taken her holiday on Skye." She eagerly opened the envelope and read:

Dear Miss Pyn,

I do hope that this note will arrive in London before your departure for America. I wish to say how much I enjoyed knowing you, and I am pleased to send a brief report of my travel to Skye.

You remember that you told me about King James and his decree about Falkland Palace. I stopped briefly at the Palace to visit the chapel that Queen Mary treasured. The chapel is very beautiful, and at the back I noticed a special icon honoring Our Lady of Czestochowa. An elderly gentleman with an Eastern European accent told me that the icon was made by Polish airmen who were stationed in the area during the Second World War. They were able to attend Mass at the chapel -- the only Roman Catholic one in the area. The icon was given in thanksgiving for the privilege of their attendance at Sunday Mass there. It is a marvelous work of art. The man said that it was made of spent shell casings. I suspect, because of his accent, that he may well have been one of those airmen.

After my discovery at The Falkland Palace, I journeyed to The Isle of Skye. At a place more or less in the middle of the island, I found a delightful fishing lodge with an excellent lunch buffet. My brief stay at the fishing lodge was even more wonderful than I could expect. Although I was not able to engage in fishing, I did walk to the fishing streams and enjoyed the surroundings and the fresh clean air. The food at the lodge was superb and provided examples of the very best taste of Scottish cookery. I shall recommend the marvelous place and give you more details when next we meet.

On the drive down from the hills of Skye to the ferry back to the mainland, I saw a sight that I'll probably not ever see again. From one end of the horizon all the way to other end, there stretched a most beautiful rainbow. All I could think of was that if a pot of gold can be found at the end of a rainbow, there must two pots of gold on Skye.

Later, along the road from Skye I was delighted to see rock formations that create a landscape just waiting for an artist to capture its magnificence on canvas. One day you must come to that place, and I too must see it again.

My friends among the young people at the Abbey all agree that your brief presence in our midst was a genuine delight. I personally look forward to seeing you again at the next International Library Association meeting, which I hope to attend and which is scheduled for Chicago in your country. Then I will be able to visit you at your library in Seven Oaks.

Affectionately, Emily

Miss Pyn was both amazed and delighted that Emily would have taken time to write such a long letter during her holiday. She left a reply with Mrs. Stabler, indicating how pleased she would be to welcome Emily to Seven Oaks.

The evening, Miss Pyn's last in England, was drawing to a close. She thought of no better location for final reflection than the place she always recalled as her introduction to London -- Waterloo Bridge. It was not, she reflected, the ornate Victorian bridge she had seen in old pictures and films, and expected to find here. The current architectural structure, best described as "modern utilitarian," provided Londoners and their many visitors with easy access to both sides of the river.

The evening breeze, coming downstream along the river, was fresh. Lights were bright, but many began to dim as theatergoers and concertgoers and wanderers began to wend their ways home. Public and private boats for tourists slowly moved upstream. On the Bridge, native Londoners and visitors walked; and busses and motor vehicles moved along -- some slowly, others briskly -- toward one side or the other of the river.

Miss Pyn stopped next to a man flying a kite from the middle of the Bridge. Neither said a word to the other. She studied the moving water and the skyline. He gazed at his kite and at the emerging stars in the heavens. The two might have been in different worlds, oblivious of all activity beside and around them. Those who walked past them apparently didn't notice the two figures standing near the middle of the Bridge -- a strange tableau -- a woman studying the water; and a middle-aged man studying his kite and the stars beyond. Where else but in robust London could one come upon a scene like this as midnight approached.

Miss Pyn looked in the direction of Waterloo Station. She could see people coming from The National Theatre Complex, and she thought about the splendid theatrical productions staged at The Olivier Theatre and elsewhere in London -- and at the Royal Shakespeare Theater in Stratford. She saw other travelers coming from the direction of the Royal Concert Hall, and she thought with awe of all the musical grandeur performed in that Hall.

She moved a little -- quite reluctantly -- toward the Temple Tube Station. She looked upstream toward Parliament and Big Ben, its lights still on. She assured herself that she need not absorb that scene, since most pictures of London feature that very same view. She did, however, record in her notebook of reflections, her thoughts about the late evening magic of the river just before "lights out."

Then, she took one final look at Saint Paul's. She lingered a while, for soon she must begin her journey by boarding the Underground -- and tomorrow take a bus, a train, a plane, a coach, and a taxi to her home on Adams Road. And so she would return to her other world of library patrons and books in her little town across the sea.

Miss Pyn sighed and shrugged, and with her book of reflections in her hand she began a slow deliberate walk toward The Temple Tube Station. She didn't realize that a page of her notes slipped out as she walked. The breeze carried the paper out over the railing of the Bridge toward a tourist boat coming up the river.

A young man, on board, leapt up in an effort to catch the paper. The tips of his fingers merely brushed the note, sending it on its way into the water and toward the sea.

It was just as well that he could not catch the fleeting note. How could such a young man -- or anyone else for that matter who had not lived a whole life of expectation and disappointment, and only now and then known joyous satisfaction -- ever begin to fathom those final thoughts now lost in the swirling waters ...

Ed. Note: The Pyn manuscript abruptly ends here. On an overleaf toward the end of the last manuscript pad, the words which follow appear. While there is no way of establishing whether or not these words were a draft of the thoughts on the lost paper drifting out to sea in the Thames, it is just possible that they were....

Final Thoughts At Waterloo

Your roses lovely I shall not soon forget
The cold dark rain happily, eagerly forgo

But if ill-fated am I to walk onward
And on, always and forever away

All your wonder-magic kindled in my sad heart
Could never ever consume nor quench

This awful rue our parting now inflames
So farewell my friend, old London town

Auf Wiedersehen and fare ye well
I fear I shall not soon return

23695279R00211

Made in the USA
Charleston, SC
31 October 2013